LAST CALL FOR JUSTICE

A MELLINGHAM MYSTERY

SUSAN OLEKSIW

Hale Street Press ◆ Prides Crossing, MA ◆ 01965

OTHER BOOKS BY SUSAN OLEKSIW

The Mellingham Series featuring Chief of Police Joe Silva

Murder in Mellingham
Double Take
Family Album
Friends and Enemies
A Murderous Innocence

The Anita Ray Series

Under the Eye of Kali
The Wrath of Shiva
For the Love of Parvati

Last Call for Justice

Cast of Characters

Mae and Pae Silva—Joe Silva's parents
Zaira Souza—Joe's oldest sister, married to Gray
Lucia Foster—Joe's younger sister, married to Larry
Rosalie Avila—Joe's younger sister, married to
    Eduardo/Eddie
Gino—Joe's younger brother, married to Melanie
Deanie—Joe's youngest sister
Sarah—Zaira's daughter and youngest child

Prologue

A Friday Evening in August
When Nixon Was President

Christina was not easy to upset. The light silk blouse
billowed and slid off the wooden slat, floating to the floor. She
snatched it up and fumbled with it, draping it lopsided on the
hanger; she shoved the hanger and blouse onto the bar between
two other blouses. She slammed the door shut and gripped the
doorknob. She was shaking.

"Stupid stupid stupid," she whispered, resting her forehead
against the door.

After a moment, she straightened up and went into the
bathroom. Her parents would be home soon and they expected
her to be ready to go out for dinner. Her aunt and uncle were
celebrating something—she couldn't remember what, something
about a new job. How could she forget something so important?
She would remember. Of course she would remember. This was
family. The minute she saw them, she'd remember. Her
breathing slowed. She took a deep breath and gave a heavy sigh.

It was all going to work out, she reassured herself as she
perched on the edge of the old claw-foot tub; she turned the hot
water tap and watched the water gush out. The water was clear,
with that tinge of aqua that made her wonder how painters
managed to capture the sense of wetness. She felt herself being
pulled into the churning bathwater. She loved color and watching
it change as the light moved across a surface, as shadows
darkened or the sun rose in the sky—she could lose herself in
thinking about it. This evening she needed to lose herself in it.
That was how she thought about life—how much light there
was—and right now, she reassured herself, her life would
brighten. She would pass through the darkness and look back on

this time as just something girls go through. She'd think back probably when she was picking out a dress for a date with a new boy.

She reached for a bar of white soap but it slid out of her hands, splashing into the tub. She stiffened, watching it bob up and down. She rubbed her hands over her face, then ran her hands along her slip. The lace was torn along the hem. Her hands trembled as she began to inspect the rest of her. A long red mark where her bra strap had pulled against her shoulder made a third red line across her pink flesh, and a thick blue-red bruise was spreading along the inside of her upper arm. It would turn dark and ugly later tonight. Her hand went to her throat, but she wasn't yet ready to move to the mirror and see what was there. She thought about her wardrobe and what she might have to wear tonight—perhaps a scarf, maybe a chunky necklace, if she could find one. It was too hot for a jacket.

When he grabbed her, her first thought had been, I'll tell Joe. But with the same speed as the thought came to her, it evaporated. Sure, she could tell Joe. But it wouldn't help in the same way. At the thought of Joe, she felt the sadness seize her again. He wasn't her Jose anymore.

The water tumbled and churned behind her, its noisy fall filling the small room, echoing off the old tiles and fixtures, the steam turning the windows opaque behind the curtains and venetian blinds. She didn't usually let the water run this long but the sound was comforting—it made her feel like there was activity in the house, something going on around her. And right now, she didn't want to feel alone, abandoned to her own thoughts and feelings.

She was just getting used to thinking about her future in a new way, one without Jose and the certainty of marriage, and trying not to dwell on what might have been. She knew a lot of other boys who had been interested in her. What was the name of that one who lived over on Georges Drive? She'd babysat for his younger sister a few times and once he drove her home. He seemed nice. Her arm began to ache and she realized she was pulling it tight and stiff against her side. She flexed her fingers, shook her arm, took a deep breath. She reached over to turn off the water—the bathtub was near to overflowing.

She slid into the water, thinking about how pink she'd be, like the first burn of summer, only this one wouldn't last. It would fade away in half an hour. She liked the high temperature—it gave her something else to think about than the soreness running up her arm and the ache that went deeper.

She'd never been ill treated before. She'd heard about couples where things didn't go well—everyone knew about the Santuccis down the street—but no one had ever touched her that way. She'd never been spanked as a child, not even as a two-year old. Her mother was the talk of the neighborhood when Christina was growing up. She hadn't known what violence was like—until today.

Christina rested her head on the back of the tub and closed her eyes, letting her legs float to the surface. Her parents bought an old house with an old bathroom, and with the exception of regrouting the tiles and painting the upper walls, the bathroom stayed the same—the old soaking tub her mother's single luxury in a life that had known none and expected none.

"You are beautiful."

The words startled her. She pushed herself up, splashing water over the side and staring at the man standing in the doorway. "How did you get in here? Get out!" She reached for a towel.

"You let me in."

"I told you to get out!" Her voice was hoarse with fear, rising with each word. She was almost screaming. The neighbors would hear her. "Get out!"

"I want you to know that I'm not the kind of person you think I am," he said, looking down at her, his face drained of color, his words sounding rote. "I'm just as nice as anyone else." He took a step into the room, his dark eyes fixed on her face. He seemed so large—too large for the little room.

Again she told him to get out, but her words were fragmenting, her voice breaking, as though she didn't have enough oxygen for every syllable. He went on talking to her as though she hadn't said a word to him, moving closer and closer to the tub. She saw the little hairs under his chin where the razor had missed during his morning shave, the way his collar folded in instead of lying flat.

"You shouldn't treat me the way you did."

"I told you to get out." She could barely catch her breath for fear. "I'm calling the police." He seemed to hear her this time. He stopped moving, stared, and she could see in his eyes she had said the wrong thing. She had threatened him. "Get out. Just go." She spoke in a quieter voice, trying to soften her threat. He didn't move. She thought he was going to stand there forever and she would sit here forever with a little hand towel covering her breasts, the water turning cold. He began to turn away. "Creep." The word came out in a sigh of relief, but he must have heard her. He stopped where he was, gazed at her over his shoulder.

She opened her mouth to say something, she didn't know what, but instead she saw his large hand rise from his side and hover over her.

"Please," she whispered. "Please."

She felt his fingers clamp down on her head, his nails dig into her scalp. His hand pressed her head down into her shoulders and she was under water, thrashing, her eyes burning, her limbs flailing. Her foot hit something; she swung her leg and slid deeper into the soapy water, twisting, the world behind her closed eyelids turning red.

One

A Thursday Evening in August This Year

At the age of seventeen Joe Silva got into his first and only brawl. There were seven of them—Joe, his older brother Paulo, Eduardo, who later married Joe's sister Rosalie, and four boys from another neighborhood. Joe couldn't remember what it was about—and that bothered him more than anything else. In his twenties he'd been secretly proud of how he and his brother and Eduardo had bloodied and beaten the others, but in his thirties he looked back on that episode with disgust, and now, facing the age of retirement, he was stymied at not being able to remember what the fight had been about. Joe couldn't remember Paulo ever getting into another fight after that, though he'd had his share of roughhousing, but Eduardo hadn't changed for years—he seemed to go from brawl to brawl, as though that were the point of his life.

Joe was thinking about this because he always did when he visited his family. The way they had been, the brawl and other encounters equally memorable, came up more often now, as though his parents, actually, mostly his father, were trying to get the details straight after all these years. His father seemed to have a few moments from his earlier years highlighted in his mind, and they flashed brighter and brighter as Joe visited less and less frequently. The brawl was sure to be a topic of a long reminiscence on Friday, after he and his dad had settled down for a talk.

It would begin with his father standing by the bookshelf rearranging the family photographs, making sure Paulo's picture in his uniform was not eclipsed by the rows of little grandchildren at their first communion, weddings, graduations, and little families of their own. Paulo, the man who never aged,

9

never grew slope-shouldered or wrinkled, never disappointed. The dead cannot disappoint us, Joe knew, but they can hold us, haunt us, and sometimes loom over us just when they should be the farthest from our minds.

Joe lowered the lid on the box, checked to make sure it was securely locked, and turned away from it. He wouldn't take his gun anywhere near his parents' home—it was a superstition he had, and he'd had it from the beginning. Getting through the police academy and onto the force had been a long, fragile dream, and once he got there, he wasn't taking any chances. If he was going to spend the night at his parents' place, his gun stayed elsewhere.

His father noticed that after a year or so. Or, maybe he noticed it earlier and just didn't say anything.

"You afraid your family not being trusted?" Pae Silva asked one day. Joe was used to his father's blunt and often awkward speech—his grasp of English hovered near but never quite reached proficiency—because Joe knew after his parents instructed the child in English they would lapse into Portuguese. His father raised his hand, and shook his head, muttering. "No, not asking." He leaned into the refrigerator and pulled out a beer and handed it to Joe, then changed the subject to his next gardening project. He could grow melons, hanging them from lattices tied to the house, tomatoes in pots, and carrots in narrow rows along the walkway. Finding a new corner in which to plant was as exciting to him as harvesting the crop. He would tell Joe all about it, as though Joe had never helped in the garden in his entire life.

Joe walked out of the Mellingham police station and climbed into his car. He would be lying to himself if he said he was facing this long weekend at his parents' home without any reservations. His father had insisted on bringing everyone together again—for one last visit for sure, he had said. But when Joe tried to get at what was behind this drive to get everyone together, the old man had insisted he wasn't sick, he wasn't in trouble, he didn't have bad news. There was no special reason for the gathering except that he wanted to do this.

And everyone was coming. Even his older sister, Zaira, was coming, leaving her husband, Gray, with a nurse just long enough to make an appearance and appease her father. She was almost 65, her husband older and trying to succumb gracefully to old age and a weakening heart while his wife rounded up therapists and specialists and hovered over him all day, every day. But if her father wanted her at the reunion, she would be there. But even she didn't know what he was up to. Joe knew because he had asked.

"I don't know, Jose," she said when she called him to ask him the same question. "Why now? What does he want?"

"He's an old man," Joe said.

"He's been an old man for years," she said. "My husband is an old man, but you don't see him trying to get all his relatives together."

"He has one brother, Zaira."

"All right, all right. But you know what I mean." His sister hung up still muttering that her father should stop imposing on all of them—they had troubles of their own.

Joe pulled into his driveway, and turned the car around, to make it easier to load the luggage. This was setting up to be a major production, no matter how hard he tried to keep it simple and low key. His father had insisted on three days—when will we have another chance, he cried over the phone—and Joe had gone about persuading Gwen, his partner, and Jennie, her daughter, that three days was entirely reasonable. Philip was off at camp—a longstanding commitment that no one dared alter—and Gwen (and Joe) would not leave Jennie home alone. But coming up with reasons for this extended visit had not been easy—Joe was pretty sure Gwen could see right through him.

But Joe was persuasive, and Gwen was agreeable, and Jennie was a teenager.

The real problem was getting at his father's intent.

"Can't a man have his family around him?" Joe's father had said to Joe the weekend before.

Of course, he can, Joe thought. But why now? And then the reason he couldn't understand—couldn't make sense of no matter how hard he pondered it.

"And Christina! Christina will come. Her mother says she can bring her. For one hour, maybe two." His father coughed, the cough of an old man who got too excited and lost his breath. Joe felt himself stiffen even when he tried to tell himself it didn't matter—what happened to Christina was over and done with. But his fist clenched and he forced himself to loosen it and shake it out.

"Pae, she doesn't know who we are anymore," Joe said. "She lives in a bed."

"Maybe so, maybe so." He heard his father sigh, deflated. "But we know who she is."

* * * * *

Gwen McDuffy tried to keep her arms loose at her side, her head casually tipped to show interest, as she listened to Jennie, her teenage daughter, go through the list of reasons why she should not have to go with Gwen and Joe to visit Joe's family. The list went on and on, and included things like age, headaches, cheerleading lessons, but in the end they could all be reduced to one thing—she was a teenager and she didn't want to spend the weekend with a bunch of old folks. Gwen carefully kept an open countenance, willing herself not to start spitting in rage. Old? Her?

"Joe wants you to go," Gwen said. "His family adores you."

This had the desired effect—if only momentarily. In Gwen's experience, no teenage girl could resist even the hint of adulation, and she watched the girl teeter on the brink of capitulation before recovering her balance. Gwen sighed; she knew it wouldn't be that easy.

"I don't really know any of them," Jennie said, her voice softening. "And besides, Philip . . ."

"Yes?" Gwen said, smiling brightly. "You have to remember that this is his first summer at camp—he was so excited about it—you saw him. It would be a shame to spoil something like that for him—he wouldn't really understand. He's a lot younger than you are." Gwen almost choked on these fatuous lies, and was briefly appalled that Jennie didn't confront her about them—Philip was only a year younger. But then she wasn't at the altruistic age yet either. In a burst of genuine feeling, Gwen reached out her hand and squeezed Jennie's shoulder. "You know how Joe loves having us all together, and I'm just as nervous as you are."

"Oh, Mom, do I have to?" Jennie twisted herself into a curlicue of passion. "Why can't I spend the weekend with Emmy?"

"Because Emmy's parents are going away," Gwen said. "And I am not allowing two teenage girls to spend the weekend alone in that house. I don't know what her parents are thinking."

"They trust her, Mom," Jennie said in her best imitation of an indignant adult.

Gwen lowered her chin and glared at her. Jennie would soon be taller than Gwen but that wasn't going to stop her from looking down at her even if she had to climb onto a chair to do it. "She's sixteen! And the answer is no and will always be no until you are much, much older."

"How much?" Jennie quickly asked, sensing a breach in the dike.

"You're entitled to a serious conversation about this, and I'm going to set aside time for just that." Relieved at having evaded Jennie's relentless drive for independence, Gwen sent her off to pack a change of clothes and whatever else she might need, then turned back to the suitcase lying open on the bed. She wasn't feeling awfully sanguine herself about this visit.

She loved Joe and his family, but this was the first time she and any of her children would be spending a whole weekend with them. They had met for family dinners, holidays, special visits, but she had never stayed over, and neither had the children. And that was what made her nervous. In her own little home, where everything had meaning and she controlled the order, she felt safe. During their short get-togethers with Joe's family, everything had been managed enough so that she had felt barely threatened—she could pick the restaurant, the departure time, the route for the drive down, the time to say goodbye—but this time it would be different. They were arriving on a Friday morning and staying until Sunday. Gwen sat down on the bed with a bounce, pushed the suitcase away, and fell onto her side.

Joe's family was big and loud and—foreign. Sometimes they didn't even speak English. And the one time she had gone into the kitchen to help with the meal Joe's mother had hovered over her every second and burst into impromptu and lengthy cooking lessons. The dinner was two hours late, Gwen was exhausted, and everyone else was hungry and annoyed—except Joe.

"She does it to every prospective daughter-in-law. She doesn't want any of her children going hungry," Joe explained. "I should have warned you."

They would have had a huge fight on the drive home if Gwen hadn't fallen asleep in the passenger seat as soon as they were on the highway.

What was it about mothers-in-law? Since Gwen had never been married before, she couldn't understand her own reactions to all of this family togetherness. She understood the fierce protective feelings of a mother, even though Jennie and Philip weren't her biological children, and she understood her own deep loyalty to Joe. But why was she falling apart just because she was going to be spending time in Joe's mother's house? And that's how she thought of it—it wasn't his parents' house, it was his mother's house.

The first time they had visited, Joe's father had stood up on his wobbly, bony legs and reached out a gnarled fist to her, then sat down on the sofa and seemed to ignore her. After some conversation during which he listened and nodded, he leaned over and began to ask Joe questions for Gwen to answer. She thought that was odd. In her family, her father had been politely but superficially direct with anyone who came into the house— conversations were always courteous, correct, and inclusive. But Joe's father was startlingly different—and not just in appearance. He asked and watched and asked some more, and Gwen, as graciously as possible, gave in to the interrogation and was even a little surprised at the words flowing out of her. Every now and then Joe told him he couldn't ask her that, and then switched into Portuguese, perhaps to explain why, or perhaps to give his own answer. Whenever she asked him later what he'd said, he replied, Oh nothing. If she pressed him, he said he couldn't remember.

But when he was at his parents' apartment, he was relaxed—more truly, deeply relaxed than she'd ever known him. It was as if he no long had to think about anything outside that small apartment with its tidy bookshelves in one corner, the row of porcelain figures of children on the top shelf, the gently worn carpeting, and the crocheted fringe on the window shades. On the way home he had asked if the apartment reminded her of her grandparents' home, expecting her to say yes. But she said no.

"My grandparents lived in a trailer and later they bought an RV and drove out west and never came back." Joe glanced over at her, frowned and shook his head.

"My cousins still live in our grandparents' house in the Azores," he said. "Most of my family has never moved farther than across the street."

Gwen slid down in the seat, struggling to smother an unexpected feeling of terror, of wanting to flee, to just get in a car and drive and drive and drive until she ran out of gas or ran out of road. Was that how her grandparents had felt? Was it in the genes? Was she doomed to be restless, unsettled, forever on the edge of bolting for a new town, a new life, a new man? No, not a new man. But could she ever get Joe to go with her? She peeked over at him: he drove with one hand on the steering wheel, the other resting on his leg. The traffic was light, the evening pleasantly warm, the surroundings still. She began to feel herself grow calm, the panic in her subsiding. They could be home in an hour.

Gwen sat up on the bed, and tugged on the suitcase. Joe had promised to show her some of the places of his childhood, take her out on the bay, and spend time with her alone. Jennie would have others her own age to spend time with. Maybe it wouldn't be so bad. After all, how often did she and Joe get to be alone, really alone, with no sirens going off, no one asking for help, no one calling in the middle of the night.

She never took the next logical step of complaining about the kinds of problems people called with—she'd been there. She remembered. And yet it seemed so far away.

If they were going out on the water, she should take a sweater, maybe a jacket too.

* * * * *

The old man unclenched his fist and stretched his fingers out, flexing his joints slowly, leaning over and listening for the sound of his bones disintegrating. He was sure he could hear the little bits of bone flaking off and falling into a vein and floating away. It was a fear he had, that little parts of himself were chipping and collapsing, until soon all that would be left of him would be disconnected bits and shreds and fragments tumbling around inside his skin, which by this time was no more than a worn satchel, ready to shred also, when all of him would flow through a tear and dribble away behind him as he tried to walk on, to go on living his life. It was a sobering thought, so he clenched and unclenched his fists to persuade himself he still had a physical body and it worked.

He turned his shoulders to get a look at his wife lying buried under a clean white sheet, not even a single curl allowed to peak out above. She had the ability to sleep when desired, to wake up when she wanted, nap when she needed to. At least she said she did. He didn't know. He never asked. He just listened to her talk to her sister and her friends. They shared their little ailments, or large ailments, and found remedies to try or life events to blame. Always the little ailments. He only wanted his body to work a little longer—he'd live with the ailments.

With a fist the size of a teapot and the hardness of a rock, he punched the pillow, then nudged it aside and pushed himself up off the bed. He should sleep. He wanted to sleep. Tomorrow he needed to be rested; he wanted to be rested. But he was uneasy. For two years he had hinted, cajoled, suggested, to get his entire family together again, and this time he had succeeded. They would all be here—every one of them. He paused in the doorway and reached out to brace himself against the doorjamb. Well, not every one of them. One would be missing.

Paulo. Paulo forever young. Paulo whose body would never age, never ail, never dwindle and fail. The old man had nothing of his oldest son, nothing except the image of him standing in the back yard stripped to his waist digging out the vegetable garden before he left the following day to report to Fort Devens. Nothing but an image that never faded. Sometimes the old man wished it would, wished it had, faded, dissolved, so that the only way he could reclaim his long-dead son was by looking at a photograph, touching the shiny surface and tracing the picture with his own finger. Instead, the picture of his son working hard on his last day, laughing at his father giving the orders and withholding the beer until the work was done, never left him. Sometimes the image seemed so real, so alive that he had to stop himself from asking his wife about it. He had to remind himself that Paulo was gone.

Once the old man had walked out onto the back porch, not so long ago, and rested his thick worn hand on another son's shoulder, and admitted the unimaginable.

"He's still here, isn't he, Jose?" The old man clenched the son's shoulder and pointed into the dark. "I can see him there." And his son the policeman had patted his hand and looked into the blackness also.

The older he got, the more real the image became, the focus sharper, the colors brighter. He was sure he knew what it meant now. At first it had troubled him. He thought he was losing his mind, his sanity, his connection to this earth, his friends, his place in the world. And then one day, he understood. The greatest light can only have one focus, and as it moved, he had to follow. Paulo was the brightest image in his life now, just as his living children had been the brightest for all these years. He knew what that meant, but he hadn't told his wife. He hadn't told anyone.

The living room was dark but he didn't need the light. Sometimes when he walked around late at night he didn't even realize he had forgotten to turn on a light as he made his way to the kitchen and back to the dining room. His wife left plates of food for him, all made up, with cutlery rolled into a napkin sitting on the kitchen counter. She didn't like to hear him rummaging in drawers for a knife and fork, or moving containers around on the kitchen counters while he tried to figure out what was in them. For years she made two or three meals a day, leaving fully made-up plates for him to eat on whim. She left tins of cookies and pastries on the counters, bowls of fruit on the table—all ready for him. And now that the children were grown, and even the grandchildren too old to eat at random whatever was left on the counter, she left all sorts of new foods for him to try. Most of them he didn't like, but sometimes a new dish caught his fancy and he would pester her about it again and again, too proud and certainly too unschooled to ask, so left to hint and hope and sulk if misunderstood.

Tonight it was a vegetable soup with celery, onions, peppers, tomatoes, and rice, all from his garden except the rice. He ladled the soup into his mouth, recalling the tastes of other dishes he had enjoyed over the years. This was a good one and he knew he'd have it again, especially in the fall when she would add chicken and perhaps sausage. A bright light from a passing car flowed over the wall and up across the ceiling before fading out the window, but in the moment of illumination the dining room stood before him still and bleak. He was eating alone. The shock of it stalled him and his spoon hung in the air, little drops of soup splattering into the bowl. He never ate alone. His wife always stood behind him, making sure he had enough, had what he wanted, was satisfied. Why was he alone?

He thought of Paulo. Paulo liked to sit with him late at night after studying or after work, and talk. He was a good boy, Paulo. So big and robust. When he came through the door he filled the apartment—it felt like the rest of the family was pushed out of the room by a sudden heavy wind. But his warmth—like a magnet pulling them back in. Paulo, the first, the biggest, the lost.

When the news came no one knew what to say. His wife went to the cemetery every day after the funeral for an entire year, and then she stopped. Something sank down where even she couldn't reach it. He watched her go out the door every morning, to catch the bus up the hill, and he refused to go with her. It wasn't right to put such a young man into the ground, and he wouldn't witness it one more time. His daughters tried to get him to accompany them on holidays, but he said no, not him. So when his Paulo grew more and more vivid, more and more real, the old man no longer had the words to articulate what was happening to him. At confession he told the priest only that he had denied his grief and now it had come for him.

He had to be careful about this lest his other children misunderstood him. He had to watch himself this weekend. The house would be full. A young cousin had cleared out the attic room, and all the young ones would stay up there—half for the boys and half for the girls. Jose and his lady friend Gwen would have one room, and Gino would stay in a motel with his wife, and Deanie would stay with one of his older girls. She had been close to Rosalie.

Deanie.

How long had it been? His little girl in a Brownie uniform, her first. He squinted in the darkness but she faded around the edges. He could barely see her.

Tires rolled on the dew-dampened road and headlights flowed across the wall and ceiling, before fading away again. He disliked the looks of the dining room at this hour; it irritated him. He should be able to see Deanie, see her as brightly as Paulo. But he couldn't. She kept slipping away, the chocolate of her uniform turning muddy. Why had she been away so long?

* * * * *

"Are you sure you can get everything in there?" Jennie asked. She was standing in a pool of light shining from the back-door lamp. Around her the neighborhood was dark and quiet. It was late, and she had surprised Joe with her fussiness about the storage compartment of the black Jeep. He had given in and cleaned it out, judging this the price of her tacit capitulation.

She rested her clenched fists on her waist and evaluated his efforts. "I mean, Philip took like four bags full of nothing to camp and you want me to leave all my clothes behind."

Joe gave Jennie a quick smile and hit the vacuum switch with his shoe—the machine roared and he leaned into the car with the hose. Jennie crossed her arms in front of her chest and glared. When Joe was finished, he switched off the vacuum and dropped the hose onto the ground.

"There's room for luggage for a long weekend." He glanced over at her as he picked up his carton of emergency equipment— a blanket, flashlight, screwdriver, water, extra batteries, a bag of energy bars, flares, and an old paperback mystery novel he had never finished reading. "You don't need anything more. Go pack."

"But Joe . . ." she began to wail. "I mean I am sixteen." Her arms akimbo again, she was ready to argue. "Everybody stays home alone sometimes. It's so normal."

"Not for your mother, it isn't." He slammed the back shut. "And not for me."

"I'd be with Emmy. You like Emmy, don't you? She's from a good family." Jennie tossed out this information as though no one had considered it before.

"You know what the answer is," Joe said with barely a smile. "Let's get moving here. Go on. We're leaving early tomorrow morning, and I'd like to pack as much as possible tonight. Take your cell. You can call Emmy and make sure she's all right. I don't like the idea of her family leaving her alone all weekend, and you can stay in touch with her."

"What? Me? You want me to spy on her?" Jennie looked genuinely shocked.

"Just in case she gets lonely and wants someone to talk to," Joe said. "She's your friend, after all."

Jennie struggled with the direction this conversation had taken and reluctantly accepted the idea, mumbling through it again while Joe worked on the luggage. He knew neither Jennie nor Emmy could admit the obvious—that no sixteen-year-old would be entirely comfortable alone for two or three nights in that big house up on the hill, no matter how confident she seemed to her parents. "Well, I suppose she might be bored."

They had been through various stages with Jennie and Philip—resentment, jealousy, defiance, and a few others—in the years since Gwen and Joe had moved in together, and were now at the normal teenager-confronting-parent stage. Joe knew what to expect, even if Jennie didn't. She had turned into a lovely young lady—polite, well behaved, mostly obedient—but something of a tester. She wanted to know why in terms that made sense to her, and she wanted to debate every single reason. Joe found it exhausting but mostly harmless, and appreciated that it was a matter of practicing, learning how to make her own decisions. But he worried sometimes that in an effort to be open-minded and responsive, he was being too easy, too willing to argue, debate and compromise.

Jennie crossed her arms again and scowled. "So, how many relatives do you have?"

Joe suppressed a smile. This was the crux of the matter. When Joe first broached the subject of a long visit to his family's place south of Boston, both Jennie and Philip seemed to think this was a great idea. They had long conversations with his mother on the telephone, sent her emails, which somehow got to her, through a path Joe didn't understand, and sometimes exchanged cards. Hungry for grandparents who acted the way teenagers thought old people should act, Jennie and Philip had readily accepted Joe's parents as surrogates and treated them accordingly. They grabbed the telephone receiver to say hello, rolled their eyes at the grandparent advice, and reminded Gwen of upcoming holidays, in case she might forget something for Joe's parents.

But when Joe mentioned that the rest of his family would be there, Jennie gave a snuffle of surprise. She knew there were a lot of them, but little more. Philip, already scheduled for camp, was less defensive, more curious.

"You never said how many?" Jennie persisted.

"I was one of seven," Joe said, turning to her. "My oldest brother, Paulo, is dead. Vietnam. He was married just before he went over, but his wife, Angela, probably won't come. She drops by to see my parents every now and then but she's got her own family." Joe was about to go down the list when he realized just how gloomy it might sound. His oldest brother dead, the oldest sister taking care of a husband after a heart attack, and then him, Joe, third on the list.

"Gee, I'm sorry," Jennie said, apparently thinking Joe's silence tied to ongoing grief.

"Forget my brothers and sisters," Joe said. "They all have kids, and some of their kids have kids. You'll have lots of your generation to talk to, and you'll probably be drafted into babysitting some of the younger ones."

"Well, I don't mind helping out," Jennie said, energized by the thought of having a purpose and being useful. "You know, it's like the whole weekend with nothing to do."

"Don't worry," he said, picking up the vacuum cleaner, "there'll be plenty to do." Just staying out of the way of the trampling hordes will keep you occupied, Joe wanted to say but decided not to. It was hard to explain to people who had grown up in small families what it was like in a large one. You had to give up your sense of order and propriety for a greater cosmic law. If you wanted something, you had to fight for it, earn it elsewhere, or give it up. Joe couldn't remember if he had ever asked his parents for anything that he couldn't earn himself, not after the age of nine or ten.

"Take that in to your mother," Joe said, handing Jennie a bag of empty soda cans and candy wrappers. "Let's finish this up. It's late."

It was a pretty good family, Joe had to admit. His brother's early death had devastated them all, but over time everyone had accepted it and moved on. He could see them standing around the open grave, the priest peeking down at his shoes for fear he'd step too close to the edge and loosen more dirt. He saw the grave, the sisters and cousins and brother huddled together, but his mind's eye swept across to only one—Deanie. It was always the same. After Joe thought about Paulo, he skipped through the relatives right down to the youngest, Deanie. She was the pebble stuck in the heel of a shoe, clicking against the macadam with each step, the draft on his neck in the movie theater. She took him out of the moment but left him nowhere.

She had fallen away early on, the youngest caught up in all the residue of a dying culture, lost and wandering and wild. She wasn't the one he would have suspected this of—she was quiet as a child, thoughtful and curious and watchful—but she had changed. One summer she seemed to go off into another world and never seemed to come back. She was fourteen then, going into high school, thinking about her future. Maybe that was what did it—the idea that she had to move on and she didn't know where to go.

When his mother told him Deanie was coming home for this reunion, Joe had been too surprised to say anything. He heard the words forming in his head, the polite, expected words, but he couldn't bring himself to say them. The dishonesty caught in his throat. He knew his mother would know he was lying, just saying the right things, and she deserved more than that. She put no veneer on reality, she wanted no soft words to ease the pain, she tolerated no dishonesty.

"It must be time," was all Joe could say. His mother had murmured agreement. "Maybe she'll tell us something."

"No, not that one. We lost her. Somehow, Jose, we lost her." His mother sighed, shed no tears for the pain she had lived with for decades, and asked him what she should make that Jennie would like.

Sometimes when Joe listened to his mother talk to Jennie he could hear the voice that had raised him—Jennie was his mother's second chance, the one who could tell her where she had gone wrong with Deanie, and perhaps what she could do to make it up. Mae Silva would never believe that Deanie's disappearance wasn't her fault, and would never accept that there was nothing she could do to alter the past. For Mae Silva, every chance to love a child was another opportunity to get it right. She didn't consider the other children and grandchildren who had turned out well, responsible adults who raised decent kids, held down good jobs and never got into trouble. The only one she saw was Deanie—her one and incomprehensible failure as a mother.

* * * * *

Deanie sailed through the red light, then remembered she had seen it and slammed on the brakes. Unfortunately, she was in the middle of the intersection, but it was nearing midnight, and no one else was around to see this. She charged the accelerator again and bolted across the street, then settled down to a sedate forty-five, ten miles over the speed limit. She hated driving in the dark. No, she hated driving in places like this— little towns bypassed by old highways. These places depressed her.

This was the time for breathing exercises—if she could just remember them. Or maybe not. Maybe she should just keep driving—she had only a few miles left anyway. The car slowed to a crawl of five miles an hour while Deanie lost herself in the vision of the house she had grown up in. She hadn't seen it in almost thirty years—hard to believe. She felt her heart beat faster, her breath moving in little gasps and puffs. It would be the same, of course. Of course it would. Oh God she hoped not. But if it was different . . . She didn't want to think about it.

The steering wheel rocked beneath her fingers and she stared at it in horror. Suddenly aware of her surroundings, she pulled over to the side of the road, coming to a stop in front of a small cape sitting back from the street. She pressed the button and the window lowered. She had driven across the country on a whim, she told herself, but it was a lie. If she had gone through all the trouble of making a plane reservation, renting a car, the whole thing, she would never have made it to the airport. No, for her, better to get into the car and just go. Besides, she felt safe in this car.

In the silence she listened for signs that the world was still out there, was still familiar to her, was still her place. The street lamp ahead of her dimmed and went off and another farther down blinked and grew brighter. The shadows seemed to slide along after the light, seeking out new corners to rest in, new shapes to distort. Deanie felt a chill though it was hot enough for her to wish she had turned on the air conditioning. But she wouldn't. If she was going back, she was going all the way back—she'd remember it all. She pulled at the placket on her blouse, waving it to circulate the air. She moved against the seat and felt the back of her shirt pull away from the leather.

If she focused on driving, just paying attention to the speed limit, the road, where she was going, she could get to her parents' house by two o'clock. They might be up, but probably not. They were early risers, and of course early to bed. She wondered if the back door would be open—unlocked, as they had always left it when she was a girl. The first time she had come home late from a party, staying out without permission, and had tried to climb in through a window opening onto the back porch, she had found her mother sitting at the kitchen table, her head resting on her arms as she watched Deanie struggle to get over the sill. She clambered over the radiator and tried to land quietly on the bare floor.

"Shhh. You'll wake your father." Her mother sat up, her bathrobe hanging open over a flannel nightgown. Deanie could only stare at her.

"You're such a smart girl. Why are you doing this?" Her mother pushed herself away from the table. "You want to sneak around? You want to throw away this good name your father gave you? You not want to be a Silva? Okay. You're smart. You're a college girl. Use the back door. It is always open—for your sister." And with that, her mother struggled to her feet and went back to bed.

Deanie hadn't dared move. She couldn't believe what she had heard. She kept waiting for her mother to return with the scolding Deanie had expected—that no decent girl stayed out late at night and then crawled in through a window. How would it look if people found out? How would it look if her brother Joe's bosses found out? He could lose his job, a good job, a policeman's job. "Do you want people to think he comes from a bad family?" She had heard her mother say this again and again until she couldn't stand to hear it anymore, as though she, Deanie, could single-handedly ruin her brother's life.

That night, so long ago, Deanie had listened in the dark for the familiar sound of someone sitting on an old mattress, the creaking of springs sinking too close to the wood frame, a soft voice, more creaking, and then silence. She got up and walked through the kitchen and tried the back door. It was unlocked.

She had forgotten about her sister Rosalie, fifth in the line of seven of them, the pretty one who had married the jerk, as the others called him. Only he was more than a jerk. Deanie quietly turned the knob and pulled open the door, checked the lock, and just as quietly shut it again.

Her hand was turning and twisting on the steering wheel, as though this were the lock and she could unlock the past, experience it again, and this time get it right. A car drove by, startling her into the present. When she had called her mother, telling her that this time, this year, she really would be there for the family summer picnic, she waited for the words of delight and warmth, but there was only silence.

"Yes, Deanie, we hope so," her mother said. And in that note of resignation and doubt came a pain Deanie didn't know she was capable of feeling; in that moment she gave her word.

"I will be there, Mae. This time I will be there." She didn't ask her mother to believe her, because she knew this time she would not disappoint her. That must have been what kept her going over the last few weeks, when she bought a new suitcase, something simple and plain, not her usual style, and told her colleagues that she did indeed have a family, a rather large one too. She tried not to think about all the relatives in too much detail for fear she'd panic and back out, and yet, no matter how tense or anxious she became, she knew that this time she would see it through. Something was pulling her back to that old city south of Boston. She would see them all.

She tried not to think about that too. What would they think of her this time? An uncle once whispered to her father that perhaps, just maybe—no, no reason to think so, but maybe—she wasn't quite right in the head. Maybe she had one of those diseases. No? Okay, not possible, he had agreed, and left the subject alone. But Deanie hadn't. She had wondered. What was wrong with her? What made her so different from the others? She was too old to care anymore—a woman in her fifties. But that question, that wondering, was part of her identity.

A well-meaning therapist had suggested suppressed memories, but Deanie had laughed, then scowled at the suggestions proffered. She was well adjusted sexually,

probably too well adjusted. Well adjusted and still Catholic at heart. No, she had no suppressed memories that fit her neuroses. And so, in the end, she had admitted that perhaps Uncle Serge was right. She was sick in the head. She hoped he wasn't going to be there this year.

Why oh why had she agreed to this visit?

Two

Early Friday Morning

It was foolish to believe in new beginnings, as though the clean air of sunrise could sweep away the bumblings, weaknesses, malice, errors of previous days, erasing them from both memory and time spent, leaving nothing but the promise of what a man wanted to be and could be if he carried no baggage but hope. Joe believed in new beginnings, but only when they followed on a closing of the past, a turn to a new direction knowing that the old one had been a failure, or worse. He didn't believe life could go on without that belief and hope—some could not breathe without the dream of being able to make a new beginning. But he wasn't one to believe that hope could erase the past.

Joe paused inside the screen door watching his father leaning forward in the old garden chair as he peered through the railings. Joe knew what he was thinking—where he would put the tomatoes next year, the strawberries, the pole beans. Every year he moved the plants a little bit here, a little bit there, thinking he could catch more sun with each move. He never stopped believing that there was a perfect location for each crop, and with determination and persistence, he would find it. Through the years he had cajoled a little more land from the downstairs neighbor, a little more from the abutters in the back, a negotiation that went on for years until an agreement was sealed with a bushel of eggplant, their purple skin so luscious and beautiful that Joe wasn't surprised when he saw his father kiss each one as he snapped the stem from the plant and laid it in a cardboard box. The older Joe's father got, the more he lived for his garden. Sometimes, near the end of the season, his conversation narrowed to the line of late planted lettuce, the last few tomatoes, the Brussels sprouts that might make it to December. Joe couldn't drag him away, and no one else even tried.

"You're there," the old man said. "I know you are." He spoke barely above a whisper. Joe looked down, as though to gather thought and strength, and pushed open the door before stepping onto the porch and easing the door shut behind him. It was barely eight-thirty, and Joe's mother was helping Gwen and Jennie get settled.

Joe lowered himself into the other chair, the one, he knew, that his mother had always used when taking a break while something was rising or cooking in the oven. For as long as he could remember she would step onto the porch and gaze over the back garden, along the driveway, into other yards, her mind on whatever she was cooking. Sometimes she didn't even notice a neighbor's wave, and other times she calmly watched a stealthy rabbit nibble through a row of beets. Joe's father shifted in his chair, now leaning closer to Joe.

"Three days is a long time," Joe said.

"You haven't anything to say to each other?" Joe's father continued to stare at the garden. "All those times I had to shut you kids up for supper." He shook his head and leaned back, resting his head against a thin pillow. He let his head fall sideways until he was looking directly at Joe.

"It's a long time," Joe said.

"Gives your mother time to fall in love with Gwen," the old man said.

"Three days, Pae."

"Yes." The old man closed his eyes and sighed. His face grew flaccid. Joe waited. "Deanie came in last night." His eyes opened, and Joe could see how watery and tired they were.

"Must have been late," Joe said.

The old man laughed, a quiet, almost resentful sound. "She has not changed. She tells her mother she is different now, but she has not changed." He ran his hand over his face as though trying to wipe away the pain. Joe reached out and took his hand.

"Angela has another grandchild," the old man said. "She sends me photos, as if they're my own and Paulo never died." He pushed himself up in his chair. "And Zaira is coming. And Bernardo will bring his mother. Lucia thinks she must work all the time, but my grandson will bring her. And Rosalie has promised to come with all three girls. Beautiful they are. How could an old fart like me have such beautiful grandchildren and great-grandchildren?" He turned to Joe with a look of amazement on his face, but then he sighed and looked away. "My sister and her family."

"How is Tia's family these days?" Joe rarely saw his cousins anymore, only at family events. He knew it was odd, or at least that others thought it was odd, that he rarely visited to keep up with everyone. But he had been so consistent in his absences over the years that his other relatives had finally stopped asking about why they saw so little of him.

The old man shrugged. He began to list the cousins and the recent changes—weddings, births, first communions, deaths. "You didn't come, did you?" The old man turned to study Joe, then, resigned, settled back in his chair.

"One wedding per cousin is enough. Otherwise I'd be down here all the time." Joe said.

"Your mother would like that." The old man sighed.

Joe was used to this conversation. Whenever he visited, or called, he heard the same thing. The litany of his siblings—how they were, who was coming (and that was always the same)—how beautiful the girls were. It never changed, including what was left out. That was perhaps the most painful part of all, but Joe had accepted it over the years, and he no longer argued or tried to fathom his father's thinking.

Suddenly his father reached over and gripped the chair arm. "You think I've forgotten, don't you? You think so, yes?" He shook his head in quick, sharp jerks. "I haven't." He stared hard at Joe, his eyes burning and widening with each passing second. "I have heard from Gino." As he delivered himself of this information, he fell back into his chair, his breath quickening. "He called me. But I heard about Deanie too."

Joe leaned forward barely noticeably so as not to distract his father. No one had heard from Gino, not really, in years, and on one level none of his family expected to really hear from Gino ever again. When he had left, he had departed with such bitterness and confusion that it almost seemed better that he go. First the news was that he was dead, then he was alive. But he had been gone for years and years, and now, no longer a teenager, no longer a wild young man, he had at long last reached out.

"Tell me what happened," Joe said.

"Yes," the old man nodded. "I tell you. Because you have to fix this once and for all." The old man frowned and began to beat his fist gently on the chair arm, as though keeping time with thoughts in his head, a silent rhythm only he could hear. Joe could feel the energy growing in him. The old man's head nodded as though in agreement with his quickening thoughts.

"Pae?" Joe laid his hand gently on his father's arm.

"Yes, I tell you." The old man turned to him, leaning closer. "You go see Christina. Yes, yes, I know. So many years. And you loved her once—you almost married her. But she is still alive. In the nursing home she listens with her eyes and she smiles. She gives so much happiness to her mother. If you go, her mother will be pleased, and Christina too."

Joe cringed. Here it was again, the love that had died, but awkwardly, inconveniently, making everyone sad and uncomfortable. "That may not be a good idea, Pae."

"I promised Christina's mother. She has always liked you. Such a good woman, Mrs. Perreira. She doesn't blame you." He raised his hand as though he expected an objection. "Just go. You should visit her." The old man gave Joe the look of a captain, not a father, and Joe felt a flicker of his youth. "Two years it has taken me." He whispered as though he were talking to himself.

"Two years to do what?"

The old man studied Joe, and Joe felt the power of his look as he had felt it when a boy. It had never been unkind or hostile or threatening, but always it had penetrated him. "Your cousin tell me that Gino tried to kill himself so many years ago, and all he does now is drink. He lives out in some place where he finds easy work, days and days from here, but he perhaps will come too."

"Gino? Coming home?" At that moment Joe first felt the wonder that perhaps his father was no longer the rational, hard thinking man he had always been. First, Gino, now Christina. It didn't make sense. His father was digging up the past as though whatever had happened had occurred only days ago and could be worked out now. "How do you know this? Why is he telling you these stories now? You don't know if you can believe him."

"Your cousin knows how I feel and he wants me to know about Gino, how he is feeling so guilty about things."

"What things?"

"He's not telling me, but I guess. I can guess and so can you."

Joe tried to take this in. The tragic turn of Christina's life had always been just that—a tragic turn. At least that was how Joe had seen it. He couldn't accept guilt for any part of it just because of the timing of their break-up, and he had never believed that anyone else could be held accountable. Things happened. And things that had happened forty years ago should be left. And now someone was passing on old rumors and half-truths, mindless gossip that should have been buried and abandoned years ago.

"There's nothing here, Pae." Joe knew if he didn't catch this fly ball the entire family would stampede onto the field to argue with the umpire.

His father tipped his head to one side and studied him, the hint of a smile poking at his lips. "I want to know. I want to know about Gino. You can find out. Do it. For me." He nodded twice, then pushed himself out of the chair. Joe rose with him.

"Pae, that was forty years ago. And I can't dig into other people's lives." He rested his hand on his father's shoulder, feeling the iron of muscle beneath the soft cotton fabric worn smooth by years of washing and ironing. "Christina's life is sad but it is her life. God takes what he wants and we must accept it. You taught us that."

"Maybe it wasn't God," the old man said, turning away.

* * * * *

"So all I have to do is take the picture and then I send it to my brother." Jennie held out her new iPhone and steadied it about a foot from her face, then pressed a button. "See?" She tipped the phone towards the other girl leaning over to stare at the image. "Not that I bother sending things to Philip."

"My older brothers are the same," the other girl said. "Wicked dumb."

"Oh, he's not so bad," Jennie said, rising to her brother's defense. "He just thinks my pictures are stupid." She began to type in a message on the keyboard. "Which one is your mom?"

"My mom is the oldest girl, and now the oldest, after Tio Paulo died. I never knew him. Tio Jose is next."

"Okay. Is that why you're called Sarah? After your mother?"

Sarah nodded, and Jennie went on typing.

"Okay, he's got it." She read the reply, then slipped the phone into her pocket. "He got out of coming but Joe wouldn't let me stay with my friend overnight because her parents are away."

Sarah shied away and her eyes opened wide. "You even asked him?"

"Well, yeah. Duh!" Jennie frowned and studied her new friend. "Wouldn't you?"

"I wouldn't bother. Not in my family. My mom would go into shock if I asked to do something like that, and my grandmother would come over and sit down and wail about where had she gone wrong and did I know how my grandfather would feel, and my dad would come into the kitchen and look confused and wander off looking for my mom because he doesn't get my mom's family. My mom says it's because he's Irish and the Irish don't talk about things. They just hunker down and hope to get through it."

"Your family's weird."

"Totally."

They walked on down the sidewalk, saw a break in the traffic, and darted across the street and into a small park in the middle of the block. On the opposite side was a drugstore, and they pushed open the door and went in. The shelves were wooden and shiny from years of cleaning, and they could easily see the grain for the lack of inventory. Along the top shelves stood old stuffed animals that no one had thought to buy when they were new, so they sat waiting for someone to need something for a last minute gift, even though in this neighborhood that was unlikely. On the lower shelves a single cereal box stood where a dozen might be expected, cans of tomato soup were lined up four deep, and two types of crackers were arranged gracefully along the depth of the shelf.

"Mom wants a pack of the generic," Sarah said to the old man behind the counter. He looked up from the newspaper he was holding open before him, the times according to O Mundo, and gave the girl a reproachful look.

"How many times I tell your mother I can not do this," he said.

"I know, Mr. Vida, and you know I tell her she shouldn't smoke too." She grimaced again. "But it's all the family together and she's so worried about my granddad." Sarah leaned over plaintively. "Can I just take one pack and tell her how much it upsets you?"

"What is it God gives you girls in this world? How is it you all know how to look at a man like that?" He tossed the paper onto the counter and spun around on the stool until he faced the glass-enclosed cases behind him. He slid open the old door and reached in for a pack of cigarettes. "Your mother was such a sweet girl. I knew her when she was in school, just before my parents bought this place and I came to work here on the weekends. I had my other job, but I came and helped out here too. Did you know that?"

"I don't think I did, Mr. Vida." Sarah handed over a ten-dollar bill and took the cigarettes. "But I'll tell my mom you remember her, okay?"

"Such a good family. You tell her I remember you all." Mr. Vida placed the change on the counter, gathered up his newspaper and settled himself on his stool again. "And your father. Such a good man." He gave the newspaper a shake and disappeared behind it.

"I didn't think you could buy cigarettes at our age," Jennie said when they were once again on the sidewalk.

Sarah shrugged as she stuffed the pack into her purse. "Last week he told me I was too young because I wasn't yet sixteen."

"What?" Jennie stopped short on the curb.

"The laws have changed so much in his lifetime that I don't think he knows what they are anymore. He's getting kind of old. Every time I come in for something he tells me he remembers my mom, but sometimes he calls her Deanie and sometimes Rosalie and sometimes Angela, which is my great-grandmother's name."

Jennie laughed and they darted back across the street.

"If I had to go through that every week I wouldn't stop laughing," Jennie said as they walked through the park.

"I don't have to go through it every week," Sarah said. "I only drop by once in a while. My mom comes every week, and Aunt Lucia does too, and Aunt Rosalie once a month or so, but she calls a lot. They gave her a cell phone—I think her husband is really tight with money and he complains about the telephone bills. That's weird in our family. They're always on the phone."

"So you guys don't have these reunions all the time?"

Sarah pulled a face and shook her head. "We don't need to. We see each other all the time anyway."

"Then why now?" Jennie frowned as she looked over at the double decker on the other side of the street. This was not what she had expected. The first time she had visited, she knew how large Joe's family was and fancifully had assumed the house would be comparable in size—perhaps a grand Victorian or an old colonial with tons of little rooms. When Joe had pulled up in front of the double decker she had blurted out, But this can't be it. Where did you all sleep? She felt awful—she wouldn't hurt Joe's feelings for the world—but she decided that he mustn't have heard her because he turned around and smiled and told her it was a good place to raise kids. She still couldn't understand where they put seven kids—except in the attic. Wasn't that illegal? Maybe one of the relatives was a really good lawyer and bribed the building inspector or someone. "Is there a lawyer in your family?"

"No." Sarah looked confused. "I don't think this reunion is because someone's in trouble. I think it has to do with how old my grandfather is now. Avô is ninety something. And Avó, my grandmother, is probably close to that. Mom said he wants things settled. You know how old people are."

"No, I don't. I don't really have grandparents, not like you do. What things do they want to settle?"

Sarah shrugged. "Dunno. But he's Avô and if he wants something, everyone jumps. So here we all are, even Tio Jose."

"And that's unusual?"

"My dad calls him the one who got away. Come on." Sarah tapped Jennie's arm and they darted through the traffic back to the house.

* * * * *

Joe could smell the coffee and bacon down in the back yard. It had been the same every morning of his childhood. Stacked by the platters of eggs and grilled tomatoes and peppers and onions were bowls of fresh fruit and baskets of toast and muffins, but none of that could compete with the fragrance of coffee followed by the smell of bacon. Every morning of his young life had been defined by the smells of the hot meal that waited for him and his brothers and sisters while they jockeyed for the one bathroom, grabbed towels out of each other's arms, and clattered down the stairs from the sleeping attic above. Where did they all sit, he wondered? How did his parents find room for them all?

That was what he missed, he realized. For all his longing to move into the larger world, discover corners he never thought about, he missed the sheer physicality of his family, the bumping of shoulders as they hurried down the hallway or up the stairs, the jostling on the porch, the easy toss of an arm over a shoulder. They'd been like pups in a basket all their lives growing up, and now they were apart and it felt unnatural, alien. Zaira's first grandson, barely ten years old, came running down the stairs from the back porch and threw himself at Joe, who wrapped his arms around him and tussled him across the ground.

"Avó has everything set out. She's looking for you," the boy said.

Joe swung the boy up the steps and followed behind. The first floor of the double decker belonged to a longstanding friend, a now elderly couple who had been young when Joe was a teenager, and still considered themselves the caretakers for Joe's parents. It was hard to tell who needed the more help, Mr. Morton or Joe's father, but they bantered about who needed what, who was the most incapacitated by age, and who should call the taxi to take them to the Portuguese American Club. Joe rapped on the open back door and called out hello as he passed by and on up the stairs.

"Jose, Jose, Jose!" A woman came towards Joe with open arms and kissed him on both cheeks when he reached the upstairs porch. "Why out so early? Gwen won't tell me anything."

"Stop pumping her for information, Lucia." He kissed his younger sister and told her she looked beautiful. And she did— her thick black hair curled around her strong face and throat, her wide-set eyes warm and mischievous, her facial bones sturdy. She would always look strong.

"She has you well trained, that Gwen, if you say such things now." Lucia slapped him on the back and went off to find a chair on the porch. "I'm eating out here. I'm too old for the pandemonium of our kitchen. You should go in and rescue Gwen before she understands what she's seeing."

Good advice, thought Joe, as he pulled open the screen door. But too late, he knew, when he saw Gwen seated at the dining table to his father's left. In front of him was arrayed his breakfast, a plate of eggs, a separate plate of bacon, toast buttered with a small dollop of peach jam nearby, and his mother holding a plate of browned potatoes spooning them gently onto his plate. He tasted each morsel and frowned, deciding if it was cooked properly or not, then looked at each plate in turn.

"My berries. Where are my berries?" he said.

"Ooh," the old woman said and walked back into the kitchen.

"Bon dia, Pae," Joe said, taking a seat. He reached for a large plate of scrambled eggs and began to serve himself. He offered Gwen what he hoped was a natural smile but he knew she was calculating just what she was going to say to him and he had no answer. Yes, he wanted to say, my nearly ninety-year-old mother waits on my father hand and foot. She'd cut up his meat for him if he asked.

"You have a good walk?" his father said. "I am having breakfast with Gwen." He gave Gwen an uncertain look as if unsure if this was allowed, and then looked down at his plate, still skeptical of his meal. His wife returned with a bowl of berries and a pitcher of cream, and set both beside his plate. He didn't acknowledge either the food or the delivery, just glanced at the bowl, nodded to himself, and picked up his fork again.

"Bernardo has a girl friend," Joe's mother said.

"What does he care about Bernardo's girlfriend," the old man said. "He has important things to think about."

"What things? He is resting this weekend. He is here for relaxation, to see his family. Bernardo is his nephew. He should be happy for him."

"And I am, Mae, I am. I'll have to ask Bernardo about her."

"Bernard," the old woman said. "Bernard he is." She gave a little snort and left the room.

"Am I the last one in for breakfast?" Joe asked Gwen.

"I'm not sure," Gwen said, glancing at the old man. "Your sister Zaira was here, with her daughter Sarah, who's just Jennie's age. I think they went off for a walk together."

"Sarah's a good girl. She'll be good company for Jennie."

"And I met Lucia and her husband, Larry, I think he said."

"Yes, Larry. I didn't see him out on the porch but he'll be back."

"I'm not going to keep all these people straight," Gwen said, resting her fork on her plate. "But then maybe I'll just eat," she said looking down.

"Yes, yes, you eat." The old man waved his fork at her and the plates scattered across the center of the table.

"Don't worry, Pae, she has a great appetite," Joe said. "Ouch!" He leaned down to massage his shin where Gwen kicked him.

"And Lucia said Rosalie was coming over later," Gwen said with a tight smile. "Her husband is off doing something."

"Ah," the old man said and frowned. Gwen looked at Joe, who barely perceptibly shook his head.

"When are you going to see Christina?" the old man asked, leaning towards Joe.

"When it's time, Pae, when it's time."

"It's time. Now it is time." The old man grew fierce and pounded his fist on the table, then his expression collapsed into a heart-rending appeal. "You must do this."

"I'll do what I can, Pae. I promise."

Joe's father stared at him for a moment, then grunted. Apparently satisfied, he again looked over his breakfast, decided he had had enough and pushed back his chair. "I am going for a walk. Mr. Morton needs the exercise." And with that he levered himself up from the chair and left the room. Joe could hear him talking to his mother in the kitchen, before he went out onto the porch and down the stairs.

"Who's Christina?" Gwen asked.

* * * * *

An hour later Joe pressed down on the gas pedal and the jeep roared up the hill and veered right onto a side street. Walking in this area was certainly good for the lungs, but he'd rather drive—his days of running up and down hills to see friends or get to school were long gone and not at all missed. He slowed at the upcoming intersection, checked the traffic on the crossroads, and continued on. It was a glorious day—the sky clear and sparkling, the air fresh as though after a rain, the city quiet. It was vacation time—with families gone to the mountains or the Cape—and the city was the better for it, with quieter streets and slower traffic. He turned another corner and pulled onto a road heading into the suburbs.

Just how long, he wondered, could he avoid looking over at Gwen, her back partly against the door so she could look straight at him. He should have known his parents were up to something. His father had never been to a reunion in his life—his most ordinary day was filled with visits from his children, grandchildren, cousins, friends. He had never spent a day away from his family except during World War II, and even then he wrote something—a letter, a postcard, a scrap of paper shoved into a tattered envelope—every day. Joe should have known. He glanced over at Gwen and started to smile.

"I'm glad it's funny," she said, "I was beginning to get worried."

"You're not the sarcastic type," Joe said.

"Maybe I've never been tested, never been given the opportunity to show what I can do." She crossed her arms and continued to study him. He smiled at her again and almost laughed.

"You'll never be the sarcastic type. You're much too curious to be that alienated."

"Are you going to tell me who this person is?"

"I'm surprised I never did." He slowed as he came to the highway, moved into traffic, and coasted to the next exit. The landscape became pastoral, with small houses clustered at bends in the road and broad and deep fields of strawberries, corn, and other crops stretching off toward the low hills.

"The woman I was expected to marry." Joe let the words hang in the air. They sounded strange even to him, even though they had flickered through his memory off and on during the years. When the magnitude of the loss for Christina and her family first became clear to him, he had tried to feel guilty, to accept that he must have had some role in the tragedy, but beyond feeling a deep and painful sympathy for Christina and the Perreiras, he couldn't find it in himself to feel anything more.

He had loved her, honestly, but mostly like a young man who wanted a girlfriend and was in awe of anyone both pretty and generous with her attentions. When they went out on dates with others he was eager to show off a new behavior, shepherding Christina through crowds of their friends who now seemed like nothing more than rowdy strangers. She was sweet and uncomplicated and the better he understood that, the more he realized he was becoming a different person, one who was moving on, following a long-held dream of another life, and she was staying the same. When they parted, he thought it was amicable and easy, closing the door on a friendship for which little feeling remained, an end to his old way of life in favor of the new. But then he decided that the old way must have had a stronger hold on him than he realized because years later, when Gwen came along, he felt at once how deeply he missed family life.

"Oh." Gwen leaned against the seat, then slid around facing forward. She tugged her skirt into place and turned to the passing view.

"Perhaps expected is too strong. More like 'assumed' I would marry," Joe said. "Either way, there were expectations, assumptions. And disappointments."

"How long ago was that?"

"I was a teenager, going off to Northeastern." He waited, listening to the engine hum.

"Should I be jealous?"

Joe pulled up to a stop sign and turned to look at her. It was her earnestness that amused him—no possessiveness, just wondering what the situation was. He shook his head. "She was a lovely girl but I had no interest in marrying her and settling into my parents' world. After we split up, a few weeks, maybe less, she had a terrible accident."

"What sort of accident?" Gwen leaned toward him, more curious now than concerned.

"She almost drowned in the bathtub."

"How can you drown in a bathtub?" Gwen wrinkled her forehead, squeezed her eyes in thought.

"You can drown in a puddle, Gwen. You only need enough water to block the air passages." He pulled onto the road and drove along at a slow pace watching the passing houses. "What you mean," he continued, in a softer voice, " is why didn't she climb out or get help. It was one of those freak things that happen more than we want to believe." He slowed the car. "Here it is." He hit the blinker and the car turned left onto a wide entryway, past a sign announcing a private nursing home. He drove to the side of the building and pulled into a space, put the car in park and shut off the engine. The silence settled onto them and Joe let his hands rest on the steering wheel.

"This is a nursing home, Joe. I don't mean to state the obvious, but why are we here?"

"Christina lives here, has since the accident." Joe pushed open the door. "Her family comes to see her every day. It's sort of a vigil, for her mother at least. Her father has never come—can't face it, I suppose. His wife talks about visiting Christina as though it were the most ordinary thing in the world, and her husband sits and listens and never says a word. I've never even seen him flinch. Sometimes when my father is there, the two of them sit there like concrete—not so much as a twitch." He opened the car door but didn't get out.

"And you visit her too?" Gwen said, looking confused.

Joe shook his head. "No, not me. After the first family visit, when she was in a coma and no one thought she'd recover, I saw her maybe once, twice. And that was well over forty years ago."

She watched his nostrils flare and wondered what he wasn't telling her. She was one to let people keep their secrets until they were ready to unload them—she thought there was nothing worse than asking someone to confide in you, thinking it would make things easier for them, and getting loaded down with a horrific story you wished you'd never heard. But this was Joe. What could be so bad? "Was the family upset by something? Was there something else?"

"Upset?" Joe rubbed his hand over the steering wheel while he thought about this. "There were a few hints that the accident wasn't an accident, that our breaking up had pushed her to try suicide."

"Oh, Joe!" Gwen cringed, feeling her shoulders stiffen as she leaned in protectively.

"It was nonsense. Christina was a good Catholic—a really good Catholic."

"But it must have hurt."

"People will say a lot of things when they're in unbearable pain or confused or desperate for a reason." He relaxed. "But no one in my family seemed to think I owed her anything—it was just a sad and terrible accident."

"So why now?"

Joe waited so long to answer that Gwen wondered if he had heard her, but of course he had—he was barely two feet away. "I

don't know," Joe said. "Pae thinks there's something we don't
know about her accident and he wants me to look into it." He
leaned back against the seat, his eyes closed. "He's old, Gwen. I
think—what goes on in his mind I think doesn't always make
sense. But he's old and he's my father, so I'm here. You don't
have to come in," he said, sitting up.

"I don't mind." Gwen opened the door and paused. "Unless
you'd rather I didn't."

They walked into the one-story nursing home, three wings
extending off from a central hall. Joe approached a reception
desk for directions. "This way," he said and headed down a
hallway. A moment later, he paused at an open doorway and
looked in.

"Give me a minute." He nodded to Gwen and walked into
the room. An older woman rose with her arms outstretched and
came toward him.

"Jose, Jose! You are so good to come." She took his face in
her hands and kissed him on both cheeks, then turned to stand
beside him, slipping her arm through his. "Look at her." She
watched him as he did so. "Come, sit here." She led him to a
chair by the bedside and pulled up another one for herself.
Through the doorway Gwen could see a figure lying in the
hospital bed, in the first bay, still and thin, a thick black braid
lying across her shoulder.

"Is she not beautiful still, Jose?" the woman asked.

"She is still beautiful, Mrs. Perreira, very beautiful." Joe
turned to the mother as he spoke, watching her as she gazed on
her daughter. He had seen such devotion when he was still living
at home, the mothers who stood vigil at the bedside of a dying
relative, a sick child, but he had never seen anything like this—
Mrs. Perreira had stayed at Christina's side for decades. It had
taken more than an iron will to continue day after day, watching
her daughter's limbs shrivel and twist, her skin grow blotchy, her
hair dull. But she was obviously loved and cared for—her head
resting on brightly flowered sheets and a yellow blanket
covering her body.

The old woman didn't bother to look at Joe—she couldn't
stop looking at her daughter. She rearranged the braid,
straightened the sheet and blanket; she settled back in her chair
as if to study her handiwork. Then, to Joe's surprise, she turned
in her chair and began to study him.

"A long time, yes?"

"Yes, a long time," Joe agreed.

"Is it true Gino is coming home?" Her delicate smile faded ever so slightly, leaving Joe wondering if it had really been there, and her dark eyes grew sharp.

"I've heard the same thing, but I don't know." Joe shifted in his chair—he was already getting restless. Sitting motionless beside Christina was harder than he imagined it would be, though he hadn't expected it to be easy. Still, he knew Mrs. Perreira was watching him, so he shoved back the chair a few inches and tried to get a better look at Christina. What he saw both surprised and unsettled him.

As he looked more closely, he noticed that Christina's skin was as pale as he always remembered it—but now it was like light shining through a window at night, thin, tinged with yellow. Her hair was black but now with streaks of gray, her limbs thin and her flesh flaccid despite what he knew were regular visits from a physical therapist. But the most startling moment was when his eyes met hers—she was looking straight at him, with a half smile on her lips, as though she couldn't control them very well. He found himself saying a soft hello.

"She hears you, she does," the old woman said. She grew animated then and Joe listened to her talk to Christina about their visitor, what Joe was doing now, how well he looked—didn't she agree?—and then the upcoming festivities. As Mrs. Perreira rattled on, Joe stood up and stretched, staring down at the bed, where once in a while a pale sickly face turned a fraction of an inch to gaze up at him. He let himself look into those eyes, but he couldn't decide if she was really there, if the old Christina knew who she was looking at.

Joe stepped away from the bed and walked to the window, looked out at the parking lot and up at the crystal blue sky. On a small night table, the only surface not littered with medical equipment, stood a large frame holding a photograph. Joe picked it up. The photo had been trimmed along the left-hand edge, cutting out a vertical row of guests at one of the family picnics several years ago.

The photograph wasn't torn—it had been carefully trimmed, so that some persons were left and others had been cut out. The scissors had turned and snipped carefully, taking away several familiar faces. Joe studied the rest of the photograph, trying to reconstruct in his mind who should have been there. Christina was in the bottom left-hand corner, but whoever had been standing behind her was missing.

He replaced the photograph on the table and looked up to see Mrs. Perreira watching him. Her expression was not friendly.

* * * * *

The cream-colored doorframe captured Joe and Mrs. Perreira leaning toward the inert figure in the hospital bed, like an image frozen in one board of a triptych; in front of Gwen was the long hall with the bustling activity of a nurses' station and a crowd of old women in wheel chairs maneuvering around each other. To her right was another doorway framing the image of a grandmother holding a child on her knee, a younger woman standing off to the side. Here it all was, thought Gwen, the passages of our lives as we prefer not to see them—the constant reminders of mortality and limited time, too little time for all we want to do. This seemed to be the theme of the weekend, she thought—with Joe's father hinting darkly about the need for him to have all his children around him, as though he were going to announce the end of his days, with date and time. And Joe's mother acting like she was bracing herself for some onslaught, something more than children and spouses and grandchildren and cousins and half the neighborhood showing up to eat in the backyard. There were so many undercurrents in this family, Gwen thought, she might as well crawl into bed and stay there until the storms were over.

She turned back to Christina's room, and suddenly felt like a voyeur, an intruder, and she felt ashamed. She had no reason to expect Joe to tell her about his previous girlfriends—she'd never asked, not because she didn't want to know but because she didn't want to look back on her own past. She didn't want to open too many creaky old doors. But here she was, staring through one of Joe's.

Gwen backed away out of sight of the people in the room, then turned and walked to the entry area, a large hall where people could gather.

Gwen pushed the door open and stepped onto the terrace and took a deep breath of fresh air. The burden that had settled on her lifted and she felt shamelessly relieved to be out of there. It unnerved her to see someone Joe's age lying so near death and yet living on year after year, the carefully controlled anguish in the mother as she found ways to make her daughter more comfortable, at least in her own mind, the futility of it all. Christina was never coming back, the tubes in her arms and stomach and throat told Gwen that.

An old man sitting in a wheel chair and wearing a cloth cap cocked to one side looked her up and down and tapped his cane on the flagstone. "Join me," he said. "Not often a pretty girl comes here without an old someone attached to her arm." He grinned and Gwen, startled out of her disorientation, smiled back. She pulled up a white plastic chair and sat down in the sun. She noticed that the nursing home was positioned so that sun would hit the entryway almost throughout the day—a kind designer did this, she thought, and gave in to the feeling of relief and delight.

"You didn't come to check the place out for someone?" the old man asked.

Gwen shook her head. "I came with a friend to see someone he knows."

The old man nodded. "Jose Silva." He continued to nod. "He looks like his father as a young man. Christina Perreira?" Gwen nodded, growing embarrassed. "Sad, sad, sad."

"So I've heard." Gwen began to look around for something to bring to the conversation—the garden perhaps, or the traffic she could hear farther away.

"I think she's waiting for the truth to come out before she dies," he said.

"What?" Gwen swung around to look at him. Her heart skipped a beat and she could feel herself growing warm. "What do you mean?" Since arriving with Joe that morning, she'd had the feeling that she had been led into something far beyond a family reunion, and even Joe had not denied that things felt odd.

"The truth. The story isn't finished," he said. "It's time to figure it out. He's a good cop, isn't he?" The old man leaned forward, spittle filling the corners of his mouth.

"What is it that's unfinished?"

"Do you know the story?"

Gwen shook her head.

The old man leaned back in his chair and smiled, the satisfied smile of a man who holds the key to a mystery and will not give it up easily. "You should know this—especially if you're walking out with someone from that family. I will tell you."

Gwen felt a frisson of disgust—how dare he imply something distasteful about Joe's family. She closed her eyes and tried to calm herself—the strain of the first day of this visit was already making her feel volatile. "I heard she drowned almost."

"She did—almost. And that's the question."

"Someone saved her?"

"Ah, that's the question." He nodded and his smile took on an unpleasant cast. "Gino found her and called the police." He paused. "That's what he said."

"Oh. Gino? That's Joe's younger brother, isn't it?" Gwen shied away from the look in the old man's eyes. "If that's what he said he was doing then I'm sure he was. And the police seem to have believed him." This sounded lame even to her and she wondered how gracefully she could back out of this conversation.

"He found her and called the police—after several minutes." He leaned forward again and whispered. "You have to wonder why, don't you?"

"No, I don't. Maybe he was giving her CPR," Gwen said. She was beginning to feel a revulsion for this old man, for the way he relished telling her the story, planting his suspicions, implying guilt and evil. He was smarmy and seedy at once. And she disliked herself for listening to it, for feeling those seeds of curiosity and doubt taking root in her when she should have stood up and walked away. She knew she should get up and tell him he was a distasteful old man spreading rumors because he was bored and lonely and resented the way his life was ending, but she knew she wouldn't. She was much too polite for that.

"I'm sure if there was anything wrong, the police would have figured it out."

"Maybe." The old man shrugged and gave her a look that made her skin shiver. "Lots of Silvas around here—lots of connections. Better for him to get away than hang around—just in case we get a new police chief or something. I was working for the city back then." His face grew dark, his lips an arc of contempt, his words a funnel for all the resentments of a lifetime. Gwen stood up and pushed the chair away, catching it before it fell over and dragging it back to the brick wall, out of the way of people coming in or going out. She would not listen to him anymore, not let him plant his suspicions about Joe's family in her. If there was something wrong, Joe would have told her—she was sure of it.

Three

Later Friday Morning

Deanie pulled a sweater out of her suitcase, then a t-shirt, and then she began ripping clothes out of her bag, muttering, "Where is it? Where is it? I put it in here. It has to be here." She was almost to the bottom of her suitcase when her older sister Lucia came up behind her and put her arms around her, holding her still. Deanie froze for a few seconds, rigid and unfeeling, then suddenly grabbed at her sister's arms and pushed her away. Lucia stood in the same spot, stiff, uncertain what to do for several minutes before she walked around in front of Deanie.

"Sit down, Deanie," Lucia said, pushing away the scattered clothes. She patted the bedspread, and the younger woman lowered herself to the bed.

"I look crazy, don't I? You think I'm crazy, don't you?" Deanie hunched her shoulders and stared hard at the floor.

Lucia shook her head and held her sister's hands in hers. "You were brave to come. I can see that. I don't know why, but I can see it took courage." She squeezed her younger sister's hands. "We've all missed you so much."

Deanie sought Lucia's face and then her eyes—yes, she thought, she means it. She understands what's happening to me even if I don't. "I shouldn't have come."

"Why not? It means so much to Pae—you know that. He's an old man, Deanie. If he is making such a big thing about having us all here formally together, then we have to do it. Something is troubling him and he wants to settle it."

"Is he dying?" Deanie's voice was suddenly higher and thin, the words catching in her throat. This was insane. What was happening to her? Two days ago she had everything—money in

46

the bank, a solid reputation in her work—no one tried to put anything over on her—and men any time she wanted. She might be over fifty, but the young ones couldn't compete with what she had to offer. But the minute she crossed the state line—it all went wrong. She had to get a grip. "I shouldn't have come. I don't belong here. If he's sick, I'll just make it worse. Hell, for years I thought he was dead and just no one put it into the papers, so I didn't know."

Lucia smiled, amusement in her eyes. "You think it wouldn't be in the newspaper?"

Deanie shook her head. "A postcard would be enough to let me know."

"Deanie, Deanie, listen to me. I'm glad you're here, even if you're not. But think of it! He's ninety, Deanie. It's amazing he's lasted this long." Lucia relaxed and leaned back on the bed, propped up on her elbows. "You don't think when you're growing up that you'll be feeling old while your parents are old. It's ludicrous, but it's happening."

"I hate coming back here," Deanie said to her own surprise. "I feel so, so, I don't know—disjointed, like something's wrong with me."

"There's nothing wrong with you," Lucia said.

Deanie studied her older sister. "You think your teen years are so far away, gone forever, but I feel just as rotten now as I did then. What was wrong with me? I couldn't stay out of trouble."

"There was nothing wrong with you," Lucia said easily.

"You didn't get into trouble." Deanie rubbed her palms against her temples as though she had a headache. She had the family's thick curly hair but it had lightened to dark brown and her bones were more delicate, as though her parents' genes reached far back into the past for something different when she was conceived.

"I know." Lucia sighed and fell back on the bed, staring up at the ceiling. "I was so good. I was sick of myself."

"And I was bad enough for all of us."

Deanie looked as miserable as she sounded, Lucia thought as she sat up. "You were just a little wild when you were young, that's all, and people weren't as forgiving in the seventies as they are now. My God, Deanie, the things kids do today—hooking up, sexting, binge drinking—it's scary. Sometimes I hear these things and I don't even understand what the words are supposed to mean."

"That's now. Back then . . ."

"Well, Pae wasn't an innocent boy all his young life either." Lucia winked at Deanie. "Oh, come on, Deanie. Don't be so serious."

"I don't like the way I feel," Deanie said.

"You just got here. Give it a chance. Give all of us a chance." Lucia studied her sister's face.

"What?" Deanie lifted her chin, cautious, ready for an argument, ready to defend herself.

"Your makeup—it's so—perfect." This seemed to confound Lucia.

"I like to cover my skin out there. The sun, you know."

"Oh, sure."

"But?"

"It's just that it looks so professional." Lucia frowned.

Deanie gave her a quizzical look. "It is."

"Oh." Lucia sat up. "So, is there a man in your life?"

Deanie thought about the question. It was inevitable—she knew that—but that didn't make it any easier. She tried to think back to their teen years when she'd pester Zaira and Lucia about their boyfriends, or want to try on their clothes or lipstick. Sometimes she even threatened to tell their parents one of them was dating on the sly if the sister refused to let her in on their secrets, such as they were. And now she was the one with the secrets—lots of them. But all of the power and none of the fun was in holding onto them, keeping them close. "A man in my life." Deanie sounded out the words, then ran her hands over her hair, pulling it into a short ponytail before letting it fall loose and springy again. "Lots, sort of. But no one special." She stretched out on the bed. "My life is good, Lucia. But when I come back here—I don't know—everything feels so creepy."

"Then you shouldn't let anything in the past upset you now. And if you want to talk about strange," she said, leaning over towards her and whispering, "there's enough here to keep you occupied." She paused, saw the flicker of interest in Deanie's eyes. "Pae pressed Jose to go see Christina in the nursing home. He wants her to come to the picnic tomorrow."

"Christina?" Deanie stared at her sister. "But she's . . . "

"Barely conscious?" Lucia nodded. "Yes, but Pae wants . . . I don't know what he wants, but Jose went."

Deanie gave a little gasp.

"What?" Lucia cocked her head, a frown spreading across her face. "Does that surprise you?"

"It gives me the creeps, to think she's alive but not alive and people going to see her."

Lucia looked her sister over from head to toe, as though she hadn't really seen her before, reached out and fingered the silk of her blouse. "It troubled you enormously back then, didn't it?"

Deanie sat up and reached for a pile of garments thrown onto the floor. "It bothered everyone." Lucia waited, saying nothing. "I have to hang these things up. I forgot a jacket I wanted to bring. I'll have to go shopping later. Are there any good stores around?"

"You can borrow anything of mine," Lucia said, standing up. "We're not so different in size." She walked to the closet door and swung it open, then ran her hand over the row of hangers. "There's an extra blanket and pillow up there on the top shelf in case you need them, and extra toiletries in the bathroom. That's all yours too—we use it only for guests." She turned around to face her younger sister sitting on the bed, clutching a mass of clothing to her chest. Deanie could feel her sister's eyes on her, saw her feet turning toward her, but refused to look up.

"Deanie, if there's anything you want to talk about, well, I'm here. We can talk any time about anything. I know things were hard for you—I don't know why but I accept that they were—and I don't want you to feel you have to go away to have life the way you want it." Lucia walked over to her sister and raised her hand to Deanie's face, brushing her palm over her cheek.

"Thanks." Deanie pulled back before Lucia could press closer and reached for the clothes strewn around her.

* * * * *

"Sarah and I are going to the beach," Jennie said. She had come up behind Gwen standing on the back porch and made the announcement. Gwen could smell the suntan lotion had already been applied. She looked over her shoulder and smiled.

"She seems like a nice girl," Gwen said.

"She's downloading some neat songs. So, okay I go? We'll be back for lunch."

"And where are you going?"

"To a beach. Sarah says she goes there all the time."

"All right. But back for lunch for sure."

"For sure." Jennie clattered down the stairs after her new friend, their pop-up syncopated chatter bouncing along the clapboards. Sometimes just listening to Jennie and Philip gave Gwen a headache—she couldn't keep up with the way words tumbled from them, seemingly without meaning or order.

In truth, though, Gwen's questions had been pro forma. She was relieved Jennie had someone to hang around with so that she, Gwen, was free of the responsibility of being upbeat and entertaining at least for a while. The trip to the nursing home and back had been emotionally exhausting, not only for her but also for Joe. She could tell even if he refused to admit it. He had fallen into that abstract state—polite, distant, as cordial as ever, but remote. He had become a policeman in his childhood home.

Gwen pulled up a chair and sat down. Below in the back yard, Mrs. Silva was shaking a hand towel to drive away flies while she chatted over the fence with a neighbor. She had been on her way to the small garage for a hoe to work in the garden but had apparently given it up when she encountered her neighbor. Between waving hands and occasional emotional bursts of foreign words, they looked back at the house and Gwen felt uncomfortably aware they were talking about her. She closed her eyes and rested her head on the back of the chair, willing herself to ignore them and her own paranoia. She wanted Joe's family to like her, really like her, but they were nearly overwhelming. Instead of trying to make a good impression, she was reduced to making sure she didn't get trampled in every conversation and in the kitchen—everywhere in fact.

But when she closed her eyes and let her mind drift, she found herself staring through a doorway at a frail inert figure in a hospital bed—Christina Perreira. As Gwen watched Joe with the woman's mother in the nursing home and earlier with his father in the dining room, she realized that this woman, barely alive, was a shadow on the family, and she had no idea why. She didn't believe the old man in the nursing home—it was too venomous, his story about Gino—and far too long in the past. Memories had a way of twisting and reforming as one's feelings grew and changed. A bitter experience in one part of life could transform an otherwise innocuous memory not at all connected. Humans weren't all that reliable, she knew.

Deanie. Gino. Why had Gwen never heard these names before? Whenever Joe talked about his family—as the middle of seven children—she had never caught on to the fact that he never named seven, just five. He told no story about a family loss or tragedy, other than Paulo's death; he never seemed secretive about it either. The two siblings had just fallen out of the picture, and so out of Joe's narrative. It made Gwen uneasy.

Gwen shifted in her chair and stared out at the garden. The tomatoes were a jungle of green with little patches of red. She imagined the pungent smell of the mature plant and the taste of the ripe homegrown fruit. She sank deeper into the experience, pushing the rest of the morning from her mind, feeling herself falling asleep, a deeply satisfying sensuous experience.

Then a shout jolted her awake and she opened her eyes to see Mrs. Silva walking along the fence with both arms raised in greeting to Mrs. Perreira. At that moment Gwen felt something slicing through her. What was it Joe had said about Christina's near drowning?

"It changed them," he said as he pulled out of the parking lot.

"Who? You mean your family?"

Joe nodded.

"And you?" Gwen said.

"Yes, but not as much. We'd broken up, quietly, weeks before. She was already dating someone else, one of my cousins, I think. I suppose I should have felt more than I did—at least I used to think so. But other than feeling sorry for her, I didn't feel anything special.

"My father was very upset about it. Not at first," Joe said, slowing at a stop sign. "But after a couple of days his feelings about it seemed to change and for a while he was quite upset."

"She must have been close to your family," Gwen said absently.

Joe turned onto the highway and drove along. Surprised at his silence, Gwen looked over at him. His face was relaxed but she could tell he was thinking about something by the way he turned his head infinitesimally to the side every few seconds, an oblique nod as it were. Every now and then he clenched and relaxed his jaw.

"Were they close—Christina and your family?"

"Well," Joe said, "that's the question. Her accident had quite an impact on Gino and Deanie, but I always thought it was because they were so young at the time. Deanie was just fourteen, I think. Gino's two years older than she is."

"I suppose it could have traumatized them." Gwen wondered how her children would have felt if a friend of the family's had nearly drowned.

"Gino found her," Joe said, driving on.

* * * * *

Joe rubbed his knuckles gently down Gwen's arm as he passed her on the way to the stairs to the third floor; one set of stairs curved narrow and tight beside the kitchen, and a second set rose outside from porch to porch. Joe and his two brothers had shared the attic, or dormitory as his parents called it, and now it was just a large room for guests—mostly family who could park their children in the attic and not have to listen to them arguing, laughing, singing along with the music, though now a quiet child didn't mean what it used to mean.

The attic was insulated and covered in bead board, from the floor to the peak, and gave off the slightly dry musty smell of all attics. At the far end, along the wall facing the street, was a long built-in series of shelves and cupboards where Paulo, Joe, and Gino had hidden their few treasures, or so they thought. It wasn't until Joe was grown and gone that he realized his mother had checked the cupboards at least once a week to make sure none of her boys was up to any mischief. And after everyone was grown, the boxes grew dustier and were forgotten.

Joe began opening the cabinets one by one, just looking and wondering what he was looking for. Whenever any one of the children moved out, he or she was encouraged to put the few remaining belongings into a cardboard box and tuck it away— and then claim it as soon as possible. His mother stated this rule once, then never mentioned it again, and they all knew she would cry if any of her children took every last personal possession out of the house. Beneath the window, where rainwater might have damaged it but had not, Joe found a box with Gino's name on it, printed in large black letters by a felt-tip pen. He pulled it out and carried it over to the nearest bed. The box smelled of dust and heat and neglect, of warm cardboard once moist now dry, and of years of neglect. He flipped open the lid and a little spray of dust sparkled in the sunlight.

The box contained a few envelopes and Joe rifled through them looking for a date on a postmark. Nothing was dated later than the late 1970s, when Gino was an older teenager. Joe poked around and found report cards (Gino was an indifferent student), a high-school yearbook for his junior year, and a history of the Supreme Court. Joe'd forgotten that—forgotten all about Gino's dream. He had wanted to be a lawyer. The edges of the dust jacket were curled and brittle and the spine creaked as Joe lifted the front cover and a wad of pages at once. Gino had stared hard at those words, trying to make sense of something even Joe, then in college, didn't want to struggle with. But Gino was dogged.

When Gino was very young, perhaps ten or eleven, a lawyer had visited the house to speak to their father about a lawsuit from a man who had shipped with him. Mr. Silva had fired him, and in no uncertain terms explained why to anyone who asked. He was passionate about his boat and because he knew his years at work were numbered, he resented anyone who spoiled them in any way. The lawyer came to talk about the suit and Gino had been transfixed by the man's demeanor, his style and voice. The boy sat in the corner, on the floor, leaning back against the wall, his knees drawn up, and just watched, never taking his eyes off the strange man. At the end of the visit, Mr. Silva walked the man to the door and shook his hand.

"Good, eh?" the old man said to Gino. "Good lawyer. Smart. No fussing, no conniving. Good." He patted the boy on the head as he passed through to the kitchen to tell his wife the results of the conference.

For days afterward Gino could talk of nothing else—to his parents, to his friends, to his siblings. They began to tease him, but instead of being embarrassed and shutting up, Gino said yes, that was exactly what he was going to do. And then it stopped. Gino simply stopped talking about the lawyer, the law, his future.

Joe turned the book over and dropped it back into the box.

Something died in Gino when he was a teenager, something no one could put his or her finger on; the boy grew to be different during those years. Unlike Paulo and Jose, Gino did little about sports, didn't hang around with a large boisterous crowd, didn't take in the movies, the beach, the races. And then one day, he was gone.

The next thing anyone heard was a rumor from a friend who said Gino had tried to kill himself somewhere, and three days later the mail delivered a barely readable but very ambiguous note. The attempt had failed, Gino lived, but he stayed away. His parents were torn to pieces but they couldn't find him to bring him home, nor could they be sure what the note meant.

Joe rifled through the box again, looking for the note. He put a collection of envelopes in order, pulled papers out of folders, sorted through letters—he found the envelope, but not the note.

"What are you doing up here, Jose?"

Joe turned at the sound of his mother's voice just as she came through the door. "How did you know I was up here?"

"Gwen. She is telling me. Why are you up here on such a day?" She walked towards him, and took in the box opened on his lap. "What are you doing, Jose?" Her voice was soft, barely audible, her footsteps slow and small. She reached the bed and looked around for somewhere to sit. As Joe rose, she placed her hand on his shoulder, telling him to sit, and moved to a nearby rocking chair.

"I was just thinking about Gino," Joe said.

The rocking chair began to squeak as Mrs. Silva placed her feet on the floor and pushed. She inhaled deeply and let her eyes rise to the ceiling. "I too think about him."

"He wanted to be a lawyer. Do you remember?"

Mrs. Silva smiled and rocked faster. "Ah, yes. A lawyer." She shook her head as if to say she couldn't imagine such a thing in her family.

"What's he doing now? Do you hear from him?"

"Only second hand, from friends." Her eyes closed, and Joe wondered how she endured the pain—one child dead, one gone missing, and another barely on the fringes of the family. "He is alive, working somewhere. Like Deanie. But at least she is coming home this time."

Joe shuffled the envelopes in his hands. There was nothing to say about a daughter, cherished, somewhat favored as the youngest, who fled and didn't come home for thirty years or more. "Well, she's here now. Whatever he said—or you said to her—she's here." He replaced the envelopes. "Why is Pae doing this? What is he looking for?"

The old woman shrugged. "How would I know?" She closed her eyes and hummed. "When children are little, we have to have all the answers. And then they grow up and find out we don't have all the answers and some of our answers were wrong because the world changes and what was true back then isn't true anymore. And they feel betrayed. Is that worse than letting a child learn too soon that we don't have any answers? Isn't that cruel?" She dusted imaginary dirt from her lap. "I don't know what he wants. I just let him do this. He's losing his mind." She scowled at the wall.

"You certainly are mad at him," Joe said, smiling.

"You live with this grumpy old man every day," she said. "He complains about everything—the government, the regulations, the weather, the street pavers; he even complains about my cooking! My cooking!" She leaned forward in the chair at the very extravagance of the insult.

"He hasn't been so bad so far," Joe said.

"Hah! You wait! Even the cousins are sick of it," she said.

"Who else has he invited to come by?"

She ran through a list of cousins and other relatives. "And his sister—bless her, Lord—can't leave the nursing home without so much help." She shook her head. "And only eighty-eight!"

Joe's was a long-lived family.

* * * * *

The driver scanned the side of the road, slowing when he came to a plaza to see if the restaurant looked okay, then pushed back in his seat and sped up. The thick green leaves encased the highway in its own tunnel, open to the sky but shut off from the surrounding world, as though the line of cars speeding back and forth along the tarmac were part of a private toy with neither beginning nor end, an infinity of restless searching and hurrying.

"I thought we were going to stop," the woman said, rolling her head to look at him. She had little black half moons under her eyes, a combination of lack of sleep and smeared eyeliner. She began every morning with a careful application of cosmetics, even after these many years. He liked that about her, appreciated the care she took with her appearance, and underneath, where he kept his fears and insecurities at bay he believed it meant that she still thought well of him, was not yet disillusioned by this fifty-something man going gray, wrinkling around the mouth, and thickening in the middle from too many beers. He never told her this, never admitted his fear that she would leave him, but when she reached over and squeezed his hand during a movie or at dinner, he thought she must know and he didn't feel so foolish.

"I need to stretch," she said after a pause. "I'm getting stiff again."

They had left Pateros, Washington, four weeks ago in a rented car and driven straight across the country, admiring the landscape, marveling at how it changed mile after mile, stopping at all the odd little places locals put up to draw in passersby—a grain elevator museum in Illinois, a little shop that sold petrified rocks imported from China, or a historic site honoring a local figure who invented something that put hundreds of people to work, a post office with WPA murals, a farm with the world's largest snow pea, well priced but too big to carry home without hearing it split in the back seat. Much of the time the man didn't know where they were except on a particular highway, usually a red squiggly line moving West to East. He sensed the change in location mostly by the change in the light. He felt the loss of the pellucid light of Pateros, and the space of the universe opening up before him as they dropped south and headed east. The sand turned to soil and rocks, and turned again.

"We'll try the next one," the man said.

"All right." She sighed and closed her eyes. "How far do you think it is?"

"Not far. Maybe an hour." He relaxed now that he knew he didn't have to stop. So far on this trip they had stopped three or four times a day—to savor the landscape—neither had taken the time to appreciate the vastness of the country before—to stretch and break the boredom of a piece of road that just went on and on and on into nothing, an existential experience that was starting to make the man think about random comments from college professors. It was disorienting, the way being lost in a new landscape tapped into seemingly irrelevant past experiences. He didn't do well in college, barely finished a course or two, so hearing an old teacher's voice rise from a forgotten memory was startling.

"It's pretty," she said, opening her eyes to the trees shifting in a light breeze along the median strip. "But smaller than I thought it would be."

"Smaller?" He turned to look at her. "How do you mean smaller?" He could feel the beads of perspiration settling on his upper lip.

"Well, things seem closer here, one town after another—all those exits."

"Yeah, I guess that's so." It was a thought he was hoping to escape, he realized, the idea that things were pushed closer together, so that it was hard to avoid what you wanted to avoid, hard to move around without bumping into unpleasant things or people. That's what he liked about Pateros, about the west in general. It wasn't so crowded, but even where there were people, all you had to do was turn and there was the Columbia in all its vastness and the high desert country rising up on all sides with scarcely a soul to be seen. In the beginning he took his truck up into the hills and just drove hour after hour, often times getting lost and wondering if what he was really doing was just driving until he went off a cliff. But then he'd find a solid shoulder, turn around and start back, taking a side road and wandering until he eventually came to a sign with a name he recognized, and then he'd follow that back to a place he knew.

It was his wife, Melanie, falling asleep now, who pointed out the humor in the landscape. And he saw it the minute she said it. Signs in New England were serious, earnest announcements of wares to be sold, services to be acquired. But where they lived now the signs seemed to remind others of how small human beings were compared to the landscape surrounding them, a gentle suggestion to remain humble. Her favorite was Whack and Yack, for the hair salon down the street from his construction office, and his was Pig in a Poke for the local thrift shop.

"Did you call anyone, Gene?" she asked. Her voice sounded sleepy, as though she were reminding him to make sure the cat was in, safe from hungry animals that might come up to the house at night. She had found the butterscotch-colored animal crouched in a crawl space between the garage wall and the house, where rain and time had forced a few stones out of the narrow wall. The wretched animal had refused to come out for

hours until Gene had given in and started chipping out rocks so
Melanie could reach in for her.

"I talked to Deanie." His mouth narrowed into a line and he
knew Melanie was staring at him. He had told her little about his
past, only that he had a family back east and never saw them.
That wasn't so strange for her; lots of people had relatives back
east and rarely saw them, she said. Families grew up and
scattered, grew apart and forgot about each other in the business
of their quotidian lives. It was nothing to get excited about, she
said. He knew she meant it in the best possible way. The west
was full of families strung miles and miles along the landscape,
never thinking about what they'd left behind. It was a strange
sensation for him and he hadn't ever felt easy about it. He knew
this distance meant nothing much to her and many others. But
for him, for someone who had grown up in a family whose
branches intertwined and protected each other generation after
generation, it meant a lot, more than he could endure sometimes.
And he would have lived with this, this sense of having only
three limbs, not four, of speaking a foreign language, not his
mother tongue, of waking up some mornings not sure where he
was, then realizing he wasn't where he assumed he was. He
would always live with it because Deanie interrupted every step
he took away from the east and she seemed to know when he
was drifting too far away.

Gene had decided to drive to the east coast rather than fly
because he could not bring himself to jump back into the past.
He persuaded himself that if he drove, he could always change
his mind, and just turn around and drive home—at the New York
border, at the Massachusetts border, at the Bristol County border.
He couldn't think farther than that, but he gripped the steering
wheel tighter, felt his shoulders ache with tension, and reminded
himself of his promise to Deanie. "You'll never face this alone, I
promise."

How old had he been? Fifteen? Sixteen? For years
afterwards he had blamed that foolish promise for changing his
life, hating himself for not knowing how to get out from under it,
and then hating himself for wanting to. But when he got up the
courage to go to confession after many years, he let a priest
comfort him, and he came to accept that the promise of a near
child wasn't what changed him. For years he didn't know if that
made it better or worse, but it was different. And then Deanie

disappeared, just disappeared, and he moved on—sort of. Whenever he caught word of her—either through a friend, a news report, or a note from her—he felt himself stumble and fall, but at least he was moving forward.

"Are we stopping here?" Melanie pushed herself up in the seat and leaned toward the dashboard. "It looks okay. They're all alike, you know. Very generic. Nothing to worry about really, as long as you like fast food. It should be okay. Whaddya say?" She turned to Gene, smiled, looked hopeful.

"Sure. Why not?" He couldn't resist her hopeful look. He told her that once, and she cocked her head to one side, gave him a quizzical look, and burst out laughing. She told him that was the funniest thing a man had ever said to her—maybe the sweetest too—and anyway, could they? He didn't remember what the request was, but he guessed he said yes. He always said yes. She rarely asked for anything.

At first he thought she was mousy, but it turned out it wasn't that. She had grown up poor—really poor, without food and sometimes living in a car with her mother, who drove around the western loop, from Montana to Arizona, and back again, always stopping in Nevada. She had a system and she was sure it would make her rich, and when it didn't she packed up her children—three of them—and headed out again, looking for work, a place to recover, and time to refine her system. She kept scraps of paper in all her pockets, stuffed in every corner of the old station wagon, stuck into books and grocery bags. She died of alcohol poisoning when Melanie was twenty-four and living in a house with half a dozen other girls working at a resort. Gene couldn't imagine that kind of life—an evening with no food on the table, no siblings jostling for room, arguing over the television, stampeding up and down stairs.

"It was just a life, honey," she said after she told him. "There are lots of ways to live." But for Gene it explained why she was so careful with her movements—there wasn't much space in a car, and the quieter the kids were, the less likely the state authorities were to take notice. In a less decent woman, Melanie's habits would have made her furtive and sly.

"How do you feel about pancakes?" Gene asked, looking at the big poster in the window.

"Food is food," she said, giving him a peck on the cheek before she pushed open the door with her shoulder.

* * * * *

Joe knew he couldn't sit in the car much longer. His oldest sister, Zaira, would have heard him drive up to the house and park, and would be listening now for his footsteps on the gravel and a knock on the door. He could pretend he was admiring the large modern colonial she and her husband, Gray, had moved into a few years ago, but she wouldn't buy that for anything longer than a few minutes. She knew he didn't care about the size of her house—he'd never cared.

Joe slipped the car keys into his pocket and walked toward the heavy mahogany door, its solid brass knocker gleaming in the sunshine. Gray Souza had done very well in life, selling insurance to anyone who needed it and for anything they owned, from a child's bicycle to a private airplane. If you bought it, he would insure it. Zaira was proud of him, and their two sons had done almost as well, fanning out into the community as lawyers, proud to be part of the life of everyone they knew. And then, at the last minute, came Sarah, the menopause baby. But through it all Zaira didn't change—she showed up at her mother's house at least twice a week, fussed over the family, and called Joe a couple times a month, just in case he'd not gotten the full story, whatever it was, from their mother. She fussed and complained and meddled, and Joe chalked it up to having so few challenges in her life. She was meant to raise a large brood under difficult circumstances with crises and catastrophes as daily fare. Instead she scratched her head over two perfect sons and one perfect husband and wondered what to do with her confused daughter— and all the energy she still had. She volunteered everywhere, visited everyone, and solved all of life's little problems—except her own—the need to be needed. Even her husband's recent illness didn't seem to sap all her energy.

"You took your time, Joe." Zaira swung open the door and scolded him. "Come on. Gray is in here." She led the way through a large entry hall and into a small library, where a man who might have been in his eighties but Joe knew to be in his late sixties sat in a wheel chair, a thick navy wool blanket tucked around his lower body.

"Hey!" the other man said, lifting his left hand a few inches off his lap. He gave Joe a lopsided grin as Joe reached out and gripped his hand. For the next few minutes, Zaira stood off to the side while Joe and his brother-in-law conducted a halting conversation.

"He's not as bad as I thought," Joe said later, after he and Zaira had moved to the living room.

"That's only because I have help all the time, getting him up, feeding him, all of it." She plumped a pillow behind her and leaned back. "I couldn't do it alone. He'd be in a home if it weren't for . . ."

"That's too bad." Joe watched a twitch beneath her eye, thinking how tired she looked, not in body but in spirit.

"But the reunion! He'll love it." She forced a smile as she turned to him again.

"Think you'll get him over there?"

"Oh, yes, I couldn't let him miss it."

Joe nodded. It would take the whole day just to get him there for a few minutes, and then he probably wouldn't be able to stay, to tolerate the congestion and noise and perhaps the weather. He was frail, frailer than seemed possible. "I hear Deanie's coming," he said.

Zaira's face collapsed, and in her eyes emerged the serious, sharp look she was known for. The family used to joke that Gray made his money by taking Zaira on sales calls with him, so she could spot the losers and frauds in the first ten seconds. Joe respected her instincts about people, but mostly he wondered why she never had any ambition to use them in the world for herself. She had been entirely content as a wife and mother, always refusing Gray's offers to find her a paid position in his business. "Why should I go to work? Am I poor?" That was her only response.

"She's here. Arrived already. Lucia called me." Zaira leaned forward and tidied a pile of magazines on the coffee table. She had brought out a tray of sandwiches and beer, which sat in front of them—for his benefit alone, Joe was sure, but he had no interest at the moment.

"You don't sound pleased."

"She shouldn't have come."

"She's family, Zaira. You of all people must understand that. Our parents have felt like a part of themselves was missing all these years, with Deanie and Gino gone." He didn't like making this appeal to her, falling into the habits of a younger brother. He had the feeling there was more to this than just a resentment of siblings falling away.

Zaira crouched over, resting her elbows on her legs and staring down at the floor. She shook her head from side to side. "I don't think she should stay here. I don't mean here at the house. I mean here, in Massachusetts. She lives mostly on the west coast now. Did you know that?"

Joe turned the tray of sandwiches and mumbled something he knew she wouldn't get. Gino was out west somewhere. Odd, he thought, that the two youngest should be the ones to go the farthest.

"I always thought you would be the one to go away and not come home." Zaira leaned back and smiled at him, then stretched her arms out, brushing her hands on the sofa fabric. She rubbed her palms over the cloth, rippling the velvet into different shades. "I suppose you have, sort of."

"I'm only in Mellingham, Zaira."

"You know what I mean."

"What's this all about?"

Zaira closed her eyes. She was old, he suddenly realized, just as he was. She was sixty-two, sixty-three—he couldn't remember. He was startled—and then chagrined—at forgetting, getting the family birthdates mixed up. But he didn't need to know her birthdates—the evidence was there in her skin, in the little pale brown spots along her cheekbones, the slackening jowls, the thinning hair. She had raised her sons and was raising her teenage daughter now; she had grandchildren to be proud of, and cared for an ailing husband. She had years left, but in essence, she had had her life and if she had regrets, she wasn't telling.

"Deanie isn't our little sister anymore, Joe. She's different." Zaira looked at him squarely, as if in that look was the rest of what she wasn't saying. It was Joe's turn to dissemble. The trouble with being a policeman was that special key to a closed world, a way of finding out, of knowing, through all those channels that opened for the brotherhood. And some years ago, to calm his parents' fears, he had begun a search. He hadn't told them where it led, only that Deanie was alive and well. He left it at that. Alive and well—compared to what? A dead woman? "I wish she hadn't come."

"Gino's coming."

Zaira frowned. "Why?" She threw up her hands and looked about her. "Those two . . . I don't understand why now, why both of them. Why couldn't they just stay away? I'm worried about Pae, Joe. He's old."

"So are we." Joe shook his head. "I'm sorry, Zaira. Look, you know as well as I do that no one can predict how someone is going to turn out. Gino and Deanie went their own way. Who knows why? But they're coming back—because either Mae or Pae begged them to. They haven't long left, so let's just make it a good time for them. They're old, you're right, so let's just let them have this time the way they want."

"Deanie won't do that." She studied Joe. "You know she won't." Her look was steady, challenging. She was strong-willed and level-headed. After Paulo died she seemed to grow into the role of oldest child, not just as the next in line, but also as the one to take on the duties and mind-set of a first-born. She was doing it now—trying to set a rule, pull rank, and push the others into line.

"If you know something, Zaira, tell me now." Joe couldn't press her as though he were interrogating her, but he knew she'd hear that tone of voice—he wasn't her younger brother right now. He was a policeman.

Zaira sighed but she didn't look away. "It's just a feeling, Jose. Just a feeling."

Yes, he thought. You have nothing more than a feeling. He hoped she'd keep it that way and not try to turn it into anything more. "Something persuaded them to come back, Zaira, and we have to make sure they don't spoil things for anyone else."

"This is Pae's doing, isn't it?"

"He wants to make his peace over Christina Perreira." Joe shook his head. "All those years and he never said a thing, and now it's eating him up."

Zaira let out a little gasp. "Christina? Oh no! This is a nightmare, Jose, a nightmare."

Four

Friday Afternoon

Somewhere beneath all the platters of food was, Gwen knew, an intricately patterned tablecloth that had faded to pale hues but still bubbled and flowed with energy and a sense of the sweeping wonder of food—a series of looping vines ending in cornucopias of vegetables and fruit. Taken in hand by Joe's mother, Gwen had chatted amiably to the old woman while she cooked and tasted and assembled and directed anyone and everyone who came into the kitchen. For the hours Gwen had spent handing things to her and hearing snippets about the family, Gwen expected a nice hot meal, but as the platters and serving bowls began to blossom on the kitchen counter, she began to wonder where the food was coming from. She couldn't quite believe she had watched all this being created, and yet she had been standing in this very room almost all morning. In the back of her mind she kept wondering if Joe's mother ever looked at a cookbook.

"Are you exhausted yet?" Joe slipped his arm around her waist and pulled her away from the door leading into the dining room. "You have that stunned look."

"Well, I'm . . . I'm not sure what."

"I haven't seen that look since my nieces and nephews were dating and brought their dates to meet Mae. She's a force of nature in the kitchen." Joe pulled her closer to him. "Let's take a ride."

"You think that's a good idea? Your parents won't mind? I'm not expected to be doing something?" Gwen said as she pulled the car door shut a few minutes later. "I have this sensation of becoming another person, Joe, someone who does

64

housework and runs around doing errands. I feel like I have an alternate being here."

Joe laughed. "Mae does that to people, but, trust me, she is now glad to be rid of us. She has a rule. A new member of the family should help cook, but not clean. And that means you— you're not allowed to do any of the hard stuff. Not yet, anyway." He smiled at her, as if to apologize for the future he had not unfurled before her—helping with dishes and other household chores. Gwen laughed, to his relief.

"Where're we going?" Gwen sank lower in the seat. "I am tired. It doesn't feel like I did very much, but I'm pooped."

"That kitchen has that effect." He turned the wheel and they were soon driving down a road that crossed a field and then opened into a dirt lot. Joe parked. "Let's walk."

A narrow but hard-packed dirt path led down to the edge of a large pond. Across the water was the city they had just left. To their right, Gwen could see large homes peeking up above the treetops. The path led along the bank before dipping away from the water to pass beneath trees where the air was noticeably cooler and still—the smell of the dirt and lower temperature made the short passage among the trees seem dank. Along the water's edge cattails grew thick, masking the openings to tunnels dug deep into the bank by muskrats; Gwen found herself watching for swampy ground beneath each step.

"We used to come fishing here when I was a kid," Joe said, "all of us, sharing the rod, falling in more than anything else." Joe pulled aside a branch and they walked slowly back along the water's edge, emerging from the trees into a broad clearing. He knew Gwen would wait while he sorted through the myriad thoughts his family usually brought up, while he decided which one he wanted to grasp and shock with the light of day.

"What is all this about?" Gwen asked when she reached him. The water had seeped into her sneakers and she shook one foot, then the other.

"My father's an old man and he wants to settle something, at least in his own mind." Joe motioned Gwen to sit on a small bench just ahead. The planks, gray and splintering, had seen better days, but the bench was still serviceable, so it had been left year after year, for anyone who might want to sit and watch the sun set over the city. "He's not telling me much." Joe sat down and rested his head in his hands.

"You looked even more tired."

Joe broke into a smile. He gazed over the water, soft in the afternoon light, pressed into stillness by the heat. Light shimmered across the surface, as though drawn to the bright buildings in the distance. "He's never been so secretive, so unwilling, maybe unable, to say what he's up to, what he's thinking."

"Maybe part of it is his age—what seems to be happening to him could be just how old he is." Gwen offered this in the most tentative manner, knowing how sensitive relatives could be when faced with a declining parent.

"Maybe. I don't know what's going on in his head. And I don't know how he got Deanie and Gino to come back, but he has. That by itself is amazing."

"So you think he told them something he didn't tell you?"

Joe stretched his arms out, resting them along the back of the bench, feeling the sun on his face and on his chest through his thin cotton shirt. He didn't remember the pond ever being this quiet—he barely heard cars on the highway over there. But then he had always come with his friends and they were anything but quiet. "If he knows something he isn't telling me, he hasn't even hinted at it."

"But you know something, too, don't you?" Gwen had a small camera that she fiddled with, but after taking one shot she was done. She carried it with her though she rarely used it. She had taken it out, thinking to take pictures of the pond, but after sighting it three of four times, she decided she wasn't really interested. She wrapped the neck cord around the camera and slipped it into her purse.

"One of the advantages of being a policeman." Joe stared at the city resting quietly in the distance. "Whenever I got a hint of where Deanie was I did a little checking, just to keep up with what was happening with her. I didn't want to meddle in her life—just make sure she was safe."

"Was she?"

Joe lifted his arms and pulled them to his sides. "I guess so."

The water lapped softly against the bank and flies buzzed across the surface, looking for their meal and unaware that they might soon be another's nourishment. The surface of a pond always seemed serene, and yet, Gwen knew, it teemed with creatures chasing, maneuvering, escaping, tricking, devouring each other, moment after moment, century after century. It never ended. A frog rose to the surface in the apparent stillness, then sank again into the muddy water.

"What does she do? What does she get up to?"

"My father worshipped his daughters. He loved us, his sons, but he believed his daughters were nearly perfect—no one could say a bad word about them." Joe turned to her with a half smile on his face.

"Oh, Joe, I'm so sorry." Gwen leaned over and gave him a light kiss on his cheek. Joe laughed.

"Exactly." He sighed and looked again at the pond. "I wouldn't have cared if she had stayed away—she has a right to her life. But when she showed up last night, I started to feel I'd have to say something if she started talking about her life."

Gwen listened, leaning in to him, nodding, frowning as he spoke but she could feel a prickling from the back of her neck down her spine. She didn't like the sound of this at all. She was tough in a lot of ways—she'd had to be—but family confrontations brought out the darkest feelings in her—they could go so badly wrong.

"I was in the attic this morning, just looking through some of what she and Gino left behind. Mae puts the family treasures into boxes, with one for each of us—things she can't bring herself to throw away—mostly horrible artwork in smeared crayons and old report cards."

"You found something in one of the boxes? In Deanie's or Gino's?"

He shook his head. "That's the problem. I thought I'd find something in Deanie's that would point me in the right direction."

"Such as?" Gwen leaned closer. What would a young teen leave behind that would or could predict a life gone awry?

"Deanie was a very thoughtful child. She kept a diary all the time, until she was maybe fourteen. And then she just stops. Nothing." Flies skated in criss-crossing patterns over the surface—quick, sharp, gone.

"And you think that means something?"

"The last entry I could find was the day before Christina had her accident."

"Oh." A fish broke the surface, the frog bolted from its hiding place, and the water churned muddy. Gwen peered into the ruffling surface but couldn't see below, couldn't divine what had happened to disrupt the apparent tranquility. "Didn't you tell me once, Joe, that was when she changed?"

"I'm not going to say there's no such thing as coincidence, but in this instance I have doubts. Somehow she's connected with Christina's accident or something about it."

"And would your father know that?"

"I don't think he does, Gwen." A light breeze flickered through the branches, and Joe leaned toward her and brushed a wisp of hair absentmindedly away from her face.

"Is that what's worrying you? That this reunion will turn up something about Christina that will upset the apple cart?" Gwen tried to get a better look at him, to see if she was reading him right.

"Maybe it is. It certainly might be part of it, now that I think about it. No, what I've been worried about is whether or not Deanie is going to, I don't know, let us see who she is now." He pulled his arm away and clasped his hands in front of him. "It would kill Pae, kill him, kill him for sure."

"But he called her, Joe. He called her and Gino."

Joe turned to her, picked up her hand, letting it rest in his palm as he ran his thumb over her fingers. "And that, Gwen, is about the most surprising thing of all—my father, getting on the telephone, and making a phone call to an estranged child."

* * * * *

Sarah crossed the hot sand, walking straight to a spot that she seemed to have chosen before she even reached the beach. Jennie lagged several feet behind, stopping every few steps to study the layout of the beach from each new angle, before dismissing the location and again following her new friend. She liked going to the beach with her friends in Mellingham, and she was used to choosing a spot according to its proximity to one or another crowd and the water. She still liked to swim when she went to the beach, though some of her friends now insisted that swimming would ruin their makeup. Jennie was still young enough emotionally to sense the conflict and ignore it—leaving her makeup off on beaching mornings.

But this beach posed none of those challenges—it seemed almost empty, with long stretches of sand and dunes and very few people. Far up ahead she spotted a number of people walking away from them, straggling across the water's edge and moving inland as the waves pushed closer before ebbing; almost beyond her range of focus, a family was sprawled across the sand beneath the dunes. The vastness left Jennie feeling that something was definitely missing—people.

Sarah squinted upwards, looked around, and spread out her blanket. She had chosen to position them for the best view of the ocean as well as the walkway onto the beach. Jennie also squinted up at the sun, shielding her eyes with the palm of her hand. She scanned the beach for other sun worshippers one more time, decided that there probably wasn't any other spot with more people around, and turned her attention to her beach towel. Hers was large, brightly colored, and lumpy, she discovered, as soon as she sat down on it—the sand underneath was not at all smooth. Jennie picked up the towel, walked a few feet, and shook it out; she returned to the spot, smoothed out the sand with her foot, working her way down and back a couple of times, before re-spreading her towel.

"You're very particular," Sarah said after watching this exercise.

"I like being comfortable."

"I guess." Sarah flopped down onto her back and pulled a cotton hat over her face.

"Our sand sings," Jennie said.

"So Uncle Joe has told us."

"It really does."

"If you say so."

Jennie let it go and began rummaging in her bag for suntan lotion. Sarah wasn't a bad sort—just different. Jennie had reached the point where she had concluded that if they went to the same school they probably wouldn't be friends, but family was different. She was okay as a distant cousin, and in that context Jennie liked her—she was different and Jennie was curious. She pulled a tube of suntan lotion out of her bag and twirled off the cap.

"I'll never look like you, Sarah, so I have to be careful. You turn brown—you're so lucky—and I just burn." Jennie squirted lotion onto her calves and began smoothing it into her skin, running her hands up and down her legs. "Mom is always warning me about getting too much sun, but, I mean, really, what's the point if I can't go to the beach once in a while? I mean, I'd look like an albino. Yuk!"

"You'd look freaky," Sarah said. "Actually, you'll look freaky anyway."

"Gee, thanks." Jennie twisted around to glare at her, but was met with the crinkled white hat covering Sarah's face.

"Take a look at my family! Everybody turns dark, except Uncle Leon and he's almost dead." Sarah sighed. "No one has skin that doesn't tan."

"Not your cousins?"

"Tia Eluara is so delicate looking, but her kids all came out looking like Uncle Serge." Sarah pulled off her hat and rolled onto her side. "You'll meet them tomorrow. Everyone's coming. Well, my dad isn't. At least, probably not."

"Why not?"

"He's pretty sick. My mom's been taking care of him for ages—his heart—and I think it's getting to her. He's okay with the wheelchair stuff but she's getting kind of weird about it."

"That's too bad." Jennie deposited another squirt in her palm and started on her thighs.

"What about your dad? Is he dead?"

Startled, Jennie stopped with her hand in midair. "No, I don't think so."

"Don't you know?"

This was probably why we wouldn't ever be friends, Jennie thought. My friends wouldn't ask me things like that, not so bluntly, anyway. The thing was, she didn't think about her parents, her birth parents, anymore. Gwen was her mother, and Joe, well, Joe was Joe, like a stepfather. But the thing with having all these relatives in a large family, Jennie concluded, was that you had to ask lots of questions or you might miss something important. "I can't remember the last time I saw my parents, my birth parents."

"You're not curious?" Sarah slipped the hat from her face and propped herself up on her elbow. "I'd be curious—I'd want to track them down."

Jennie shook her head. She didn't want to track them down—she had an inkling of how things had come to be the way they were and she didn't want to lose what she had. No, she wasn't one for digging things up if she didn't have to. "I have a mother."

"Yeah, but . . . " Sarah flopped back down. "You must be Irish or something. My mom is always going on about how the Irish are so different and that's why Uncle Larry lets Aunt Lucia do whatever she wants or something like that."

Jennie paused in her ministrations, intrigued by the family tree leafing out in front of her. It sounded odd, but she couldn't quite figure out which part was throwing the whole thing off. "That's weird."

"Was he like Joe?" Sarah asked.

"Who?"

"Your birth dad."

"I don't think so."

"No one's like Joe, not really." Sarah peeked out to check the position of the sun, then rearranged the hat over her face again. "I wanna be like him."

"A policeman?" Jennie looked up at the clouds drifting overhead, large white bundles tumbling over each other like little polar bears.

"No, dummie. Independent. He just picked up and left and no one could get him back." She stretched out her arms, turning them over so the undersides got more sun. "He comes back when he wants and goes when he wants."

Jennie screwed on the cap and dropped the tube of lotion back into her bag. "I thought it was the other two who did that—Deanie and Gino. Didn't they go away and never come back? Aren't they the ones who have been away for so long—years and years and years?"

"It's not the same."

Jennie looked down at the supine figure. "How could it not be the same?"

"There's something screwy about them. You know, like secrets and stuff."

"Secrets? What kind of secrets?"

"You know, family stuff."

"I thought everyone in your family knew everything there was to know about everyone else." Jennie tucked her legs beneath her and studied Sarah—this was entirely different from what Joe had suggested about his family. How could anyone keep any secrets in this family? "What kind of secrets?"

"I dunno. Things we're not supposed to talk about."

"Oh. Everyone has those." Disappointed, Jennie stretched out her legs again, deciding how to settle on her towel.

"You don't understand, Jennie." Sarah pushed herself up on her arm and grew serious. "No one does that in this family—go away. It's all about family—and that's good. I really like that. But no one really leaves. We all are supposed to stay and take care of each other, no matter how you feel, but sometimes . . ."

"Sometimes what?" Jennie tilted her head to one side. She hadn't known anything like Joe's family—she was painfully curious.

"Well, you're not supposed to admit how you feel about some people. Like Tio Eddie. He and Joe grew up together and I think they got into fights or something—no one will really talk about it—but Tio Eddie always makes little jokes about Tio Joe and my aunt glares at him, but more like she's embarrassed than angry. And we're not supposed to disagree with him."

"Why not?" Jennie unconsciously pulled away from her friend, her head back as though ready to bolt. "I would."

"I don't know. Something to do with Tia Rosalie." Sarah grew thoughtful, frowned, and turned her attentions to the waves crashing and rushing up the incline. "I asked my mom once why they didn't like Tio Eddie the way everyone liked Tio Larry, Lucia's husband."

"What'd she say?"

"She said he was jealous of Joe and that made it hard for them all to be together, so it was better not to bring up Joe when he was around." Sarah sighed. "Stupid."

"So why do you think everyone agreed to come this time?"

"I don't know." Sarah flipped the edge of her blanket to remove a wrinkle. "Sometimes you wish the ones who didn't go away would and the ones who did go would hang around. Things work out so weird sometimes." Sarah twisted around to Jennie and gave her a big smile. "But it's going to be wild—just you wait. We're gonna have a great time."

* * * * *

Mrs. Perreira rolled the white laminated case across the floor of her daughter's room and nudged it into place alongside the bed. "There we are, darling." She patted her daughter's arm and began to pull the sheet down to her waist. When she leaned over the figure in the bed, to push the pillow up, revealing the slender neck, for a moment her eyes locked on her daughter's face, and a barely perceptible tremor flowed across her features. Her shoulders flinched and she pressed her face into a smile.

"You know I'm here, don't you, Christina." The older woman peered into her daughter's eyes, a painful studying look as though she wasn't sure of the answer. "Nurse said you were restless, kind of uncomfortable—she wasn't sure why." Mrs. Perreira drew back and dispassionately looked over her daughter's body, slowly examining the nearly flattened blanket and sheets where her legs were stretched out, little more than thin sticks beneath the coverings. "Don't worry." She spoke with new energy and determination. "We'll just get you feeling so much better." On the rolling case sat a flat-bottomed yellow plastic bowl filled with warm water and bath oil. Mrs. Perreira reached in for the coral sponge, picked it up and squeezed. Warm water thick with fragrance of violets dribbled into the bowl.

"Hello, Mrs. P." A young woman in pink slacks and a brightly patterned overblouse walked up to the foot of the bed and stood with her hands on her hips. "Any time to you want us to help, just let us know. We do this for everyone, you know."

"Yes, Peggy, I know." Mrs. Perreira glanced at her over her shoulder and smiled. "But she is my daughter. Christina knows I'm here; she knows I'm taking care of her."

The nurse's aide watched but seemed to have no response to the mother's comments. This was her job—to stand at the ready in case Mrs. Perreira needed her, whether she wanted help or not. Peggy had been working at the nursing home long enough to accept the surprising ways family members responded to death and dying, and Christina Perreira had been dying for as long as Peggy had been on this earth. But it seemed as though no one else acknowledged it. Mrs. Perreira came in every day to visit her daughter, give her a sponge bath, talk to the nurses, sit by her daughter's side and read to her, or just talk. Sometimes Peggy was embarrassed by the kinds of things she heard Mrs. P saying as she passed the open door—the way she talked about her family, especially her husband, and her friends, as though the woman lying in the bed was one of the mother's own friends and wanted to hear the latest gossip about divorces and arrests and bankruptcies and how strongly the mother felt about all these people. Right now Christina had the room to herself, but in another day or so someone new would move in. Beds never stayed empty for long—the nursing home couldn't afford it, even if it was privately owned.

"She's going out with us tomorrow," Mrs. Perreira said, lifting Christina's arm. She laid a towel underneath. Gently she rubbed the coral sponge along the flaccid arm, washing away the wasted day.

"Out?" Peggy clamped her mouth shut as soon as she heard the word fly out. Christina had enough motor skills left to sit in a wheelchair and hold her neck up while being moved about the nursing home, to sit at a table while others ate and sometimes hold a piece of bread. But her diet consisted of nothing more than pureed food and thickened juices, in case she aspirated her drink and choked to death. She wouldn't be able to manage even that much longer. Peggy hadn't thought the patient was strong enough to ride in a van, or that she would even want to. One of the nurses told her Christina's family occasionally took her home for holidays, but since Peggy had never actually seen the van take her away, she remained skeptical.

"Our good friends are having the summer family get-together." Mrs. Perreira moved the cart to the other side of the bed and began arranging the towel again. "They have them all the time, but it is such a large family so many can't come every time, but this time all the children are coming and their children and even their grandchildren. Such a large family." The sponge hung poised in midair, water dripping onto the bed covers. Mrs. Perreira seemed to have forgotten what she was doing.

"Mrs. P?" Peggy took a step toward her.

"What? Oh, sorry." Mrs. Perreira lowered the sponge. "That was going to be my daughter's family too. She was going to marry one of the boys, but it didn't work out. I don't know why. And then . . . " She ran her eyes over Christina's entire body as though she were a stranger lying there being assessed for a new blanket.

"I'm sorry." Peggy couldn't hear herself speak but Mrs. Perreira must have because she lifted her shoulders and waved off the words of comfort.

"I hold nothing against them."

Peggy believed her, the sound of her words coming in a soft, relaxed voice, like someone ordering a loaf of bread in a bakery with still another hour to kill while shopping. And yet, Peggy found it hard to believe that anyone could be so forgiving.

Could Peggy herself if it had happened to her sister? Would she be able to do the same thing if it had been her only child? Mrs. Perreira was always pleasant to the staff, kind and loving to her daughter, but sometimes Peggy felt a holding back, as though this aging, now-creaking and sometimes hobbling old woman concealed more than she or anyone else suspected, and someday would let it all out.

"I mustn't say too much," Mrs. Perreira said. "She can hear us. I don't want you to have troubled sleep, Christina. Past is past. Yes?"

Peggy wasn't sure Christina could make out very much. Yes, it was true there was some brain activity, but no one could say what that meant, if anything. The doctor had been reluctant to draw any conclusions, but Mrs. Perreira had been different after that, almost dancing down the hallway the first few days after the tests.

"It's wonderful what medicine can do," Peggy said. She racked her brain for something else to say, to change the subject. "Do you have your own van, or do you use the Ride?"

"A friend." Mrs. Perreira turned slightly and smiled again. "A friend has one. He will come. His son needs to use a van, cerebral palsy, so he will take us and bring us back. A good friend." Mrs. Perreira gently uncurled her daughter's fingers and ran the sponge over each one and along the palm. "It tickles her. Can you see?"

Peggy watched Christina's face, leaning toward her, but she couldn't see anything happening. She was glad she wasn't going to be here tomorrow—she knew getting Christina into the van was going to take a lot of extra work and she also knew that if the sick woman became upset or confused, the nurses might even have to give it up and not let her go. Sometimes, for no reason that Peggy could see, Christina got upset—waving her arms like flippers, her eyes rolling up into her head, moaning and whining. Peggy had run down the corridor to Christina's room once on hearing the cries, but Mrs. P put her off, saying nothing was wrong, nothing was wrong. That was odd because little things upset Mrs. P and Peggy thought this would upset her too. But Mrs. P didn't say anything, just got down on her knees and scraped up the old photos and crumpled them in her hand as she heaved herself up onto her feet.

Peggy waited, resigned and grumpy, for the warnings to come. She was sure Mrs. P would complain to the head nurse, saying Peggy had failed to do something that led to the outburst. Mrs. Perreira would be upset and angry. Once, when the puree hadn't been smooth enough, the old woman, only seventy back then, had marched into the kitchen, opened the refrigerator, pulled out one of the pies meant for dessert, and mashed it up. She turned to the cook who had been watching her in horror and yelled at him. "How do you like it? Do you want to eat something like that? You think you can give my daughter something like that?" She threw the puree onto the floor, the plastic cup bouncing against the tile and splattering puree all over the stainless steel cupboards. "Never give her something like that again. Never!" The incident was famous in the history of the nursing home—repeated to every new employee, partly as warning, partly as gossip.

"It'll be nice to see so many of your old friends again, won't it?" Peggy was a cheerful young woman with a new boyfriend. An only child, she delighted in his family dinners on Thursday nights; she couldn't imagine what a truly large family must be like—chaos, she suspected.

"He never married." Mrs. Perreira ran the sponge over her daughter's face. "Never married. The boy Christina almost married, I mean. Now he lives with a woman who has children of her own I'm told." She patted the towel over her daughter's face. "Such beautiful skin she has even now. Always it was beautiful, as a child, as a teenager, as a young woman, and now, even now."

"Oh." Peggy gripped the footboard and leaned against it. "Pretty hair too. I always like brushing it for her."

"You're a good girl, Peggy. You wouldn't run away if something happened to your boyfriend." Mrs. Perreira slid the sponge into the bowl and folded the towel. "What does it take to love someone? So little. So little. You have to love all you can, Peggy." Mrs. Perreira pushed the cart towards the nurse's aide and leaned over it. "All you can. Life can change in an instant. Just like that." She snapped her fingers just in front of Peggy's nose, startling the girl so that she jerked backwards. The fierce expression on the old woman's face faded so quickly that Peggy wasn't sure she had seen it or just imagined it. "But that won't happen to you, not to you, Peggy. You're a good girl. Life won't ask that of you."

* * * * *

Joe walked down the short driveway towards the street, waiting for the dark green pickup to get into position. The driver swung the wheel and the big tires cut onto the dirt driveway, and the truck started coming toward Joe. He stepped backwards, waited for the driver to glance in the rear-view mirror for Joe's signals.

"Straighten out, Eddie," Joe heard himself saying. He wasn't one for talking to himself but sometimes when he got really frustrated, it was better than swearing or telling someone off. "Just straighten out." He winced as the driver swung wide and brushed against an old rose bush whose long stalks hung over the narrow grass verge. Thorns scratched delicate lines in the shiny paint and light red petals fluttered onto the ground as the pickup swerved back onto the dirt and headed toward Joe.

Walking backwards, Joe did his best to guide the truck with his hands raised, waving one way then the other. But despite his best efforts, including several shouts to the driver, Joe knew he wasn't getting anywhere. Eddie seemed set on getting down the driveway on his own, swerving wide and sharp, swinging back, as though he were rocking the steering wheel with one finger in time to the radio. Near the end of the driveway, when he was parallel with the back porch, the driver flung his arm out, gave a wave, then slapped the side of the door twice. Joe moved aside and the pickup sped straight back to the old garage, a row of three open bays, one for each floor of the apartment building.

"If you tried that where I live, you'd have a couple of tickets by now." Joe caught the truck door as it swung open.

"Hey, Jose." The driver jumped down and threw out his hand. Joe was slow to meet it, and wondered that Eddie never seemed to notice, year after year, Joe's lessening enthusiasm for their encounters. Eddie was turning loud and brash, or louder and brasher, a caricature of the twenty-something who had started his own construction business with one truck, one worker, and sheer bravado. But he worked like a demon and soon was building houses all over southern Massachusetts, getting a reputation for being quick and good on pricing. "So loosen up. It's a driveway!"

"Those all the tables?"

Eddie walked around to the back of the truck and unlatched the tailgate, pulling it open. Six long tables were stacked in the bed of the truck, with a few boxes and canvas bags stuffed in the far corners. "Give me a hand." Eddie moved to the side and began to pull the top table towards him. Joe went to work on the other side, and the two men unloaded and stacked the long tables against the back porch.

"Where's Mr. Morton?" Eddie asked. "He's usually out here telling me where to put everything."

"Gone out with Pae, maybe." Joe pushed the last table into place and walked back to the truck. He began pulling out the bags, sliding them to the back.

"It's good to see you, Joe. But, you know, I'm surprised. Didn't think you'd bother." Eddie sat on the edge of the tailgate, resting one arm on his raised leg. "I mean, what's down here for you? Hear you're nicely set up where you are now— Mellingham? Nice little town, I hear. Haven't been up there myself. Maybe sometime."

"Let me know." Joe pulled out a number of bags and carted them over to the tables. He knew Eddie was watching him, waiting for him to return. Eddie liked to poke and prod, looking for soft spots, weak spots, sore spots—he'd been like that all his life. First as a kid when he wanted to see if one of the younger ones had candy he'd give up without a fight; then as a teen when he liked to see if someone would give up something without even being asked. Menacing, Joe later learned, and chargeable. But Eddie was family now, and he never actually did anything wrong—he was smart that way. Even so, Joe liked him less and less each year, and Eddie seemed to know it—hence the poking and prodding. Joe figured Eddie's ego couldn't take rejection, so he'd keep after Joe till he got what he wanted—recognition, acknowledgment that they'd been friends, something.

"You'll show me around?" Eddie continued smiling while Joe carried another clutch of bags and returned.

"Not much to see." Joe looked up when Eddie didn't answer and found him staring up towards the second floor porch, Joe's family's porch. Joe followed his gaze and saw Gwen draping a number of dish towels over the railing.

Eddie glanced back at Joe. "Just looking, Joe. Just looking." He laughed. Joe didn't. "Hey, how long you staying?" Eddie climbed down from the tailgate, slammed it shut, and followed

Joe into the first bay, where a number of folding chairs were stacked. Joe began to count, considered the total, and pulled out a cell phone.

"Zaira?" Joe said into the phone. "What's the usual number of chairs?" He listened. "All right. Another ten, just in case. Okay. I'll pick them up." He flipped the phone shut.

"Thought you'd have something fancier, Joe." Eddie eyed the phone as Joe slipped it into its case on his belt. "Is it safe carrying it like that? I mean, it doesn't get in the way of your gun or anything?"

"I have another one for work, carries different." Joe turned towards the house.

"You'd lose it in a fight out here." Eddie began to fall into step beside him.

"I'm a little old to get into fights, Eddie."

The other man slapped Joe on the shoulder and rested his hand there. "Never too old, Jose, never. But you never took to it, did you? Just that one time." Eddie laughed and shook his head but Joe shifted to throw off his hand. "You remember that?"

"Eddie, I have to pick up some chairs. I told Zaira I'd do it—she's got enough on her hands right now."

"Hey, they'll deliver." Eddie threw out his hands. "I can go. I owe you—since I whupped you so bad that one time. Don't you remember?"

"Yeah, Eddie, I remember the fight, but I don't recall your beating me." Joe could feel himself growing increasingly impatient. He didn't like Eddie's forced familiarity and wanted to get away from him before it went too far.

"Sure I did. You and Paulo and some other guy against me and my brothers. You don't remember? Course not. Who'd want to remember losing so bad?" Eddie rested his hands on his hips. "But it was fair."

"Sure, Eddie."

"Hurts to remember, yeah. Paulo was touchy about it too."

Joe swung around to face him directly. "Paulo was never touchy."

"He was that day. What do you think the fight was about?"

Joe could feel the iron setting in his shoulders, the way it had when he was a teen and he knew someone wanted a fight, that he could win, but he still didn't want to have anything to do with the guy. It was happening because he didn't recall what the fight was about, and now that Eddie had brought it up, he wasn't sure he had ever known. What was that brawl about? What was it supposed to settle? "It seems to be more important what you thought it was about."

Eddie grabbed Joe by the arm. "He never told you?" Eddie looked at him in disbelief, and stepped back, studying Joe. "You know, I'll bet he didn't tell you."

"Tell me what, Eddie." Joe was bored with Eddie's manipulations. He hated the way Eddie had kept all the ploys of the teenager, adapting them to his age, but using them just the same.

"Nothing, Joe, nothing." Eddie seemed caught in doubt, his humor deflated, and he backed away from Joe. "I was just razzing you, Joe. It's good to see you. Really is. You don't get down here enough. Tomorrow will be packed—everyone will be here, I'm hearing. Good to have a moment of peace with an old friend" He punched Joe on the arm.

"How's Rosalie?" Joe stepped away from him to push the bags into a tighter pile.

"I know you think I'm not good enough for your sister, Jose, but she has everything a woman could want. I made sure of that. She has no complaints." His arms stiffened and moved away from his sides, a change Joe couldn't fail to notice.

"My sisters could always speak for themselves."

"She never complained to you, never." He waited, his arms away from his sides, in that stance that tells his opponent he's ready, willing, very willing.

"She can tell me herself."

"Nothing to complain about, nothing." Eddie pointed his finger at Joe, coming within a hair's breadth of the other man's chest before pumping his hand in the air, making his point. Then he walked over to his pickup, climbed in, and drove down the dirt driveway, bouncing over the deep ruts.

* * * * *

Jennie followed her new friend down the driveway to the back of the double decker. She liked Sarah—she wasn't at all what Jennie expected. Sarah was normal, like a real person. Jennie wouldn't want Joe to know, but she'd wondered if there was something wrong with his family that kept her and Philip and Gwen on the other side of Boston, away from them. But now she decided Joe was probably just like everyone else—he loved his family but didn't really want to live next door to them. Jennie understood exactly how he felt. Sometimes she wanted to push her brother Philip down the stairs and the only thing that stopped her was the threat of facing her mother's anger. She didn't want to deal with that, so Philip lived on. Maybe some day she'd poison him and write about it. "Oh, what a good idea," Jennie said aloud.

"What is?" Sarah turned around.

"I was just thinking about my brother, Philip, and what I might do to him someday." Jennie blushed when she realized what she'd said. "Not that I'd really hurt him."

"Once when I was little I used to cover bars of soap with chocolate for Easter morning. Not very original, but I was just a kid." Sarah preened just a bit with the confession.

"I never tried that one."

"When I was ten I borrowed this beach ball that squealed when you caught it and squeezed it, and I stuck it under my dad's car just so, so that when he started to back out of the garage it'd make all this noise."

"Did it?"

"Oh yeah. Then it blew up. And that really was a racket."

Jennie giggled. "I'll have to remember that one. I don't think we have any beach balls, but I'd like to see it—or hear it."

"Once, when my dad was having a neighborhood meeting at our house, I put out Romney for President signs." Sarah almost doubled over laughing. "I thought he was going to chase me down the street with them!"

"Was he mad?" Jennie was mesmerized by this sort-of-cousin's stories—she was a one-woman earthquake.

"Oh, no, not really." Sarah waved off Jennie's question. "That wasn't the worst thing I've ever done. Once, when he was away for a few days, I got a twin bed that was just like his but smaller and put it in their room, so when he got home he thought he'd grown or put on weight. He couldn't understand what had happened—why his bed was too small for him! It drove him nuts! But then he noticed that mom's bed was bigger and he figured it out."

"That is way better than thinking up ways to get revenge on your younger brother and not being able to do anything," Jennie said, clearly impressed.

"Then I put a teabag into the shower head and everyone thought something was wrong with the water. It took the plumber hours to figure it out! Dad was really angry about that so then I just put soap in the garden hose—that was awesome. And once I bought my mom a sweater for her birthday and after she tried it on and wore it a couple of times I replaced it with one that was a smaller size." Sarah laughed out loud, then sobered quickly. "She was really pissed at me for that one."

"I don't blame her. I would've freaked! What else have you done?"

"I filled a cupboard with popcorn—that was messy—and I filled my grandfather's umbrella with scraps of newspaper, like confetti. But that's small stuff. I have some really good ideas for us, Jennie." Sarah leaned over and whispered. "But first . . . Come on. We have work to do."

"Sure." Jennie tucked away the delicious thought for a later time. "What work? What are we going to do?"

"Help with the cooking. Avó likes to have a helper, and she really likes having two." Sarah grinned. "Okay with you?"

Jennie shrugged. "Sure. I like to cook."

"You don't get to cook, Jennie. You get to help. My grandmother is very serious about her meals." Sarah waved to the men working in the back yard. "Much too serious if you ask me." She waited for Jennie to catch up and then said softly, "My entire family is much too serious. They need to lighten up."

"Other than driving them nuts with pranks, do you tell them that?"

Sarah rolled her head back on her shoulders and closed her eyes. "All the time. Do they listen?" She pulled Jennie aside. "But I have an idea. You can help."

Sarah jumped up the first two steps to the porch. Jennie followed her. She waved to Joe across the backyard and accepted a nod in return as he carried a long table over to a tree and began to unlatch the metal legs.

"We're here, Avó." Sarah pulled open the screen door and called out as she marched down the hallway. "Where are you?"

"I'm here, right here. Where would I be?" The old woman came to the kitchen doorway with a wooden ladle in her hand, a once neatly pressed but now stained apron around her middle. "Where have you been? You are here to help? Yes?"

"Yes, we are. Both of us." Sarah gave the old woman a quick kiss and dropped her canvas bag on a chair. "So, what should we do?" She dropped her hands on her hips and looked around while Jennie lingered in the doorway, trying to figure out just how this was all going to play out. She liked Sarah, yes, but she wasn't sure she wanted to be dragged into a family squabble. And from the expression on her grandmother's face, Sarah was about to be put in her place.

"Over there," the old woman said. "Chop those carrots very fine." She pointed to a wooden cutting board on the counter and a stack of carrots sitting nearby.

"Oh." Sarah's face dropped. "I could help you make cookies."

"I don't need help with that. Carrots." The old woman pointed again, extending a still muscular thick arm. Sarah sighed, cast a resigned look at Jennie and marched over to the counter. Jennie glanced back at the old woman, who looked her up and down. "And you," the old woman said, reaching out her arm and pinching Jennie's upper arm. "Hmm. Good. You can mix butter and sugar. Over there." Jennie hustled over to her station and picked up a wooden spoon.

"I told you everyone was way too serious," Sarah whispered. "She can't hear me. She's deaf."

Jennie opened her mouth to say something, but thought better of it. She was used to old women who said they were deaf when they didn't want to talk about something. Mrs. Alesandro, who lived upstairs in the building where Joe used to live, used that trick all the time. Jennie knew better than to believe Sarah when she said Mrs. Silva couldn't hear, and clamped her mouth shut. Jennie focused on her mixing and forgot about Sarah and her plans. After a while she fell into the rhythm of her work and began humming to herself. She was caught off guard when she felt Sarah nudging her.

"Wait till she sees what we do tomorrow morning!" Sarah nudged Jennie again and quickly returned to her chopping when she saw the old woman turn around and frown at her.

Five

Friday Evening

Joe turned the corner and scanned the block ahead of him. He quickened his step while the two old men ahead slowed as they approached a wooden bench. They stopped in front of it, chatting and touching it as though they had never encountered such an object before when in fact the bench was nearly as old as they were and had been nailed to the ground at this spot for just as long. The bench was set in a small park one street away from a neighborhood tavern Joe's father had frequented in his younger days. Joe's father waved Mr. Morton to sit and he did. The downstairs neighbor was a pale figure in pale clothing, a man who had over the decades been drained of all independence and absorbed into the Silva family like a strange, remote cousin who was accepted and loved even though he looked like someone's illegitimate child. Mrs. Morton was the cagey one, superficially docile but, Joe suspected, quietly independent, able to disappear into her own life beyond the prying eyes of neighbors.

Joe's father crouched over and craned his neck at the sound of Joe's sharp footsteps, then nodded to him to take a seat at the end of the bench. Mr. Morton leaned forward and looked around his friend, nodding with a lugubrious look of approval, shook his head with apparent resignation, and then leaned back; not a word passed his lips. The two old men stared at the cracked walk in front of them, where little bunches of grass had pushed their way up along the seams. The park was really no more than a narrow strip too small for building, but the addition of another bench, three flowering trees, and some grass had changed the landscape, and old men claimed it throughout the day—three Italian men in the morning, two Portuguese in the afternoon before supper, and Mr. Silva and Mr. Morton after the evening meal.

"Such an important event you are having." Mr. Morton's thin head with its wispy white hair bobbed gently in the breeze. "Again."

Mr. Silva considered this before replying, waiting for a line of cars to pass before speaking. "All family events are important." Joe crossed his legs and leaned back against the bench. "You tell him, Jose."

"I think he's heard enough from all of us over the years, Pae." Joe grinned. "I left Gwen washing dishes—I shouldn't leave her there too long."

"You worry too much," his father said.

"He's a cop. He's paid to worry," Mr. Morton said.

"He's on vacation—here with his family, to rest."

"When is a dog not a dog? When he sleeps with chickens?" Mr. Morton snorted and tapped his cane on the walkway. "Your mother will love her," the old man said to Joe.

"Better not leave her too long." Joe reached his arms up and stretched. He was tired, sleepy, which surprised him. He hadn't noticed he was tired earlier in the day—it came upon him all of a sudden—but he felt like he hadn't had a good night's sleep all week. "She might not like it."

"What not like? She is there with your mother and your sister. Yes?" The old man shrugged and tipped his head towards Mr. Morton. "Women. Always they have something to say— leave them to talk."

"I was hoping to see Deanie, and I hear Gino is coming." Joe rested his arm across the back of the bench and turned to his father. "They are coming, you said."

"Yes, yes, coming."

"You must have worked hard to get them here." Joe watched his father's profile. How much more delicately could he have put it? Joe wouldn't have believed anyone could get those two to show up at anything, let alone a family gathering. Part of him accepted without question the longing of one child or another to flee the family world and find a new place, build a new life in a different world. But something always kept him from going any further with it and imagining what those lives might be like. He knew better than he wanted to know what Deanie's life had been like, might still be like. And Gino—what had propelled him westward?—remained the mystery he became as a teenager, quiet, still, taciturn.

"I am an old man," Mr. Silva said. "They know that."

"They know that he is an old man," Mr. Morton said.

Two pairs of gnarled, rock-hard hands motioned stiffly in the evening air, the way old men's hands got after the softening flesh of youth and middle age had faded away and the only thing left was the bare strength. All the things that smoothed out the roughness of life—the gentle hands, the kind words, the diplomatic explanations—disappeared in old age, when pure brute strength to survive was all that was needed and the rest was frivolous and time wasting and false.

"That's why they come," Mr. Morton said. "Even the cousins will come."

"They always come," Joe said, "even the ones we don't like."

"You mean Eddie," Mr. Silva said.

The statement was blunt, even for Joe's father, and Joe had to stifle the urge to laugh. Even more, the name sounded strange to Joe's ears, even stranger in his father's voice. Sometime back, a few or perhaps several years ago, the family had taken to calling Eduardo by the name Eddie, as though another person had emerged and a new name was required. Sometimes, to Joe's surprise, the new name sounded right.

"You beat him once," Pae Silva said.

"Hmm?" Joe squinted at his father.

"You beat him in a fight."

Joe racked his brain trying to remember what he had told his father but he had this uneasy feeling he had told him nothing out of a sense of misgiving for the whole affair.

"Bad thing, fighting. Sometimes." Mr. Morton began to nod again. "Sometimes."

"I don't think I ever fought Eddie exactly," Joe said, thinking he sounded like someone trying to cover up something. "I wasn't a fighter, remember?"

Joe's father shifted in his seat and twisted his shoulders around to get a better look at his son. "You didn't fight him?" Joe shook his head. The old man grew confused and turned to Mr. Morton. "You hear?"

"Of course I hear. He's not a fighter. I knew that."

"It wasn't that kind of . . ."

His father waited.

"That was quite a while ago, Pae. I don't remember what it was about and quite how it happened. Why do you care about something so long ago?"

"Hmmmp." Pae Silva's hands grew loose in his lap and the old man tipped his head one way and then another as though trying to hear better. He frowned and glanced at Joe, then frowned again. "I want to walk." He reached out his hand to Joe, then said again to Mr. Morton, "I want to walk."

Joe helped his father up, then Mr. Morton, and with the two men limping along in front of him, followed them out of the park. To his surprise they turned to the right and headed down a narrow side street where the porches sat close to the sidewalk and small but overflowing window boxes made up for the lack of lawn and garden.

"We'll stop to see Mrs. Perreira," Pae Silva said.

Startled, Joe reached out and laid his hand on his father's shoulder. "The Perreiras don't live on this street anymore, Pae. They moved, out to Cedar Street. On the other side of the lake."

The old man stopped and scanned the street, looking for the familiar house. "They didn't tell me that." He stepped into the road and walked to the center to get a better look at the houses lining the street on both sides. "It's a green house." He turned around slowly, noticing fully each house. No house was painted green.

"Why did no one tell me?" Pae Silva said. Mr. Morton turned around to stare at Joe, as if waiting for a good explanation, which his expression said didn't exist.

"I'll ask Eddie. He'll tell me. He's a good boy. He knows where everyone is. He pays attention." Pae Silva began to retrace his steps. Mr. Morton fell into step behind him, and Joe behind him.

The journey home was confused. Joe stopped and started behind his father, unable to walk slowly enough to maintain a steady pace behind the two men. The motion seemed to match his feelings of the moment, the sudden jolt of awareness of the extent of his father's decline, and then the swift fall into apparent normality. He hadn't expected his father to decline so rapidly, and so erratically. At some moments he seemed as sharp and as incisive as ever, and at others, as tonight, he didn't seem to know what year it was or who those outside his family were. Eduardo was now Eddie, a good boy, which he hadn't been since he was a small child, not yet into mischief and scrapping, but with that big ready-to-laugh expression and those shoulders ready to charge forward.

Pae Silva came to the driveway and his neighbor lightly touched his sleeve before turning onto the dirt and gravel. Pae followed him. Mr. Morton lumbered up his back steps and pulled open the screen door as Joe and his father passed to the next flight. As Pae Silva mounted the steps, Mr. Morton let the screen door slam shut and reached for Joe's arm.

"He tells me such stories, Joe." He pulled Joe closer and Joe felt spittle on his face. "But he thinks they're true. I tell him, only tell the true. Tell me one true thing, nothing more. But he goes on and on and he tells me it's true." Mr. Morton shook his head, the light glinting on the waxy shiny pink skin on his nose, the liver spots sprinkling his cheeks and forehead.

"What stories?" Joe asked.

"I only want one true thing. The others . . ." The old man shook his head. "I cannot listen. I cannot believe him. Just tell me something that's true, and he tells me such a story." He let go of Joe's arm and leaned away. "I'm too old for such stories."

"What stories?" Joe moved closer.

"I'm too old for these things." He pulled at the screen door and stumbled inside.

* * * * *

Gwen was used to feeling like a fifth wheel—it was the state of mind that seemed to be required for being a parent. Her two charges, Jennie and Philip, had no trouble letting her know that when their friends were around she shouldn't be. But Gwen was not one to give in, and Jennie and Philip knew it, their faces crumpling in resignation and annoyance. Gwen simply refused to believe them when they told her what other parents allowed, and she certainly never told them that Joe often confirmed their stories. But Jennie was deep into plans with her new friend, Sarah, and Philip moaned on the telephone about camp and then suddenly perked up when he realized he wanted something that Gwen could provide even long distance over the phone. Life was chugging along on its normal track. Except for Joe.

"Which one is Lucia?" Gwen asked as the car sped down the road. When Joe was thinking hard he had a tendency to drive hard. She was getting ready to poke him to get his attention—and make him slow down.

"What? Oh, sorry." He gave her a quick smile. "Lucia? She's number four in the list, two years younger than me."

"So you were close?"

"Hmmm."

"What does that mean?"

"We were all close, remember?"

"Okay, okay."

Joe turned down another road, this one meandering among small houses.

"You're very abstracted now." Gwen flopped against the back of the seat trying to get comfortable again. "This isn't an ordinary family reunion—anyone can see that— but I just hope it goes all right. I don't feel I should be here—there are way too many undercurrents for me. I prefer family life to be simple and stupid." Gwen pealed the front of her blouse away from her body, and adjusted the blower for the ac.

She had promised herself she would do everything she could to help make this weekend a success. She loved Joe's parents not only for accepting her but also for who they were as people, and she wanted to keep that good will alive. But she had sensed the weekend might somehow endanger her relationship with Joe and she hadn't been able to shake the feeling of insecurity and defensiveness, no matter how much she cajoled herself into thinking positively. Then, as the hours unfolded, she began to feel the danger had nothing to do with her and Joe. She didn't know if that made the whole thing better or worse. It left her uneasy in a wary and watchful way, waiting for the proverbial monster to fling itself out of the closet and terrorize the victim.

Joe pulled up at a white line and stopped, turning to face Gwen. "Simple and stupid?"

"You know how I feel about drama. I can put up with anything but . . ."

Joe began to laugh, letting his foot sit on the brake. "I know how you feel. Something's in the air."

Gwen nodded. The impertinent honk of the car behind them pulled Joe from the moment, and the car moved forward.

"Do you want to talk about it?" Gwen punched a button on the ac and the blower fell silent.

"With you? Sure. If I knew what to talk about." Joe slowed and the car crawled past a number of small 1950s bungalows. "You must have noticed my dad is losing his mental faculties."

"Yes, I noticed." It was her secret fear. She wasn't a great intellect and had a nagging suspicion that her brain would give out when she was barely sixty, and then she'd be locked up for the rest of her life by well-meaning folks afraid she'd wander off into traffic or get lost in Boston. She knew it was irrational, but that didn't ease the fear. "Your mother's all right."

"Yes, she is." This seemed to sober Joe and he drove more intently. "He's up to something and she's distanced from things. She's the same but not the same."

Joe turned off onto a dirt lane and pulled the car onto the verge. Gwen looked around her, saw nothing of particular interest beyond the lake in the distance, and looked to Joe for an explanation.

"Lucia and her husband own a cottage farther down. I wanted to see her when we could maybe talk in quiet for a while, without all the craziness of the whole family around." Joe put the car in park and stared out towards the lake.

"And that's why we're sitting here, waiting for her to come to us?" Gwen lowered the window and felt the warm air rushing in against the cooler inside air. Joe reached out his hand and Gwen took it.

"Lucia's husband is all right, Larry Foster. Actually he's a pretty decent sort, but the last time I talked to him he told me, probably without realizing what he was saying, that Lucia had just been talking to Deanie." Gwen felt Joe's grip tighten, then relax. He gave her hand a gentle bounce on the center panel.

"And?"

"Deanie took off when she was in college and just disappeared. No one seemed to know what happened to her, and the family seemed to accept it."

"I don't believe that." Gwen shifted in her seat to get a better look at Joe. "Do you?"

"I was stunned. I couldn't believe that anyone in my family would do something like that. And certainly not Deanie. But no one would talk about it—the tension in the family was surreal. So, I figured if I found Deanie, I'd find the answer."

"It sounds like sorrow, like everyone was overcome with pain and grief."

"Probably." Joe turned as though listening for something to emerge in the quiet. "I wasn't really thinking about it that way— I was too busy tracking her down, to make sure she was all right, just in case."

"Did you find her?"

"I did." His mouth crumpled flat, like smoothed over paper.

"Oh." It can't be good, she thought. Why would you keep track of your sister and not let anyone else know where she was and then be surprised when another sibling seemed to know about her?

"Lucia's been a good sister. She's helped our Rosalie when she needed it but didn't want to say anything."

"Money?"

Joe shook his head. "Her husband's a jerk—he gets all wrought up if he thinks she's lied to him."

"Oh, Joe."

"Don't worry. I made it clear to Eddie that if he ever laid a hand on her he'd never see the sun rise again." His hand tightened and again relaxed. "But she won't leave him. And she seems to have made her peace with it." Joe pulled his hand away and grabbed the steering wheel. "She shows up at Lucia's sometimes, and Mae leaves the back door unlocked—has done so for probably thirty years—just in case."

"That must be awful for your mother." Sometimes Gwen thought she knew how families went wrong, but then someone would tell her something—in confidence, of course—and she was stunned once again at the things she hadn't imagined about people who had seemed so ordinary or so blessed.

"I have to remind myself not to think of her as a frail old lady." He leaned his head back and closed his eyes.

"Joe, she is a frail old lady."

"If she knew what Deanie has been up to, it would kill her."

Gwen tried to take in the way the corners of his mouth stretched downward, the way his fingers pushed through his hair and rubbed the back of his neck, the way his jaw tightened and didn't relax. "That bad? What's she been up to?"

"A lot of things, more than I care to know about." He rubbed his palm along the steering wheel, up and down, up and down. "She spent some time in LA with a crowd that seemed to be in the movie business but on the low end, the very low end. Soft porn."

"Oh, Joe!" Gwen felt her mouth fall open, and felt incredibly stupid, like a hick suddenly getting a first look at a skyscraper, as though she really were that naïve.

"And then she found another line of work."

"You don't sound relieved."

"She was beautiful. I didn't realize what her looks might mean until she disappeared." His expression softened as he seemed to recall the child Deanie.

"I don't understand—what do you mean, about her looks?"

Joe slid in his seat so he was facing her. "That kind of beauty—it makes everything seem easy. Whatever a woman wants comes easily to her. The problem is, it's easy to get things that aren't good for you in the long run—the attention, the easy entrée, the easy yes."

Gwen was silent, thinking about the sister who sounded like she bore no relation at all to the rest of the family. "It got her into trouble?"

"Some. That's why we're here. I want to get a look at Deanie, to make sure she behaves herself with our parents. I want to know up front how much she's changed—and how bad it is." Joe put the car in gear and tapped the gas pedal; the car moved forward. He followed the dirt lane, swinging wide of deep ruts, riding the ridge down the center. The small houses gave way to seasonal cottages, with large decks facing the lake, and stacks of folding chairs along the railings, bird feeders dangling among the branches, weed-infested patches of ground that no one bothered to mow because the sun rarely penetrated there, and solid winter shutters leaning against garage walls.

The road narrowed still more and the cottages seemed smaller but now with small docks poking into the water.

"There." Joe indicated a small blue cottage with stacks of white shutters near the front door and a Jaguar XK with the top up parked on a patch of grass.

"Your brother-in-law does well," Gwen said, admiring the car.

"He does but he's not the type for that." Joe nodded at the Jaguar. "That's Deanie's." He pulled up beside the sleek black car. "That's Larry's, the Toyota. He's the frugal sort, convinced the next famine is just around the corner ready to ambush him. Everything he buys has to have long-term resale value."

"Oh."

Joe began to laugh.

"What?"

"My family has reduced you to inarticulateness. Oh seems to be your default reply for the weekend."

Gwen gave him a gentle slap and laughed. "I thought this was going to be a nice if slightly chaotic family weekend. It's turning out to be anything but. Anyway, I promise not to go around with my mouth hanging open and embarrass you."

"Not you." He leaned over and kissed her and for a moment they forgot what had brought them there and lost themselves in the fading glow of the sunset on the lake.

* * * * *

"Oh, Jose!" The tall dark-haired woman pulled open the door and threw her arms around Joe's neck, giving him loud kisses on both cheeks. Her face glowed pink and her dark eyes were warm and fixed on her older brother. She stepped away and turned to Gwen, swinging her arms to include her. "I'm so glad you've come, Gwen. We have barely said more than hello all these years you've known Joe." Lucia took Gwen's hands in hers and kissed her lightly on both cheeks. Gwen returned the warmth with a gentle squeeze of the other woman's fingers and she and Joe followed his sister into the house. Gwen liked Lucia—even though Lucia and Zaira and Gwen had never drawn close, she had been comfortable and open with the two sisters and counted them as friends in the family.

The cottage was so plain and simple outside that Gwen was unprepared for what greeted her inside—an interior that could have been taken out of a popular decorating magazine illustrating the best-appointed summer cottage. The long plush sofas covered in bubbly white cotton were complemented with antique wicker chairs and bright throw pillows. A gnarled and twisted piece of driftwood, shellacked and polished sat under a large piece of glass with a tray of drinks on top. An oil painting of children playing at a beach hung over the gas fireplace. Wherever Gwen looked, a thousand-dollar antique or object d'art looked back at her.

"Hmm? Sorry, I was taking in the view." Gwen nodded to the wall of windows when she realized Lucia had been talking to her.

"Lovely, isn't it?" Lucia didn't bother turning to look; she gave Gwen a warm smile, sat down on the sofa, and patted the seat next to her. "Deanie's just gone out, but she won't be long. Just wanted to stroll down to the old dock and back—sentimental journeys and all that."

Joe slid onto the sofa opposite them and began to tell his sister about his visit with their dad, his obvious mental deterioration compared to that of a few weeks ago, and his conversations with their mother. Lucia threw her arm across the sofa, crossed her legs, and nodded as he went along. When he seemed to be finished, she began to speak in Portuguese, then stopped.

"I'm so sorry, Gwen, that was so rude. I forget sometimes. And I should remember—Larry hasn't picked up a word after all these years." She turned to Joe again. "What do you want to do? I will do anything you want me to do—just tell me. I can't ask Zaira—Gray isn't doing well, you know. But Pae, well, Mr. Morton watches over him, Mae watches over him, I watch over him—"

"I get it, Lucia, I get it." Joe rubbed his hand across his face and Gwen guessed he was getting restless. He didn't really like talking about family problems—he was a very pragmatic man. You had a problem? You came up with a solution and went for it. But this was different, and everyone knew it. His father's decline would weigh heavily because the only solution, other than the nursing home, was the ultimate one—and that wasn't up to anyone here to decide. At least that was how Joe had put it to her a few weeks ago. "We can move him around," Joe had said after a call from his mother, "but we're just marking time now. We know the ending."

"We have to come up with something better, Joe, I agree. He is our dad and how can he be happy if he doesn't know who we are and if he has to live among strangers?" The thought seemed to sober her, and she slid forward on the sofa and began to pour out drinks. "We will all be strangers to him soon, won't we? Here. A nice gin punch," she said, handing Gwen a glass, then Joe. "I talked to a doctor friend and there are medications he could be taking. I don't know why he isn't taking something."

"Lucia—"

"He should be on medication, Joe." She leaned over and grew intense as she repeated this. "And he should have a nurse coming in every day to help him so Mae doesn't have to do everything. Think how old she is." Abruptly, she turned to

Gwen. "You'd want someone coming in to help your parents, wouldn't you?" She didn't wait for an answer before shifting again to Joe. "Think of Mae. She should have help. God knows she's waited on that man for enough years. Do you realize, Jose, she has stood behind his chair at supper for over seventy years. Seventy years!"

"And for how many years have you stood behind Larry's chair?"

"Very funny, Joe, very funny. I'd divorce him if he ever asked such a thing, Pope or no Pope." She fell back against the sofa, her drink in one hand. "But we can decide together, all of us. Right?"

"How do you mean?" Joe asked. He didn't sound suspicious but Gwen's ears perked up when she heard the phrasing. He never spoke so casually, so awkwardly. It was like listening to a teenager's voice coming out of Joe's body.

"Well, we're all here together for the first time in years. We can all talk about it." Lucia tried to smile but her heart didn't seem to be in it. "I don't want to be the one, Jose. Zaira is so worried about Gray—I don't want to be the one to step in and make decisions and then everyone's mad at me because they would have done it differently. It won't be much longer now, Jose. We have to help Mae and work this out. Please."

"Lucia, are we talking about you and me and Zaira and Rosalie, or do you really think Deanie and Gino will want to weigh in on how we manage Pae's health?" Joe set his glass on the table.

"You can ask Deanie herself." Lucia raised the glass to her lip at the sound of the door opening. "That must be her now." She pushed herself deeper into the cushions and Gwen felt an unmistakable change in the room, as though a person had disappeared, leaving behind the shell that was Lucia.

Joe stood at the sound of a woman's heels clicking across the bamboo wood flooring. Gwen placed her glass on the table, prepared to greet the newcomer but there her plan ended as she struggled to take in the image of Joe's youngest sister. She was tall like the rest of the family, but probably the tallest of the girls at close to six feet, with black hair that glowed and swirled and cuddled her neck.

Gwen knew how it felt to feel eclipsed by a beautiful or powerful or rich woman, that sense of inferiority, of drabness, of disappearing like a light breeze—she saw the makeup or jewelry or wardrobe that captured the eye and imagination of those around her—but Deanie was different. Gwen felt like she had entered into another realm where everyone was larger, richer, smarter—more different from her than a tornado was from a summer breeze.

"It is me, Jose." Deanie walked up to her brother and threw her arms around his neck and kissed either cheek, before pulling away and looking him up and down. "You're the same, you really are."

"You're not." Joe held her hands lightly in front of him.

"I should hope not." She ducked her head. "It's been a long time."

He shook both her hands, told her how good it was to see her after so many years, and gracefully segued into an introduction to Gwen. Almost robotically Gwen reached up to offer her hand and Deanie took it, giving it a quick examination as though she were wearing an especially interesting piece of jewelry. Gwen was startled by how strong Deanie's grip was. After a moment, Deanie pulled her hand away and settled herself at the end of the sofa, tucking one leg beneath her.

"That your car out there, Jose? I was thinking of getting an SUV when I got home. Do you like it?"

Gwen couldn't recall what Joe answered; she was trying to keep herself from massaging her right hand. It wasn't that it hurt—the grip had been strong but not threatening—it was that she didn't want to have had this woman touch her. Gwen knew, instinctively, that something more than an introduction had taken place, and Gwen had lost something in the transaction.

"I haven't seen you in years, Deanie, years. If you really want to know about my car, I'll get you the specs." Joe was facing her now on the sofa, his hand reaching across the back, his fingers splayed. "I am surprised that you've come, but very glad too."

"I walked down to the dock—it's been repaired, hasn't it, Lucia?"

"Several times, Deanie, several times." Lucia nodded.

"So." Deanie seemed at a loss until she looked across at Gwen. "She's lovely, Jose." Deanie said, nodding at Gwen, who struggled to remind herself that she was looking at a woman in her fifties.

"Thank you," Gwen said, feeling like she'd been patted on the head.

The conversation meandered through all the years that had passed, arriving at those in Mellingham. For a second time, Deanie turned to Gwen, and said, "She's lovely, Jose." That was enough for Gwen.

"You know, you guys really have a lot of family things to talk about. Why not set up a time for just that? I don't want to prevent you from speaking freely or thinking that you have to entertain me or include me in the conversation." She gave Deanie an encouraging smile as she began to stand up.

"Great idea." Lucia put her glass down.

"They're only looks—from a good hairstylist and a make-up artist," Gwen told herself as she crossed in front of Deanie and moved to the front door. Behind her she could hear Joe agreeing to a time to meet in the morning. She reached the door and turned to thank Lucia for the drink.

"It's wonderful to see you, Gwen." Lucia followed her to the door and kissed her and Joe as they left.

Not until Gwen was outside did she feel her knees wobbling beneath her and her heart tingling. Sometimes she surprised herself.

* * * * *

"Are you ready?" Sarah grabbed a pillow off the twin bed, threw it across the room onto a pile of laundry, and dropped her jean-clad body onto the bed. "This will be sooo cool. Wicked good." She stretched her legs up straight into the air and reached up her hands to grab at her toes. "Do you think I have thick ankles?"

Jennie looked up from the search through her purse and studied the ankles in question waving above her. "No. They're fine. Good, actually." Then she looked down at her own ankles. "They're normal."

"Is that good?"

Jennie checked her own ankles again, repeated her opinion, and continued rummaging in her purse. She pulled out a plastic lip gloss case and shoved the purse onto the bed. When she had finished administering the lip gloss, she capped it and slipped it back into the purse. "Don't you think this is bad timing? I mean, with so many of your relatives around."

"Nah. Besides, what you really mean is will you get into lots of trouble and Tio Jose will be mad at you." Sarah rolled over onto her side and propped herself up on her arm. "He's got other things to think about."

"But I promised my mother I wouldn't do anything to upset him. She doesn't want him distracted from what he's thinking about. It's because he wants to have a good family reunion, since it's been so long."

"Oh, no, it isn't." Sarah sat up and pulled her legs into a lotus position. "He didn't tell you what all this is about, but it's nothing like an ordinary reunion." She lowered her voice and glanced back at the open door, then spun around on her behind and kicked the door shut with the tip of her toe. "That's what he told you, isn't it?"

Jennie nodded. "My mom said it was important because everyone was going to be here." Jennie rearranged the pillows, settling in for an intense chat. She wanted to know what was going on, and Sarah seemed to be the one who knew it all.

"It's important because no one really knows what's going to happen."

Jennie's interest perked up. "What's really going to happen?"

"Well, first of all, they're bringing Christina Perreira." Sarah gave her a knowing look, her mouth in a crooked smile. "Mrs. Perreira's still upset that Uncle Joe didn't hang around and sort of still marry her."

"I thought she was in a coma. How can you marry someone in a coma? And why would you?" Jennie's face crinkled in disgust as she struggled to reconcile the Joe she had come to love as a father with the image of a man abandoning a woman who needed him. She was way too romantic for the complications life was throwing at her this weekend.

Sarah shook her head and her dark brown hair fluffed up into little wings. "For a while she was, in the beginning. But not anymore—not for years. She can follow you with her eyes and sometimes she can lift her hands and she makes noises. Can you imagine living with someone who can't talk to you? You'd never know if they understood you or not."

"Gee." Both Jennie and Sarah paused to consider the tragedy they couldn't understand.

"Anyway, she's coming. Avô asked Mrs. Perreira and she said yes." Sarah seemed to lose a sense of excitement and tipped her head up, gazing at the ceiling. "I don't get that one, actually. He never really talks about them. He feels bad for her and the family, but inviting her is kind of weird. Anyway, they're coming. Even Mr. Perreira, and he never says anything about his daughter—like she's not really alive."

"That's creepy."

"My mother says it's because it's too painful for him because he never had to learn to deal with it like Mrs. Perreira, or something like that."

"And your grandfather—he can do whatever he wants?"

"Are you kidding? My dad once said to me, When Avô asks you to jump, you say, How high." She pulled a face and shrugged.

"Wow." Jennie looked uncertain about that and ran those words through her head again. "How high?" she muttered.

"It's not a big deal. He's an old man—he's entitled." Sarah waved away her friend's hesitation. "Anyway, he insisted that everyone come home. He wrote everyone and called everyone telling them he was an old man and he wasn't going to live forever."

"He is old."

"Yes, he is. He's at least 90 something. But he's not sure. If I ask him he gets confused. He thinks I'm Zaira, my mother, sometimes." Sarah began to giggle, then quickly sobered. "So, they're all coming. It's hard to say no to Avô."

"Does he do this every year?"

"Never did it before. Just this year. Every year we have lots of family picnics but he never tells us when to come and sometimes we have to miss the event. Lucia Tia was in the Azores last summer and two of my cousins were hiking in New Hampshire. But this year he wrote us and called us." Sarah picked at the blanket. "It was weird."

"He's up to something."

"You're not kidding! He got up in the middle of the night a couple of months ago and called someplace long distance—he had the telephone operator make the call for him. He told her he couldn't see the address book and she had to help him."

"Who did he call?"

"Tia Deanie. She's the youngest sister—I never met her, I don't think. If I did I don't remember her."

"You were here?"

"I had the flu so I was staying here so Avó could take care of me. It's way better to be sick here than at home."

"What did he say to her? Did you hear?"

"He kept calling her by a name I never heard before—Daniellita, or something—and telling her this was his last chance and Paulo told him to do this."

"Who's Paulo?"

"He's my dead uncle. I never knew him."

Jennie shifted on the bed. She didn't like the sound of an old man pleading with his daughter because a dead relative told him to—as much as she liked to get around her mother sometimes, she didn't ever want to do anything weird like that—it sounded embarrassing. "I don't like the sound of this."

"It was okay." Sarah threw her hands out, waving her palms in the air. "He always talks like that. He says this is the situation, this is what I want, do this."

"So what did he say after that? Did she answer him?"

"Good, he said. This is right. Then he slammed down the receiver." Sarah sighed. "Good thing he doesn't have a cell phone—he'd never get his point across. He uses the phone like a weapon."

"But what about your grandmother? What does she think?"

"Avó? Hard to tell. I don't think she knows about the phone calls. Avô has a friend pay the bills, his accountant, so she would never see the call. She probably doesn't know he called Tia Deanie, just that she's coming. Besides, she won't have time to worry about that. She'll have other things to think about. Come on." Sarah hung over one side of the bed looking underneath for her sandals. "This is the time—she's gone to bed and she really sleeps for the first few hours. After that she starts to wake up if she hears anything."

"Are you sure about this?" Jennie eyed her new friend. She liked Sarah, but she had this habit of taking a fun idea and twisting it at the last moment—she gave Jennie the feeling that at any moment they could both go careening over a cliff.

"What's with you? Don't you ever have any fun?" Sarah jumped up and cocked her hip to one side, her arms akimbo.

"Of course, I do." Challenged, Jennie bolted from the bed and tugged at her jersey. "Make this good, Sarah." It sounded braver than she felt, and Jennie avoided Sarah's eyes as she gathered up her things and followed her out of the room.

* * * * *

Joe walked around the Jaguar, giving it a slow study, until he came to the driver's side. He pulled open the door and slid onto the seat. The interior overhead light illuminated the dashboard. The car was new, and looked it. He ran his eye along the console and dashboard, which looked like tortoiseshell, craned his neck to see into the back seat. The beige leather upholstery had a soft sheen in the pale light. Out of the corner of his eye he could see Gwen standing by the driver's side door of his jeep. He couldn't help wondering what she thought of this entire family, where everyone seemed so different, so unpredictable. He climbed out of the car and shut the door. It closed with the quiet solid sound of an expensive car.

"She's done well in life," Gwen said climbing into the front seat of the Jeep. She smiled at Joe—for a second. "Ohhhkaaay."

"Yeah." Joe started up the car and headed back down the dirt lane. They didn't speak until they reached the highway.

"Why is everyone so estranged, Joe?" Gwen was glad they were sitting in the dark; she was hoping it would encourage Joe to speak more freely because she was getting more and more worried about how this was affecting him. "This isn't at all what I'm used to with your family, at least the relatives I've known so far."

Joe drove along in the travel lane, letting other cars pass him going way past the speed limit. "There was some sort of crisis years ago—both Deanie and Gino going off and staying away—so the family sort of became a family of five children, not seven. You start to live around what is here, not what's missing."

Gwen listened—she knew what it was like to build a family that was nothing like what you expected in life, holding on, making it work because the alternative was too devastating to imagine.

"Paulo died, Zaira married a good man and raised a good family, I had my big-city career—for a while," he said with a smile, "and Lucia married Larry, also a good man, and Rosalie married Eddie."

Gwen waited. "I notice you don't say anything positive about that one."

He glanced at her and kept driving. "You can't like everyone."

"This isn't like you, Joe. 'You can't like everyone.' You don't talk in platitudes."

"I'm thinking of taking it up—it's a good defense, don't you think?"

"No. What about Deanie and Gino?"

"What about them?" Joe slowed even more as they came into the old city Joe knew well. He took unexpected side streets, driving past old homes in neighborhoods that might be going up in the world, or going down. A neighborhood in transition meant different things to different people—the way people see the water glass. Joe couldn't have said if some of the streets were improving or not—they had already been through so many cycles in the years since he'd left. Nothing looked the same, but nothing was very different either. He wondered about those who had stayed and those who had arrived, and had they found their dreams here, or a substitute, something that would do and perhaps make up just a little for the disappointment that awaited everyone.

"What does Deanie do now? Did she ever get married?"

Joe laughed, a sound so harsh that Gwen jerked her head around to look at him.

"No, she's not married, and probably never will be."

"I've never heard you sound so bitter, Joe."

He reached over and squeezed her hand. "She's had a . . . an unusual life. I don't want our parents to find out about it."

"That bad?"

Joe swung the steering wheel and the car cut through an empty parking lot and turned onto the street behind his parents' home. He turned again and pulled into the driveway, letting the car drift off the street and along the neighbor's fence. He parked, turned off the ignition, and stared through the windshield. "It's easy to be nonjudgmental, accepting, tolerant of strangers, the people you meet in my line of work. But to find some of that in your own family, from someone who had choices, as we say . . ." He paused, and seemed to rethink his comments. "I suppose it's not so bad as things go."

"Are you going to tell me?"

"She's a professional gambler."

"Oh." Gwen didn't know what to make of this. She'd never even realized there was such a profession as gambler, but of course there would be. But it didn't sound that bad.

"And she takes high rollers around. That's probably how she got started in it—an escort for . . ."

"She's a hooker?" She clapped her hand over her mouth. "I'm sorry, I'm sorry. It just . . ."

Joe began to laugh again, but this time without bitterness, this time a laugh of absurdity. "That's it." He gripped the steering wheel. "There's intent in her line of work, and she has a reputation for what she does. And no, I don't approve. But I guess I didn't realize just how much I disapproved until it showed up in my own family. I surprised myself with how I feel about it. Deanie—of all people."

"So that's where the car comes from." Gwen felt something like a disk turning in her gut, like a door closing, something beyond her conscious control, as though someone else were dialing the disk moving inside her. She raised her hand to her stomach. "I'm so sorry, Joe."

"The escort work isn't where she's made most of her money. It's the gambling." Joe leaned into the corner made by the seat back and the door. "She's good. She wins—and it's all legal from what I can tell. They watch her like a hawk in the casinos. Roulette and Blackjack."

"I thought they were games of chance, just luck."

"Blackjack takes brains and skill, but roulette is supposed to be pure chance. But she was so good at it that some of the casino owners started dogging her and double and triple checking the dealers."

"Oh. Did she get caught?"

Joe shook his head. "They couldn't find anything." The backyard lay quiet in the darkness—the tables and chairs set in the watery light of a single overhead bulb hanging in a tree, its power line strung from the nearest porch corner. "Once in a while she's barred from a casino for a while, but then they let her back in. No one ever finds anything."

"She must have a system—a partner, maybe."

Joe shook his head again. "No, I don't think so. We took our parents down to a casino once—it was what they wanted for an anniversary present—and I walked around watching the tables trying to figure out what she could be doing. I tried to see things the way Deanie would see them."

"She was the quiet one, you once told me."

"She was. Quiet. Observant. Better than perfect eyesight— she could have been in the air force. She could read a matchbook cover from the other side of a room."

"Or take up needlework. Okay, okay, okay. Just a thought." Gwen smiled when Joe winked at her, glad to have the tension eased.

"She used to keep a diary all the time, but that stopped."

"They do when they get older."

"She wasn't older. She stopped about the time Christina had her accident. I wondered if that had something to do with it—too much reality for a teenager, maybe." He paused. "But she was always the one who was watching, and she'd come out with some of the most embarrassing comments when she was small, before she learned not to. And she didn't actually stop as she got older, just timed her revelations better."

"And that helps her in gambling?"

"We're human, all of us. Each of us has a unique walk, a few mannerisms that we don't really notice in ourselves, and often not in others. I think what she did was something she used to do when she played softball. She wasn't a great player but she was great at anticipating what others were going to do by the way they stood before a pitch or whatever." Joe pulled the keys from the ignition. "I think she watches the dealer and she can tell by the way he spins the ball where it's going to go, how it's going to land." He paused. "Well, how they used to spin the ball. It's all mechanized now, I guess. She moved on to poker too."

"Have you been following her long distance?" Gwen felt his eyes on her fully for the first time that evening. It made her worry that maybe she had gone too far. He looked away. "It's not my business. I'm sorry I asked."

"Don't be." She could hear him breathing in the darkness. "The answer is yes. At first I was afraid she'd get into trouble— like a runaway. I suppose that's how I thought about her—a young girl running away from home. And she was, sort of. So I wanted to be able to help her. In the police you have friends. I tried to keep tabs on her but in the end I wasn't expecting to hear what I heard."

"Did she ever get into trouble?"

"Let me just say she never needed my help." Joe pushed open the door and climbed out. Gwen felt a part of her old life slipping away as she rearranged her impressions of Joe's family.

Six

Early Saturday Morning

Melanie knew she should still be sleepy but she felt ready to go out for a run or just do something strenuous, like loading a truck. Even so, she lay there in the dark staring at the man silhouetted against the open window. The bit of breeze that moved past him came to rest on the rumpled sheet beside her. She was hot, but not as hot as she got at home in the summer.

Gino could have been a statue he stood so motionlessly. His white undershirt was taut across his back and his chinos were wrinkled from the long drive. His unbuckled belt hung from a single loop at one side. He hadn't been going anywhere, she was pretty sure, except in his mind. Since they'd started the drive across country to this family reunion, he'd gone lots of places—and mostly without her. She had never thought of him as a moody man, but this morning, lying here in the early hours, waiting for the first light to wash away the night sky, she wondered how well she really knew him.

"I know you know I'm awake over here." Melanie raised her head a couple of inches to speak, then lowered it again onto the pillow, clasping her hands atop her tousled hair. Gino's head turned a few inches, but not enough to look over his shoulder. When he still didn't answer, Melanie sat up and pushed herself back until she could lean against the headboard. "Maybe coming here wasn't such a good idea." She spoke as much to herself as to him.

Gino dropped his crossed arms and walked over to the bed, sitting down on the edge. He reached out and rubbed her leg under the sheets. "I'm sorry, Mel."

"If you dislike your family that much we shouldn't have come." Melanie took his hand and held it in both of hers. "And we can get back in the car and drive home."

"I don't dislike my family. I have a great family." Gino pulled away and went to sit in a small upholstered chair near the window. "My brothers were these great guys. It was a great family. Paulo and Joe were older, a lot older than me, but it didn't matter. We weren't one of those families where the older ones don't want to hang around with the young ones. Joe was always taking me to games with him—I even went on a date with him a couple of times."

"You're making this up." Melanie curled her legs beneath her and waited.

"No one else thought it was strange at the time. My parents didn't think I should be hanging out at home one Saturday evening—actually quite a few Saturday evenings—so they sent me off with Joe. Once in a while with Paulo."

"Maybe you were the chaperone?" Melanie was grinning now, settling in for a run of reminiscences.

"Maybe. I thought I was just lucky." He put his stockinged feet up onto the bed, the gray soles dotted with green threads from the carpeting. "Probably. My parents were very old-fashioned. Probably still are."

"You really want to see them, don't you?"

"I won't have many more chances, I guess." He stretched out and settled deeper into the chair.

"So why didn't you come earlier?"

"I couldn't." He hadn't been looking at her through the desultory conversation—she noticed something like that, and in past years it would have made her aggressive. She might have called out, Hey you! Can't you see me over here? Want an answer? Talk to me! But she wasn't that aggressive woman anymore; she didn't need to be. She could feel the little bubble of resentment and aggression pushing to get out of her gut, but that was then, this was now. This was Gene.

"Couldn't?"

"Melanie." He gazed at her, a half smile tugging at the corners of his mouth. "I promised Deanie I'd stay with her, make sure nothing happened to her."

"Which is why we live in Pateros and she lives in Vegas."

"Yeah."

"So, will I meet her? Is she here?"

"Yeah. She's coming. Might even be here already."

"You must have decided she didn't need your protection. Or am I wrong?"

Gino sat up, drawing his feet slowly off the bed, placing them on the floor, and leaning toward Melanie. She could feel it coming. Whatever it was that had been eating at him all these years was finally going to burst out or die—one way or the other it was coming to an end. Curious, she held herself still.

"I finally got the message that she didn't need me. She was hiding for a while, in the beginning, but then she found her way, sort of, and by then I couldn't go back. No, I didn't want to go back. I liked it out there."

Little chills ran through Melanie. She learned young not to look happiness in the face, but she could feel it, like the electricity in the air before a storm, like the smell of water coming down a creek bed when the snow melts. "What was she hiding from?"

"I was the one they probably thought was hiding."

Melanie threw off the sheet and slid across the bed. "Gene, this is far too cryptic. You've got to tell me what this is all about." She grabbed his hands and pulled them to her chest. "Gene, please!" Whenever he looked into her eyes like that, she worried more about what he'd see than what he'd say, but not this time. She wanted to know so bad she'd risk anything to get the story.

"There's a girl my family was close to. Actually she was Joe's girlfriend for a long time—she was the one he was dating when I went along. Like a chaperone, as you said, I guess. Anyway, she had an accident. That night someone saw me and thought I'd been with her and people were talking about maybe I had something to do with it. But they couldn't prove anything. People thought that was why I took off eventually—like I couldn't take the suspicion and talk." He sighed. "It was hard on Pae—he knew something was going on, but everyone thought too highly of him to say anything to his face."

Melanie held her breath, too tense to speak, to breathe, to even think. This couldn't be Gene talking, not her Gene, not the man who never raised his voice, never could get angry without going off for a long walk to cool down and then apologizing sincerely and calmly. Not her Gene. She waited—for the words she didn't need but wanted to hear anyway. Don't take that trust away from me, God, she prayed over and over again. "And you told them you had nothing to do with it, right?"

"I was with Deanie—the whole time."

"Oh." Melanie slowly exhaled, squeezed her eyes shut. Thank you, thank you, thank you, she heard running through her head.

"She was afraid to be alone. She was hysterical."

"She was hysterical? Why? What happened?"

"She wouldn't say too much."

"How long ago was this? When exactly did this happen?"

"She musta been fourteen maybe? She was so upset. I promised her I'd stick by her, and without even thinking about it, no matter what, and I did. She was so grateful I began to think what I'd done really mattered. I never questioned it."

"No, Gene, you wouldn't." She kissed his knuckles, still hearing the litany of thank-yous in her head.

"I became her protector after that, as though she needed looking after, as though she couldn't be alone."

"Typical big brother stuff."

"Not later." He shook his head. She couldn't see his face, the way he was bent over holding her hands, staring down at the worn and decaying carpet. "When she ran off, I went after her and then I stayed with her. It was my promise to her—I talked myself into believing she couldn't make it without me. But we were a pair of kids—really, kids—but I promised her. I was her big brother the way the others were my big brothers. And back then, I had a real thing about living up to what they were."

"Oh, Gene, all these years." Melanie lifted his hands to her lips and kissed them.

"But, hey. I met you, didn't I? See how well it worked out for me?"

"Gene, Gene. But the day she was so upset—the accident. Did she tell you anything? Did you talk to the police?"

He shook his head. "Ironical, isn't it? Joe was set on becoming a cop even then, but we didn't tell him anything." He released her hands and sat up in the chair. "It's a relief to have it over with. That's really why I came—to put this all to bed, to feel that I closed the door on all that."

"That's a good reason." Melanie rested her chin on her knees and smiled.

"But now I want more, Melanie. Now I want to know what happened. I was too young to really get what had happened, but she must have been raped." He gave a slight shudder. "She looked awful—messed up, crying, red, sorta bruised. She made me promise not to say anything and to stay with her always. So I did. She moved, I followed. But then, after a few years, I fell to what she was up to. It wasn't good. I told her she had to get back on track."

"Drugs?"

He laughed. "She might have sold them but she never used them. I'm sure of that about her. Anyway, she disappeared for a while, but we got together later, months later, and she had money, real money. That's when I decided she didn't need me and I needed to move on and make something happen for me. I couldn't come back here, at least I didn't think I could, so I went west and eventually landed in Pateros with a construction crew."

Gene rested his head against the back of the chair and closed his eyes just as the sky began to turn a milky white tinged with dark blue. It would be hot today—she could tell. The little breeze had been cool but heavy, and it would heat up fast. She watched him fall asleep in the chair, thinking he at long last sounded relaxed, at peace, settled in himself. He'd never told her so much about his family and himself—she hadn't felt the need to know—and now she almost wished he hadn't. But then, that thought shattered and she was glad. She wanted to know all about him because she loved everything about him, and this was part of him too. She felt that bubble of aggression again, tickling at her insides, looking for a way out. She could ignore it.

* * * * *

Joe pulled on his pants, picked up his shoes in the dark, and slipped, bare foot, out of the room. Gwen lay still in the twin bed next to him, not asleep—he knew that—but for once he was going to pretend she wasn't awake. He wanted to keep her out of this as much as possible.

As he stood at the beginning of the hallway he remembered at once from his childhood which floor boards creaked and which gave a sigh. But it didn't matter this time. His parents were probably up, passing snatches of conversation back and forth, as old married couples do, as they moved slowly into the day. Partly deaf, partly sour, his parents didn't always bother to make sure the other understand what was said. It was said, the words were spoken, sent into the world, and that was enough; he or she moved on. One was responsible for making the statement, getting it out into reality. Someone else was responsible for hearing it even if that someone was deaf. Deafness notwithstanding, somehow the world would get the information where it needed to go, their behavior seemed to say.

Joe went at once to the kitchen, dropped his shoes on the floor, and slipped his sockless feet into them. He hadn't bothered with a shirt—this wouldn't take long—and he felt sticky in his undershirt. He went straight to the back door and tried the handle—unlocked. He pulled the door open and pushed on the screen door, looking out on the back porch. No one else was there. He walked over to the slider and settled down to wait, taking care not to make it slide, though he had loved to do so as a boy. In time a car without headlights drove into the back yard, moving so slowly over the driveway it sounded like someone folding crinkled paper. The car drifted to a stop near the tables and chairs set up for today's reunion. The driver cut the engine. When no one stepped out of the car, Joe stood and went down the back stairs, walked over to the passenger side window and tapped on the glass. Startled, the driver stared at him in the gray light, then pressed a button to lower the window.

"Joe." Rosalie held a small jar of pancake makeup in her left hand, the index finger on her right hand poised near her eye. "What're you doing up so early?"

"Let me see." Joe reached in and took her chin in his hand, turning her head toward him. "Minha Carida Rosie."

"Knock if off, Joe."

"That doesn't suit you, Rosie."

"Maybe you don't know me anymore."

"I'll always know you." He leaned on the car door and watched her cover the bruises around her eye with makeup, apply eye shadow and eyeliner. He could feel his breathing change, growing heavier and harder and deeper. She pulled out a tube of lip gloss and tipped the rearview mirror to a lower angle. "You're here early."

"I told Mae I'd help her. I always do."

"At four-thirty in the morning?"

She poked the gloss stick back into the tube, screwed it shut, and dropped it into her purse. "What's it to you? You're not one of us anymore." The words flew out of her mouth in a soft growl that cut through the dying darkness.

"Why don't you leave him?"

"What business is it of yours?"

"Your boys are grown—they've got good lives. They wouldn't want you to stay like this." He couldn't stop thinking of what he had promised her. "I'll help you, Rosie."

Rosalie tugged the zipper across the top of her makeup bag and stuffed it into her red leather carryall. She pushed open the car door and clambered out, then slammed the door shut. "Look, Joe . . ."

He stepped back and watched, and waited—for the excuses, the explanations, the rationalizations, the distractions, whatever had kept her mind astir and so disoriented for all these years that she'd stay with him. He worried now about the future. What if something happened to him? Who would be there for her, who would watch her back? Who in the family would make sure nothing got worse for her?

"Eddie's a bully, Rosie. I'll help you however you need." There were other things he could say—you're still a young woman, you're still attractive, you can still have a full life, a much better life—but they were platitudes that were insulting to a woman living in her kind of prison. And mostly they weren't really true. How many women in their mid fifties could start over, especially someone who believed in family as devoutly as in the Holy Ghost and all the sacraments?

"You don't understand." She spoke without conviction, leaning against the car, staring at the ground, as though she had lost an argument out of weariness. "Leave it alone, Joe."

"What kind of man would I be if I left it alone? What kind of brother?" He moved closer to her and put his arm around her. He was doing this all wrong. Instead of supporting her, drawing her out, listening to her own special fears and allaying those, he was putting her under as much pressure as Eddie probably did. But he couldn't stop himself—Rosalie would always be his little sister, and the words came on their own. "The money isn't worth it, Rosie."

She tossed her head and her still luxuriant black hair trembled in the cool morning air. "You think it's about money?"

The dead time of the night was coming to an end. Joe could hear a car driving down a main road nearby, and soon there would one or two more, and then the early morning traffic of those who reported to work at six a.m. But he knew that this was also the time when the ugliest things happened inside a home—when a family was captive and never thought of fleeing into the street, screaming out a window, running to a neighbor. The night quiet left some people feeling that the world had abandoned them to their fate. Rosalie was one of those.

"I think it doesn't matter, but it's killing you and it's killing the rest of us. What will it take? What do I have to do? Tell me. I'll do it."

Rosalie gave her head another toss, as though she could shake off all this misery and turn away to another day, give things a chance to disappear so she could start over. Joe could tell she was trying not to cry, but it was a struggle she wouldn't win, had never won. She was a good decent woman and had been a good decent girl—the transformation into a stranger who drove expensive cars and bought expensive furniture was an aberration that her family watched, mystified, waiting for it to come to an end.

"Most of the time, Rosie, I thought Eddie was a jerk—loud, pushy, too full of himself. But I know people are different with someone they love, and I figured he was different with you. That you saw in him something the rest of us couldn't—and that he let you see the better side of himself. For a long time I hung on that that was true. But that isn't true, is it?"

She gave a single shake of her head, before turning to him with a half smile. "You're sort of right." She pushed away from him. "He wasn't moody with me . . . not until just before we got married. I thought it was the pressure of such a big change in our lives. I didn't pay much attention. I was so excited. Getting married was such a big deal. Mae was so happy, and so was I—for a while." She turned to face him, leaning in close to him. "It's not like he comes at me, Joe. It's not like that at all. He gets upset about something and it's like he can't separate those towering feelings he has from the little thing that really happened—the car needs some extra maintenance, somebody says no to a party invitation. And he says such awful things."

"Like what."

"He calls me names. It's like he hates all women. He thinks we're all sluts." She began to turn away, then back again. "I know lots of men are like that. Mrs. Lanetti told us at dinner once that her husband—and he was sitting right there—didn't like women, never had, didn't like listening to them talk. And he was a judge!"

"Rosie." Gently, Joe laid his hand on her arm, calling her back.

She pulled out a tissue and began wiping away the tears and the makeup, eyeing the tissue as it filled with a beige residue, folding and refolding it as she went over her face. "I can't start over, Joe. I'm too tired. I don't think I really care anymore anyway. Mae's been carrying on this private battle since the very beginning—she caught it right away—but look at all the years that have passed. Eddie and I have been married almost thirty-five years. You had just stopped dating Christina when we got engaged. You remember? Mae so wanted another wedding."

Joe listened. He always listened—and cringed at the way human beings thought, at the ideas that flashed across the mind as we try to make decisions, try to find the path that will lead us in the right direction, take us through to a measure of happiness while we endure the rest of being alive.

"Maybe he'd like to let go too." Joe dipped down to see her face. "Have you thought of that? He'd let you go, wouldn't he? With all of us here?"

"And then what?"

"Then you get a life, Rosie, a life. Then you belong to yourself." He watched her listen to him, knowing she wasn't really taking in what he was saying. She wasn't one of those beaten women who could no longer think for themselves—he'd seen her stand up to Eddie with the impatience typical of the long-married, knew she had her own friends, lived her own life with family and civic groups. Her staying married had nothing to do with fear, as far as Joe could tell, at least not the typical fear of a battered wife. And to his surprise and confusion, Eddie's violence had never escalated beyond a punch in the face. She never had a broken bone, a concussion, a shut eye. Bruises on her arms and face where her husband grabbed her—and as bad as that was, that was the extent of it—for over thirty years. Joe despised Eddie.

"I can't do that, Joe. He needs me."

"Aye, minha carida, Rosie. You are crazy." Joe crushed her to him in a hug, hearing himself pray in a way he hadn't prayed in forty years.

* * * * *

Joe followed his sister Rosalie up the stairs to the apartment. He could hear his mother opening cupboards in the kitchen, getting ready for breakfast. Rosalie went to her, rubbed her back, and promised to help as soon as she fixed her face. Mae Silva turned to her and kissed her on both cheeks, then dropped her hands. Joe walked on to the living room, willing himself to let Rosalie go her own way.

The sound of something hitting the front porch floor drew Joe to the living room. He opened the door onto the porch and stepped out to pick up the newspaper wrapped in a plastic bag. On the street below a young boy ran up the steps to the next house and threw a newspaper onto the porch. He ran back out into the middle of the street and tossed a newspaper up onto a second-story porch, then hurried on, not bothering to wait to see if the newspaper landed at its intended spot. Joe peered over the railing to see a second newspaper lying on the walk to Mr. Morton's.

Joe returned to the living room, heading for the chair near the fireplace, in front of the upright piano. He wasn't usually so unsettled, and blamed himself for confronting Rosalie when he knew nothing good could come of it. Whenever he visited his parents and his siblings, he did his best to think like family instead of a police officer but perhaps this time he had been too successful, too good at feeling like the older brother who didn't really like his sister's husband. Joe tossed the newspaper onto a chair and stopped to look at the rows of photographs sitting atop the piano.

Dozens of photographs recorded more than ninety years of family history, of relatives in every stage of life. Joe reached up to straighten a photo of the three boys—Paulo, Joe, and Gino. He pulled it from its spot and examined it, turning it back and forth to catch the light on what appeared to be creases. He turned it over and noted the stubs of broken pins that had been bent and rebent to accommodate the removal of the cardboard backing. The photograph had been removed and mishandled fairly recently.

Joe replaced the photograph and began checking the others. Four additional photographs appeared to have been removed from their frames, handled so roughly they had cracked and crumpled, and then been replaced. Nothing else was different about them. Two photos depicted the three boys still in school; Rosalie, Gino, and Deanie appeared in one; Paulo and Angela in one; and Zaira, Lucia, and Rosalie with their respective husbands in the last one. The last of the damaged photos held just about the entire family, including in-laws. None of the other photographs had been touched.

"Tell me about the photos, Mae." Joe found his mother staring into the refrigerator.

She stood up and gazed at him, her thoughts clearly elsewhere.

"Before Rosalie comes back."

"What do you want about photographs?"

"The family photos in the living room look like they've been damaged. Anything to this?"

"Oh that." She slammed the refrigerator door. "Did you hear the girls this morning?"

"I don't know, I can't remember—just tell me about the photographs."

"The girls. I want to know what they're doing." She rested her hands on her hips and looked around her—she seemed worn out, scattered, and hopeful that some respite lay nearby, but saw nothing, and sighed with resignation. She looked old to Joe. He thought this every time he saw her, but today it seemed different. She seemed old without the surge of energy to vanquish time that seemed to define her.

"Mae, the photos?"

"That's nothing. Mrs. Perreira wanted to borrow them so we let her take them. That's all it is. She was here one day going on about Christina being lonely. Maybe if she had photographs to look at she'd be less lonely."

"Mae—"

"I know, I know, Jose, but she's an old woman and her daughter is, well, she is as she is. What is a little kindness, eh?"

"She was very selective," Joe said.

"Yeah, that's her way, isn't it?" She began to turn in a circle looking over the kitchen.

"Mae, what are you doing?"

"I'm looking for my eggs."

"What?"

"Did you hear the girls this morning? Were they up early?" She turned to Joe. "Sarah is a good girl, but she has such ideas!"

"Mae, are you putting me off about the photographs?"

"I need my eggs! Why is this so hard to understand? You want to eat, don't you? Well, find my eggs. You're a policeman—you can find them."

"Find your eggs?"

"The girls have taken them—I know it. Sarah has such ideas. She gave me a mirror once but it wasn't a real one. When I looked into it I wasn't there! All I saw was the opposite side of the room! She put a large photograph in it so you didn't see yourself. I thought I was dead! I am standing in front of the mirror as though I am a ghost—I thought I would see my mother behind me but not even that! Such a fright I had! Find my eggs. Your father is getting up and he will want his breakfast."

Eggs, thought Joe. Mirrors. Oh, god, Sarah. He'd forgotten what a prankster she was.

Joe ran up the back stairs and knocked loudly on the attic door. No one answered. He knocked a second time, then opened the door and went in. The girls' beds were in disarray but neither teenager was there. Joe slammed the door shut and headed back down stairs. He was beginning to think bringing Jennie was not the best idea he'd ever had.

"Ah, Joseph!" Mr. Morton extended his hand and bent over slightly in the echo of a bow. "For your mother." In his other hand sat a yellow rubber ducky, its bright red eyes and black beak shining with fanatical fatuousness in the morning light, and beneath that peeked out an egg sitting in a yellow Easter basket. "I found it in the garden."

Joe took the basket with its treasure and stared at it for a long minute. Sarah. He sorely hoped this was the only one. He leaned over the railing for the second time that morning and gazed down at the back yard. In a sudden rush of anger, he gripped the railing, then let go, realizing he was about to start laughing. There, dotted throughout, along the back of the double decker, along the garage wall, beside the tires of his car, around the trees, in the gardens among the beans and onions, beneath the corner of the steps were arrayed little yellow Easter baskets with rubber duckies sitting on them.

"What did Mr. Morton want so early?" Mae Silva opened the screen door and came out.

Joe was torn between anger and amusement. "I must be getting old. Take a look, Mae." He pointed to the back yard with its sparkling yellow splotches.

"My eggs!" Mae Silva slapped her cheeks with her hands. "That Sarah! Why can't she be like other teenagers and get a crush on a nice boy! She could be rude to her mother or she could steal little things from me! But no! She has to make jokes all the time. Why does she do these things! Jose, go get my eggs! I'm calling her mother." She threw up her hands and tramped back into the kitchen.

* * * * *

Jennie peered through the attic window at the scene below. She so wanted to laugh out loud, but then someone was sure to look up at the sound and catch her. So, instead of enjoying the scene to the full, she felt the pressure of near hysterical delight as she watched Joe going from basket to basket plucking out the eggs.

"You know he's going to come back," Jennie said. When she had first heard him coming up the stairs, she had steeled herself to face him and tried to think of some explanation that would put him off. But Sarah didn't waver for a second. She grabbed Jennie's hand and pulled her into a closet in the eaves, drawing the door shut behind them. They squatted in the dark, listening to Joe knock and walk a few steps into the room before heading back down to the kitchen.

"No, he won't. It's too late now." Sarah spoke without looking up from her task.

"Oh." Jennie pressed her face against the glass. "Do you think they're all right? The eggs, I mean."

"They're probably still cold. They haven't been out there very long."

"I wouldn't want them to be wasted." Jennie turned back to the window. Because if they weren't wasted, then Joe really wouldn't have any reason to be angry. She pressed her nose to the glass and followed Gwen's path, right behind Joe, as she gathered up the rubber ducks and tossed them into a black trash bag. Behind her came Joe's mother, picking up the yellow baskets and dropping them into a white trash bag—but not before she examined each one, perhaps deciding if she'd keep it or not for the grandchildren and great-grandchildren. Mr. Morton moved ceremoniously around the yard to help in the search,

looking under cars, under bushes, up in tree branches, among the
weeds, even under the squash. As the last in the line of searchers,
he merely had to locate and then stand and point. Eventually Joe
found him.

"I really hope he's not angry." Jennie drew away from the
window.

"Who?"

"Joe. It'll be a horrible ride home if he is."

"Why would he be angry?"

Jennie leaned against the wall, taking the time to study her
new friend. It amazed her that Sarah could think up prank after
prank after prank and never worry about people's reactions. She
seemed not to care. She just wanted to work out her prank and
then move on to the next one. This is what having ADD must be
like, Jennie decided. You jumped from one project to the next,
not even stopping to notice if the idea was a good one or not, and
not even thinking about how other people felt about it. She tried
to imagine doing something in the same way. It gave her a
headache. "Does anybody ever get mad at you?"

"My mom used to but it didn't go any good." Sarah pulled
on the rope she'd been working on. "My dad told her I'd grow
out of it if they just left me alone." She dropped the rope and
grinned at Jennie. "That was so wicked cool! No one bothers me
anymore! I love my dad."

"Wow." Jennie slid down to the floor, drawing up her
knees. "My mom would never do that. She'd make me feel like
I'd ruined her life."

Sarah paused in her task. "Weird."

"So what're you doing?"

"Oh, this is so cool. Totally."

"What is it?"

"A swing."

"What's it for?"

"I'm going to put two mannequins on it dressed in my
grandparents' clothes and then drop it over the side of the porch
during the picnic." She returned to tying knots.

"That's not much of a prank." Jennie propped her elbow on
her knees and tried to conceal her disappointment. The egg prank
had been a treat—she loved sneaking down in the middle of the
night and hiding them and then watching Joe and Gwen go
searching for them. She could barely keep from squealing in

delight. Sarah barely noticed. Once the eggs and baskets and ducks were out there, she was done—she immediately lost interest. She was eager to move on to the next idea. Jennie wanted to enjoy the prank and watch the others, and then later think up another one, but the swing idea just seemed dull. She had to admit, she was disappointed. She was looking forward to another good one.

"They'll be kissing!" Sarah choked back a giggle and held up the knot she'd been working on.

"So?" Jennie frowned. Maybe she should try to think up a better one for Sarah.

"For my grandparents that's a very big deal. They didn't even hold hands until they were engaged."

"Oh that's so weird." Jennie let her mouth fall open.

"We have to get it done and then hide it. If we're not down there, they'll figure out we're up to something." Sarah held up one rope, looked it over and decided it would pass, and threw it onto a bed. She then picked up another rope and resettled herself cross-legged on the floor, resuming her work.

"Who all is coming today?" Jennie walked over to the nearest bed and began sorting through the pile of clothes. "Are these the ones you're going to use?"

Sarah nodded. "They won't miss them. Everyone's coming—at least that's what I've heard. Even Joe's old girlfriend Christina. You've probably never heard about her." Sarah looked up at her, to check.

Jennie shook her head.

"They were supposed to get married, but then either they changed their minds or Christina had her accident. Anyway, she ended up almost dead. She's like a vegetable, but her mother says she recognizes people and understands what she says to her. It's so pathetic."

"That's creepy." Jennie began arranging the clothes on the bed in the form of two people, male and female.

"Her mother visits her every day. That's her life."

"Oh, that's so sad." Jennie held up a lacy blouse. "How old are these clothes?"

"Oh, they're probably antiques—at least from the 1930s."

"Wow! I've never seen anything this old. Is it all right to touch them?"

"Sure. Avó still wears that." Sarah glanced at the blouse.

Jennie blinked and laid the blouse delicately onto the bed.

"Even Tio Gino and Tia Deanie are coming," Sarah said, pausing in her work. "I've never met them. That is so strange— to have relatives I've never met."

"You probably have a lot of relatives you've never met." Jennie flopped across the bed, and began fingering the old fabric.

"Not in this family. We know everyone. And we know everything about everyone." Sarah bent over her work, tugging on the knots. "These are good, just right."

"I don't think I'd like that," Jennie said.

"It's a good thing," Sarah said. "For instance, we all know that Eddie knocks Tia Rosalie around—and she puts up with it. But she only had two kids, both boys, and they're grown—my cousins. They're nice, in their late twenties, I guess, and they don't come around very much. Mom says she's traded money for family, or something like that."

Jennie could feel herself go cold. She hated it when families turned out to be nightmares. She couldn't say why, but something about it made her uneasy, and she started to get edgy and nervous, afraid she'd freak and start screaming.

"And Tia Lucia." Sarah continued to check her work—she wanted the ropes holding the swing to be strong. "I like her. She married way outside the family circle—that's what Mom told me—an Irish guy. But people really like Uncle Larry and he's really easygoing. Whatever you ask him, he says, Sure, if you want. Their grandchildren are my age." Sarah jumped up. "Now we have to dress the dummies."

The two girls pulled up the floppy cloth figures and began arranging the clothing over the loose limbs. Jennie was lost in the task, imagining the surprised and animated faces of everyone at lunch later today.

"How many do you think will come?" she asked.

"Well, from what I keep hearing, about forty, maybe fifty, maybe more. It's going to be all the siblings, except Paulo, of course—he's dead. And then their kids and grandkids, so that's a lot. That's why Avó has been doing nothing but cooking. Of course, everyone's bringing something, so she doesn't have to do it all. But she's always cooking."

Jennie admired the figure of Avó dressed in a black skirt, black stockings, white blouse, black shawl, and a gray felt hat with a bright red feather. The outfit looked so foreign, made her feel peculiar. She tugged at her tank top and wondered how anyone lived in clothes like this, especially in the summer.

"I can't wait to see the looks on their faces. My mom thinks just like Avó. I used to think that after Avó dies, which is going to happen sooner rather than later—I mean she's ancient—I can do all this stuff to my mom. But she's on to me. She's the suspicious type. After Avó dies, I won't have nearly as much fun."

"So your grandmother doesn't mind when you do this stuff?" Jennie fingered the blouse again. "Doesn't she say anything?"

"Not really. Sometimes she complains she doesn't have time, but I'm not hurting anyone."

Jennie stepped back to view both figures, and take another look at her friend. She liked the other teen, but every now and then Sarah said something that reminded her of just how different they were. She almost wondered how Sarah felt about her family, like, maybe Jennie shouldn't make any assumptions about Sarah and her relatives. "You're going to go on with pranks?" Jennie watched her new friend. "Aren't you expecting to give this up for something else?"

"Oh, no!" Sarah drew herself up to her full height and plopped her hands on her hips. "This is like performance art— you create a situation, set it up and set it moving and then let people react and draw them in and that makes them part of the whole thing—they're in it and they can't get out. They're part of the prank. They are the prank. This is real art. This is me. This is what I'm going to do forever. And I'm going to be famous for it. You wait. This is my future."

"This is art?"

"Oh for sure. It's creative, enlightening. It requires planning, lots of skills, thought. It has purpose. It educates people. This is totally art."

"What about the eggs?"

"What about them? They were art too. Didn't you realize that?"

Jennie's eyes opened wide. She gawked and swallowed, then managed to slip out a bit of a sound that might have been construed to mean, Sure, I get it. And then she hunched her shoulders and picked up the Mae dummy, resisting an urge to crush it to her in a great big hug.

* * * * *

Gwen dragged the plastic trash bag up the porch steps and deposited it at the far end, in a corner behind a wicker chair. She hardly knew if she wanted to laugh or scream—this was not at all what she was expecting from Jennie this weekend. Jennie was a good girl, a truly, deep-down good person. She got into that compassionate phase early and stayed there—she'd sooner kill her best friend than see a dog or cat run over, give half of everything she owned to someone who was homeless, step into danger to protect her younger brother. But pranks? In Gwen's view these were one step ahead of vandalism, where her daughter was sure to go if Gwen didn't bring a halt to it—and it was up to her not to give in to the humor in the situation. But Gwen had to admit, she was losing ground on this one—part of her, a small part she insisted to herself, was tickled that Jennie was showing so much imagination and fun. Teens could be way too serious. Still, if this got out of hand . . .

Gwen shook her head and brushed the hair away from her eyes. What she really felt was a tingling worry that Jennie would do something perfectly innocent, like this prank, and Joe's family would take an instant dislike to her and Gwen. Oh, Lordy, she thought, I'm losing my mind. She'd be glad when Sunday afternoon came. Whatever happened to the nice traditional visit where the in-laws didn't like the newcomer and the spouse proved chivalrous and loyal?

A black SUV, shiny and sleek, drove into the driveway and parked along the fence. Gwen waited, drawn to the obviously expensive car, marveling at how out of place it looked in the Silvas' back yard, parked on a mixed dirt and gravel driveway, near a wooden fence leaning drunkenly back and forth as it staggered along the boundary, weeds growing thick along the bottom edge, thrusting up into knotty clumps around the posts. For a moment she imagined the driver was lost and would soon open the door and call out for help. But the figure that emerged was not at all lost.

The car door swung open, and a dark head appeared on the other side of the SUV. A moment later Rosalie walked around the back of the car and looked up at the porch. She waved, and Gwen automatically waved back. She had once been considered pretty, she reminded herself—young and pretty and attractive. The thought kept coming to mind whenever Gwen thought of

Rosalie, who for reasons Gwen slithered away from every time they neared her conscious thought made her feel frumpy and dumpy and lumpy. And she couldn't shake it off. She watched Rosalie walk toward the back steps—her white slacks perfectly pressed, her light silk blouse billowing out in the little breeze she created as she walked, her sandaled heels still white despite the dust of the paths, her hair perfectly coiffed. Gwen busied herself with the bag of rubber ducks.

"Another one of Sarah's pranks?" Rosalie said as she came up the back steps.

Gwen turned, surprised. "How'd you guess?"

"I know Sarah. It's always something with her. There's no other reason for anyone else to be up and working out back here. Too bad. You're supposed to be a guest." Rosalie gave Gwen a wink, then pulled open the screen door, but just before she escaped inside, she leaned around the door. "Someone should talk to her. Maybe I'll ask Joe to do it."

"Why not your husband, Eddie?" Gwen said. The last thing she wanted was to see Joe pulled into a family quarrel. She couldn't read the look on Rosalie's face.

"I promised to help Mae with the sweets." Rosalie let the screen door slam shut behind her, leaving Gwen alone on the porch.

Somewhere below, still in the back yard, was Joe moving chairs and tables back into place after the early morning disruption. The calm, quiet way he went about undoing Sarah's prank hadn't really surprised her, but the steely way he looked at his mother as she half chuckled while following them about did make her wonder. On one level he didn't seem to approve of Sarah's pranks, but on the other he loved his family and he understood the kinds of odd behaviors that serve as the glue among relatives.

Gwen leaned on the porch railing and took in the entire scene. Mr. and Mrs. Morton were talking quietly to each other, with long pauses between comments; across the back yard the neighbors were moving about, leaving for work or other appointments, making as little noise as possible out of consideration for others. She liked that about old neighborhoods—the closeness but also the unwritten rules that allowed people to live so closely together, rules that allowed you to ignore someone under some circumstances but required you to acknowledge them under others. And people understood those rules and accepted them.

All of that made Gwen wonder how Joe's large rambunctious family had managed in that small two-floor apartment. She tried to imagine them in their younger days all together, with Pae Silva ruling and Mae Silva managing it all. Paulo seemed the least hard to imagine because his photographs were so consistent—always the young man ready to go to war. Zaira blossomed into a capable, strong-willed woman who seemed to know from the first what she wanted. Lucia had a quiet confidence and certainty. Rosalie, Gino, and Deanie were the mysteries—Rosalie because she seemed to have traded all she had been born with, all the opportunities and blessings of her family, for a fancy home (or two), and Gino and Deanie because Joe never said a word about them; they were the ghosts in the house.

And the spouses. What about them? Zaira's husband was a good sort, from the sounds of it, and Lucia's Larry was loved even if he was an outsider. Eddie was one of them, a lifelong family friend and then an in-law, which meant his meanness was tolerated. But what about Gino's wife? And what about Deanie? She must have had someone in her life at some time. Gwen closed her eyes, going through a mental list of names and faces, trying to keep them all straight. She had given up trying to sort through the children and grandchildren and great-grandchildren—that was too much for her. They were just a list of names as far as she was concerned—no matter how many times someone pointed to each one while reciting names—they were all a blur. Except for Sarah. That was one family member she was going to remember.

The image of Sarah being chastened by Gwen formed in the mists of her imagination and she felt the pleasure of her mastery of the situation—the sheer power of her character pulling Sarah into line, making her a more serious and earnest person. The fantasy was laughable. It wouldn't happen, but it sure made her feel good. Someone's hands on her shoulders startled her back to the present.

Joe nuzzled her ear.

"I was wondering where you'd got to," he said. She leaned into him and grasped his hands. "I forgot about Sarah—and her idea of fun."

"You mean the pranks? It wasn't bad, sort of cute, but disruptive. That kind of thing would drive me nuts. How does her mother stand it?" Gwen looked over her shoulder at him.

"Sarah was a menopause baby, and Zaira was so glad about having a daughter that she overindulged the girl. The boys sure did—they thought she was a toy."

"Well, I'm ready for breakfast. We have a lot of work to do, from what your mother tells me." Gwen turned around and Joe slipped his arms around her, and for a moment they forgot where they were—until Gwen heard the screen door slam, twice.

Seven

Saturday Midday

Pae Silva leaned against the old wooden picnic table and pressed down hard. He felt the legs wobble beneath his hand and pushed himself away, then craned his neck to study the other tables. He spotted one beneath the old silver poplar tree and headed for it. He tested this table also, found it sturdy and bent back and forth looking for a chair. He saw the one he wanted at the next table and dragged it over, setting it just below a low hanging branch of the poplar. He shook the chair to make sure it was evenly settled, and tested the sight lines from it to make sure it was strategically placed. He drew the branch toward him and ran his thumb over a cluster of leaves; he had planted this tree more than twenty years ago, and it had flourished under his care. The leaves turned silver and shimmered and flickered even in a light breeze, as though to warn the world that here, at the foot of this tree, lies a treasure. He liked to sit beneath it during summer evenings and always during a family gathering. This was his last great tree planting—others since then had been more mundane, more ordinary, sturdy but ordinary. The poplar was special. He pressed the chair legs into soil and lowered himself onto the seat.

Paulo had visited him last night as he lay in bed listening to the whisperings of his granddaughter and her friend. He wasn't sure about them, what they were up to, but they were good girls, he was sure of it. One was Joe's and he knew Joe would never let a girl in his charge come out wrong. Joe was special. The thought of his middle son caught in his throat—Joe was different. The old man's mind drifted off to a memory of his boys playing in the back yard, their easy affectionate manner, their gentleness with the youngest, Gino. He could not hold his

127

sons tight enough he loved them so much. He would have liked more sons—they were such good boys.

What had Paulo told him last night? Something about compassion and old times long gone. Perhaps if he concentrated, forced himself to think hard, it would all come back to him. He tried, truly, he tried. But he didn't have what he needed to think hard anymore—and he couldn't force himself to do it. His mind had shifted gears and wouldn't change back again. He'd have to wait for another visit from Paulo. He wished his first-born son would come during the day, when the light was better and he could see more clearly, but Paulo was vague on this and drifted off as daylight came. It was a sorrow for the old man, but one he was used to.

"Pae, you're all ready, huh?" Zaira leaned over and kissed her father on the forehead and gave him a quick pat on the back.

All of a sudden the yard was filled with people and their voices. He couldn't understand how they had all gotten there so fast, without his even noticing. Had he nodded off, just for a second? No, no, he stayed awake, always. Underneath his hands was a clean white table cloth, and down the center of the table was a row of bowls and platters and little rolled paper napkins with utensils sticking out of them at one end. On the next table was a row of pitchers containing liquids in many different colors—the red of cranberry juice, and the gold of apple juice, and iced tea and lime drink. Little plastic cups were stacked among them. The colors were so rich, even the sunlight was drawn to them.

Lucia was there, over there, with her large hands wrapped around a bowl of paella with chicken and snails—he could smell it. It was her favorite party dish because he asked her to make it again and again—and she always did. He watched the hands—such hands, not like a woman's at all, a farmer's hands, but she wasn't a farmer's wife. A happy woman, a satisfied woman, a stranger to him no matter how often he saw her, how close she sat to him when he was sick and worried, how little she criticized him.

He wondered more and more if these people could have once been his children. They were people he didn't understand, couldn't understand. Larry, Lucia's husband, such a cheerful man, so easy going, Lucia said. He seemed soft, giving in to Lucia whenever she wanted something, never arguing, never saying no, just taking on more work. How could you raise a son like that? But he had. Bernard was a good boy, though not a boy for a long time. Larry would take the bowl from Lucia—yes, there it was, he would take the bowl from her and put it on another table. And there, she tells him it's the wrong table and he moves it. How can she do this? Why does he let her? But she has always done this, yes, he remembers. She has always done this.

"I'm going for a beer, Pae." Larry leaned over the old man, speaking softly but precisely into his ear. "Can I bring you one?"

The old man shook his head, no, no. That was his wife's job. She always brought him beer—she knew how he liked it. But where was she? She should be here by now—all this food and no plate yet for him. Something was wrong. No beer, no food. I can send Rosalie for my beer, he thought. He pushed himself up in his chair and began searching the crowd of children and grandchildren, cousins and aunts and uncles and nieces and nephews, for his daughter Rosalie. She was tall and beautiful—he should be able to spot her.

"What're you looking for, Pae?" Joe leaned over and moved his face and shoulders into his father's line of vision.

"Huh?" The old man started and looked hard at him. Joe repeated his question. "I want Rosalie. I want her to bring me a beer. Are you all eating now?"

"I'll send out Rosalie," Joe said, moving away.

A good boy, the old man thought. So different from me, so quiet and thoughtful, but a good boy. Unbidden was the thought, I can lean on him when I have to, when I'm old. He shook away the thought and again scanned the crowd, checking off in his own mind who was there and who was not. A woman he wasn't sure about came toward him and smiled.

"I'm Gwen, Pae," she said, placing a glass of beer in front of him. He grabbed her hand and pulled it to his mouth and kissed it hard.

"You are Joe's lady friend." He could feel his eyes watering as he looked at her—so young still, so fresh and clean and uncomplicated. Yes, she was uncomplicated. He could tell that in her open, accepting face. Joe was a lucky man. But the others— where were the others? Larry, Lucia's husband, was sitting down with Zaira's husband—ah, they would talk the rest of the afternoon away, as long as Zaira let her husband stay. He didn't look good. The old man didn't want to see that—it pained him to see the end coming in another man. A promise of a breeze entangled a branch, and silver light flickered across his vision.

This is so hard, he thought, even with Paulo helping me. The old man longed for the comfort of his oldest son, the way he looked up at his father and gave that reassuring smile, the little nudge that said the two of them could do it all, even this, even this. He searched the crowds around him—the children running between tables before being sent off to a corner of the yard, the cousins greeting each other as though they hadn't seen each other only last week, the ones who were still in the middle of a year-long argument over whose farm team was better, the high cost of a new train line supposed to be coming to the area—all those things that didn't matter but took over the moment. Utensils clattered in bowls and on platters, food appeared on a white plate with a blue-flowered border in front of him—Lucia's paella, Zaira's spinach with raisins and pine nuts, his wife's stuffed onions, her cod and potato salad, and her bread. He loved her bread. His hand rose involuntarily to take up the light golden loaf and he held it in his palm—so light, so soft, warm and sweet, like life itself.

"Do you want butter, Pae?" Zaira leaned over him.

"No, no, go away." He jerked his head away and crushed the bread to his chest. Why were they bothering him? Didn't they know how important today was? And where was everyone? He counted the cousins and dismissed them, counted the grandchildren and forgot them, counted nieces and nephews.

He craned his neck to see around the jostling and joking and calling crowd. They were always like this—a man couldn't sleep in his house with so many children. Some nights he had snuck onto the back porch and lain down on the settee, to have the quiet of the night and the sounds of the world around him. The girls should be quiet and ladylike but sometimes they rolled and tussled and fought like boys, even worse, like dogs. And here they were, like ordinary folk you might meet anywhere. How did it happen? He asked his wife once, if she thought it strange the way the little ones turned into these adults we hardly knew.

"Of course not. That's what they're supposed to do. We only feed them."

He couldn't understand her. But then he couldn't understand himself. It was only Paulo he could talk to. And now there was even more of a ruckus. He pushed himself up in his seat to get a better look. Someone walked in front of him and stopped, and the old man reached out and pushed him aside— someone's nephew—and jostled through the crowd a few feet.

He couldn't see as well as he wanted because all these people kept walking in front of him, blocking his view, reaching into bowls of food and joking and talking too loud. Why couldn't they get out of the way?

"Oh, Pae, it's Mrs. Perreira and Christina!" Lucia tucked her arm through his and pulled him toward her. "Mae said you asked them to come." He felt her looking at him, but who was she to ask him this? It was his home, his house. He could do what he wanted, couldn't he?

"Where are they?" He strained to move forward, felt his knees weaken and threaten to buckle, and stretched out his hand to the tree trunk.

"Here, sit, Pae. I'll make sure they come over here."

"I have waited so long." He fell into his chair.

"Mrs. Perreira just needs someone to help her with Christina's chair in the van."

"Ask Paulo. He can do it." The old man fell back into his seat, exhausted, sweating, but with a quiet smile trembling on his lips.

"Pae, Paulo is . . ." Lucia stood up behind him, kneading his shoulders with her strong fingers.

At last, he thought. I will have all my family together.

* * * * *

"Don't worry about me, Joe." He felt Gwen's arm slip around his waist and for a moment he forgot where he was and what else was going on—all he could see or think about was his father teetering beside his chair as he poked and prodded this relative or that one to move out of his way.

"I'm afraid this isn't what you bargained for, is it?" He lifted his arm over her head and rested it on her shoulder. The crowd was turning into the mayhem of his childhood and if he'd had greater presence of mind he'd worry about how Gwen felt about it all. But all he could see was his father—more crippled by some secret emotion than old age.

"I bargained for meeting your family and I'm meeting them." She whispered into his shirt collar as one of his sisters hurried by with another platter. "Do the women in this family eat or do they just rush around with a lot of food?" When she glanced up at Joe she was startled to see a frown instead of a smile. She followed his eyes to find out what was turning his mood. There, her arms waving a path through the crowd, was Mrs. Perreira. "Joe, I think I'm going to track down Jennie and make sure she's not getting into any trouble. You do what you have to do and forget about me." She tapped him lightly on the chest to get his attention and slipped away from his embrace.

"Sure," he said, still watching his father. Then, startled by her quick movements, he pulled her back to him and kissed her lightly. "Save me some of my sister's fish balls. Over there." He nodded to where Lucia was just then arranging a serving tray on another table.

He warmed with gratitude for Gwen's kindness and turned his attention back to Mrs. Perreira. Someone he didn't recognize was helping her push a wheelchair, and he didn't have to look any closer to know that it was Christina getting the ride.

What in the name of all that was holy was the point of this? he heard himself saying. He closed his eyes, took a deep breath, and took a moment to compose himself. He'd better get over there—it was expected—and make Mrs. Perreira and Christina feel welcome. Wheels within wheels, his father used to say about an argument among the fishermen, wheels within wheels. That was how this situation felt to Joe—nothing was what it seemed, and his father and Mrs. Perreira were driving toward something, and not the same thing.

Joe moved among the cousins, drawing closer, watching one relative after another dart in to say hello and hug Mrs. Perreira; he could see Christina bundled into the wheelchair as though it were close to freezing instead of nearing eighty degrees. Her hands were tightly curled in her lap, and her head tipped to one side, then back as she seemed to follow the sounds of people's voices. Her black hair, though showing signs of gray, had been carefully washed and arranged—he still marveled that no one had taken the easy route of cutting it short.

He saw the left hand twitch as someone leaned over her— he'd been so focused on her contorted body that he hadn't paid any attention to those who were approaching her. He was surprised to see Lucia lean over Christina, give her a light kiss on the forehead while the seated woman's left hand twitched and flipped over, back and forth, back and forth, like a fish left on a sunny dock. Even more surprising was the pang of grief he felt for her as he watched this.

He had put the relationship behind him just before her accident and never felt the devastation that might have overwhelmed him if this had befallen her a few weeks earlier. He wondered at the timing, at how so few weeks could have altered his life so much. Seeing her now, strapped into a wheelchair, her expression one of near vacancy and confusion, didn't bring the pangs he had once expected. But he felt in the nursing home odors that reached him the loss of what had been her life. She had been such a vibrant, exuberant woman that he hated to see her as she was now, reduced to a twitch of her hand to express her feelings. Lucia knelt down and began to speak quietly to Christina.

"You see, Joe, we have come." Mrs. Perreira grasped his hand. "She is so excited to be here, to see everyone." Joe listened to her go on in this vein, wondering how much of this, if any of it, Christina really understood. Perhaps for her it was the pleasure of being around other people, of being outdoors in a festive atmosphere, and the rest of it—well, who we all were, Joe thought, meant nothing.

"She looks wonderful, doesn't she, Joe?" Lucia stood up and moved closer to him. "I can't believe it. Just wonderful!"

"Yes." He couldn't bring himself to offer anything more. He leaned over and took Christina's hand and whispered hello. Her faced twisted into the semblance of a smile—mouth stretched wide, eyes searching and moving on their own; a little drool gathered in the corner of her lips. He straightened up and stepped back, making way for a cousin.

"Hello, Joe."

The voice captured him before the face became familiar. He knew the voice. "Gino." For a moment he couldn't move. The younger brother he hadn't seen in so many years he'd stopped thinking about it held onto the handles of the wheelchair, keeping it in balance as Christina rocked back and forth, side to side. Gino. Grown tall and thick in the shoulders, and still with the lightest hair in the family, as if after six children the genes had simply run out of color. Gino with a steady glance like the boy, but not like the young man who had disappeared at a time when he scowled, jumped at little sounds, and wouldn't look at anyone or talk to anyone. Joe pushed through the crowd and threw his arms around Gino. The wheelchair rocked.

"I promised Mrs. Perreira I'd give her a hand," Gino said looking over his shoulder as Joe pulled him away. "She caught me at the sidewalk, while they were getting Christina out of the van." He stood rooted to the spot, watching the relatives crowd in around the woman, until she was blocked from his view. "I don't really want to leave her."

"Gino." Joe stepped in front of his younger brother, breaking his view of the others. "She's okay. I can't believe you're here."

"Are you sure it's okay?"

"Larry is in his element," Joe said, wondering if he should worry at Gino's unexpected solicitude. "Leave him to it. I haven't seen you in . . . "

"Doesn't matter, Joe," Gino said as they moved away from the crowd to the garage where someone had piled empty boxes and bags.

Joe held onto his younger brother's hand as he took in the man before him. Joe could see the muscles beneath the thin cotton shirt, feel the calluses on the fastidiously clean rough fingers that said this man worked with his hands for a living, saw the neck that had thickened and turned brown in the sun.

"Where do you want to begin?" Gino said. "You look just how I imagined you would."

Joe laughed. "I have no questions, Gino. I just want to get a good look at you, to fill the blanks of all these years." Joe knew he should see an older man, a middle-aged man who was probably growing tired of working and perhaps thinking about retirement or what his next career move might be. He should notice the wrinkles and gray hair and thickening waistline. But he could only see his younger brother when he was sixteen and grew rebellious and then a few years later took off. As Joe studied him now, he still couldn't see in him anything that said this had been a reckless boy and now he was a reckless man, or a man with regrets. No, this was a man who had made a life far away and had no regrets, at least not any that showed.

"You don't want to say anything, Joe?"

"Am I making you uncomfortable? Sorry. I'm just glad to see you, Gino. Really glad. Okay, tell me about yourself."

"I brought my wife with me, Melanie."

Joe nodded. Good, he thought. A man should be married. Then he thought of his own situation with Gwen and swallowed his smile. "Children?"

Gino shook his head. "You'll like Melanie. She's a wonderful woman."

"I'm sure she is." Joe grabbed Gino's shoulder and squeezed. "Where would we be without these meaningless phrases?"

"She really is wonderful."

"Yes, I'm sure she is, really. I'm just thinking how glad I am to see you."

"How's Pae?"

"He's okay. He's getting on, you know. He's over ninety. This was his idea." Joe nodded to the family filling the back yard. "You coming will mean a lot to him." This was the crux of it, the visit, the reunion, the calling everyone together at one time. "He wanted this." He waved his hand at the crowd around the tables, the steady stream of women going up and down the porch stairs carrying food, the children helping, then disappearing for a burst of fun. "He probably senses something—something about his time coming. His mind fails every now and then."

"And Mae?"

"Older too, but more like she always was." He paused. "You haven't seen them?"

Gino shook his head. He looked around him and spotted a bench, walked over to it, sat down. He leaned forward, resting his arms on his thighs. "I should have stayed in touch. Sorry." He swung his head to look at Joe, making no statement, asking no question, just looking, before resuming his watch of the back yard.

"It doesn't matter. You wanted a different life."

"No, that wasn't it at all. I meant I wish I hadn't done things the way I did—there wasn't any point to it in the end."

Joe waited for him to continue, but when he didn't, he asked, "Why did you disappear? What did you think was the point then? I couldn't figure it out—I figured you had a right to do what you wanted, Pae always gave us that, but you just up and left. No one ever did that in our family—no one just picked up and went. I always thought it was because of Deanie—when she ran off you thought you should too. But that didn't make any sense."

"Well, you're half right—on both counts." He sat up and Joe sensed an easing of tension in the other man. "Deanie's coming, isn't she?"

"You don't sound pleased."

"She should have stayed away."

* * * * *

Deanie drew up to the curb and guided her jaguar into the open parking space. She put the car in park but kept her hand on the shift. The engine hummed barely enough for her to know it was running. She shut down the engine and the air conditioning and leaned back in the leather seat. With the door cracked open she could hear the voices, spurts of shouting and laughing and cries of one calling another—just as she expected. She didn't have to see them to know who was there and what they were doing. She hadn't been here for years but she knew some things weren't going to change—she knew that.

At first she'd been scared, coming east after so many years. She felt herself breaking apart inside, as though the person she had become wasn't real and the true soul she had thought dead and buried decades ago was shoving to get out. It made her think of a conversation she had with her father years ago—why had she thought about that now? On the way home from school one afternoon she picked the flower of a yellow weed growing out of the sidewalk near a dying tree and held it pinched between her thumb and forefinger all the way home, worrying she wouldn't get it into water in time to save it. Her father came in later and picked up the vase.

"Ah, Deanie, I know where you got this." And he named the spot. "I have been watching it grow and grow, right through the concrete." He held the vase away from him and placed it on the shelf, as though it were the finest crystal instead of an old jar. "Nothing stops a flower. Not even concrete." She thought it was just his way to tease her, but the next afternoon she stopped at the weed growing along the sidewalk, and bent down to examine the crack. And there it was, a long thin line of dirt between the broken slabs, the green stalk standing straight up, jagged where she'd torn off the flower. How was it possible, she thought, that something so delicate as a plant can break concrete? She pondered this, and then her father's awareness of it. He wanted her to learn the lesson of gentleness, but instead she learned the eternity of wonder—and the weakness of what seems hard.

Unconsciously, Deanie's hand moved to her chest, and her long thin fingers splayed across her cotton blouse. She looked down at her white blouse and black slacks, at her red sandals, and across the seat at her red purse. Her outfit must have cost her close to two thousand dollars and it suddenly seemed foreign, as though she were wearing someone else's clothing. The flower she had picked that day had been yellow, but she never wore yellow. Nothing in her home was yellow. She never liked yellow, but she used to, when she'd been younger.

Deanie locked the car and climbed the steps to the house. It was the same yet strange. She wouldn't be caught dead living in such a place in Nevada, not that they had double deckers out there. She loved high rises, where she could look out over the city, across the desert, where everything was new and only the best—where she could view the world from the balcony of a condo she wouldn't be able to explain to her family.

On the front porch she peered into the first floor bay window. Those were Mrs. Morton's curtains, the ones her grandmother made and brought over with her from Ireland. So the Mortons were still here, Deanie muttered to herself. I was right. Nothing changes here, not really. The two doors to the double decker, standing side by side, were still painted black, both still showing lace curtains in the windows. She pulled open the door to the second floor apartment and climbed the narrow stairs, running her fingers along the bumps in the wall where she and her brothers had carried in furniture, carried up boxes of books for school, groceries, guests' baby carriages, and carried down her aunt's coffin, her brother's broken toys. The hall had been painted a bright green, but the gouges and slashes were there, beneath the layers of paint. She reached the top of the stairs and peeked into the living room. The voices were farther away now, down the hall and out on the back porch and in the back yard, their upward drift muffled by heavy upholstered furniture and thick drapes.

The room was the same—her father's chair, a new throw covering the worn patches, the photographs on the piano, the neat row of books, probably the same ones, knowing her frugal parents.

"Well, as I live and breathe."

Deanie started at the sound of the familiar voice. The little girl who had hunched her shoulders as she tiptoed through the family living room transformed into a tall, lean, statuesque woman of means, her dark hair swept back and clipped in a twist with a silver barrette. A necklace of large blue stones pulled in the light. Deanie tilted her head to one side, then the other, a half smile, not warm, forming on her lips. She took a few steps deeper into the room, looked around, not yet ready to acknowledge the speaker, and continued on closer to the dining room door.

"You come to family picnics, do you, Eddie?"

"Of course. I'm part of the family."

"Oh, yes, I heard. You married my sister."

"Rosalie is a very happy woman—she has everything she could possibly desire."

Deanie reached out to straighten a photograph on the piano, moving another one aside to adjust the space between them. "Yes, I saw your cottage. Very nice."

"You look great, Deanie."

She had to look at him then, not a casual glance that allowed her to avoid his eyes, but an appraising look as though she wanted to remember him—the last thing she really wanted. But she turned her dark eyes on him anyway, as though he were an insect to be studied. Eddie swiveled towards the door, and she felt a little burst of delight at the effect she had on him. Even so, he wasn't as she remembered him. He was old now, with the beefiness of middle-aged men who continue to eat and drink at lot but no longer play football or soccer or any other games as they did when they were young. They just head straight to the bar after work, skipping the earlier stop at the diamond on the edge of town. His hair was thinning, but at least he hadn't taken to coloring it. "You look like your father."

Eddie frowned and his eyes darkened, but he tightened his smile and let his hands drift into his pockets. "Well, I can't say you look like your mother." He took a step towards her.

Her hand moved to her purse, and she saw that he watched and saw that.

"What's in there?"

"If I were a different sort of person, I'd say, Come one step closer and I'll scream. But I'm not that kind of person. I'm a different kind of person." She slipped her hand into her purse.

Eddie laughed. "Maybe I shouldn't ask what kind of person. You are something else, Deanie."

She kept watching him, her smile tight and more a warning than a welcome. His joviality faded and he cast his eyes around the room. She turned as though to walk through to the other room, but paused. "If you knew I was coming, why didn't you stay away?"

"I'm part of the family now, remember?"

"You said that." She kept her hand in her purse, watching him, eyeing the little beads of sweat forming on his upper lip, sparkling. He was a loser, she suddenly realized, in her sense of the word. This wasn't a man who had good luck—she couldn't take him into a casino and steer him from one game to another, amplifying his luck with her skill. No, he was the kind of man who would always pick the wrong horse, put down too much money at the roulette table, pick the wrong team for the Super Bowl. His luck was different—he'd slide through a police checkpoint during the holidays when they were looking for drunk drivers; he'd get his traffic ticket fixed without much effort; he'd get a great pickup for a good price because he'd pick the one in the lot that had a few dings on the driver side door; he'd win a ten-dollar lottery ticket but nothing more; he'd get to his father's death bed with five minutes to spare, able to say for the rest of his life that he was with the old man when he died. Eddie's luck wasn't worth much, like the man himself. He'd never left here because he'd be even less somewhere else.

"What?" He jerked his chin upward and took a step toward her.

"Watch it," she said. He must have caught her smiling, she realized, caught her thoughts and misread them. She could imagine the smug look on her face as she realized what he'd become; she should have remembered that was the kind of thing that set him off, any little act of defiance, any refusal to be impressed with his male prowess, any lack of interest in his masculinity. Any slight to his manhood made him violent. She squeezed her purse and began to pull her hand out, and watched his distorted face as he worked to calm himself, his glance moving from her face to her purse and back and forth again and again.

* * * * *

Deanie slipped her purse strap over her shoulder and walked around the corner of the house. Someone really should have paved the driveway, she thought. It was a waste of energy to rake the gravel—what was left of it—back into the lane after every winter, sweeping it out of the shrubbery and back onto the dirt path. Maybe she'd do it for them, for her parents, sort of a gift— she could afford it. That and a new roof, perhaps. She looked up at the eaves, wondering about the hidden condition of the old house.

The tables were full, families settled for a meal on one end, someone serving at the other, mothers trying to get their children to sit still while they wandered here and there filling plates for them, husbands and fathers gathered in clusters by the trees, beer cans in hand, an occasional burst of laughter reminding everyone else where they were. No one seemed to notice her, and at first she was miffed, then confused, and by the time she reached the first table she was relieved. It was possible, she thought, they'd welcome her back as though she'd done nothing more than take an extra hour or two at the store. She wanted to giggle and pressed her lips shut, swallowing her hysteria.

"Deanie?" A woman touched her arm. "Deanie, is it you?"

Deanie turned to the voice and tried to bring order to the disconnected features of the woman's face appearing before her. She lived in a world where the women she knew all had brown or blonde or red hair—it might not be real, but no one had gray hair. This woman's gray hair was untidy, its permanent wave faltering in the heat and old age. Her red lipstick barely marked a thin line below her nose, and her large button earrings eclipsed the lower half of her ears.

"It's me, Deanie. Mrs. Perreira. You remember me, don't you?" The old woman leaned forward, her eyes soft and curious and warm. "My, Deanie, you look wonderful. Just wonderful. Your parents will be so pleased to see you. How we've missed you."

"Mrs. Perreira . . ." Deanie knew she should say hello, return the warm greetings, and perhaps she did. She must have said something because Mrs. Perreira was nodding her head and smiling, and then she raised her hand and pressed it against Deanie's cheek, and leaned in and kissed her other cheek. Deanie couldn't hear what she was saying in response to this warmth— she seemed to have fallen deaf to her own voice. But then Mrs.

Perreira moved to the side and motioned to someone behind her. Deanie looked, confused, then saw, lower down, a woman about her age in a wheel chair.

"You remember Christina?"

"Of course. Christina, how are you?" Deanie bent down to hear her reply just as she realized there would be none, that the noise that emerged from the throat could have been a cough, a bleat out of fear, or a croak for water. The eyes that had been once so beautiful that her older brother fell in love when he felt them on him were still there but no longer had that spark. Deanie had forgotten this, all of this—until this moment, as all the feelings of her adolescent self, envious of a gorgeous older girl dating her brother, took fire inside her. "She looks great, Mrs. Perreira. How wonderful she could come today." A sense of panic threatened to overwhelm Deanie but she forced out a smile and repeated to herself that no one could read her thoughts, no one could read her thoughts.

"Your father helped me." Mrs. Perreira let her head fall before turning to gaze on her daughter. "Every day I visit her in the nursing home and every day she's better."

"What's that in her hand?" Deanie tugged at the old photograph.

"Don't touch that. It's your father's—I'm using it."

"For what?" Deanie moved Christina's hand to get a better look. In the old black and white photograph four people stood alongside a pickup filled with what looked like camping gear— Paulo, Joe, Eddie, and one other boy she could barely remember. It was one of those weekend camping trips they waited for all summer long, until the fall hunting season started. "I just saw Eddie—in the house." Deanie pulled the photo from Christina's lap.

Christina began to writhe in her chair and keen, her head swinging wildly back and forth.

"What's happening? What should I do?" Deanie jumped back, then stepped forward.

"Nothing, nothing, she's all right. You're all right, Christina. I'm here. Everything's all right. You're safe, you're safe." She began to purr to her daughter in Portuguese and gradually Christina grew calm, her voice little more than whimpers and sniffles.

"You were inside, did you say?" Mrs. Perreira moved in front of her daughter and peered up at Deanie. Deanie nodded. "I think I need to put her in the shade—this sun may be too much for her."

Deanie looked up at the leafy branches above them, the green lacelike canopy filtering the sunlight and the breezes.

"I'll take her, if you want, Mrs. Perreira. Hello, Deanie." Rosalie materialized behind Deanie, rubbed her hand along her back, and quickly moved behind the wheelchair. "Let me do this."

"Thank you, dear. I'll just go get some water for her." Mrs. Perreira took one last look at her daughter and started toward the house. "I'll be right back," she said over her shoulder.

Rosalie began to push the wheelchair over the grass toward the fence and a low-hanging branch from a neighbor's tree. She turned the chair around to face the crowd and knelt down beside it, fingering the photograph.

"It went missing about a year ago," Rosalie said.

"She said Pae loaned it to her." Deanie met her glance, then looked away. A few feet behind them the party was going well, just the way family gatherings should go—lots of food, lots of joking, children mischievous but not troublesome, parents tired but tolerant, everyone happy if weary. No one had looked in their direction, no one was the least bit curious about who the stranger in the black slacks and red sandals was—Deanie felt she could walk back to her car and drive away and no one would ever know she'd been here, and no one would miss her, not really.

"They don't know it's you," Rosalie said. She tugged again on the photograph and when Christina began to keen quickly calmed her. "Are you married?"

"Me? No." Deanie shook her head.

"I am." Rosalie continued to kneel by Christina. "I married Eddie."

"I know." A corner of the photograph dangled and Rosalie ripped it off and let it fall into her palm—it contained half of the head of Paulo. Christina rocked herself against the soft back of the wheelchair.

"I heard there was talk about Gino and . . ." Deanie paused, watching her sister.

Rosalie nodded. "Yes, but no one really believed he'd do such a thing. It went nowhere."

"Except against him. It ate him up."

Rosalie looked over her shoulder where Gino was sitting at one end of a picnic table with his wife, Melanie. "He came this morning, with her. She's nice—quiet. Pae grabbed hold of her hand and wouldn't let go, maybe thinking he could hold onto Gino that way. It's been hard on him."

"I haven't seen him in years either—I guess I didn't need him after a while. I guess when you grow up you don't need a big brother." Deanie shrugged and dug her red fingernails into her palm, feeling them cut deep.

"We had no idea what happened to you," Rosalie said, still kneeling in front of Christina.

"Joe knew."

"What? What're you talking about?"

"Nothing. Forget it."

"No. Deanie, did you stay in touch with Jose?"

Deanie let her head fall back and laughed. "Well, not exactly. If I got—" She seemed to remember who she was talking to. "He sort of knew what I was up to, that's all. We never talked or anything. Jesus, Rosie, he's a cop. They like have their own network." She scowled and brushed a stray curl away from her face.

Rosalie gazed up at her, then at Christina, then at her sister. "If I'd known . . ."

"Known what?" Deanie hadn't meant to sound so harsh, so brittle. "Jesus, I'm hungry. Let's wheel her over to a table or something."

"Is it true, what you do in Nevada?" Rosalie rose effortlessly to stand beside her sister.

"You mean would any church around here let me take communion?" Deanie laughed. "Come on, let's eat."

"Deanie," Rosalie said, laying her hand on her sister's arm, "are you all right?"

"Of course. Jesus, Rosie."

Rosie tightened her grip. "I mean, really all right."

"Are you? You're the one married to Eddie." Deanie winced as soon as she said it. "I'm sorry—I just meant—I don't know what I meant. Are you happy, Rosie? Nothing else matters if you're really happy."

144 / Susan Oleksiw

"Paulo was happy right up until he shipped out," Rosalie said. "Zaira's been pretty happy—she worries a lot, but Mae says she fretted when she was barely three months old. And Lucia—she really lucked out—Larry's a doll and he adores her. Even after all these years. I like Gino's wife, so I guess he's happy too. And Joe. He's got a live-in girlfriend, but they'll probably get married. He has the look. She's good for him—very down to earth and calm. He likes that."

"So that leaves the two of us—just you and me."

Rosalie nodded, her eyes vacant as she looked down at Christina mewling softly to herself. "What went wrong? You can't really be . . ."

Deanie rested her hand on her sister's shoulder. "I'm just here for a visit, nothing more. It's for Pae. He's old. Don't get all worked up about anything."

"Christina lost everything that afternoon." Rosalie brushed back the sick woman's wispy hair. "And you . . ."

"I'm hungry. Let's eat." Deanie set her jaw and turned away.

"Mrs. Perreira's coming. Let's wait for her." Rosalie began to turn the wheelchair.

* * * * *

Jennie loaded her plate with food she had never seen before, stuck her index finger into each little sample on her plate to taste it before moving on to the next dish. She was used to family picnics and town events, but the amount of food on these tables compared to the number of people shocked her. She couldn't imagine where it all came from. And she had no idea what most of it was—but it was delicious.

Sarah had taken a plate over to two chairs set up near the garage, as far away as she could get from her parents without being obvious. She'd told Jennie when to get in line, which dishes were the best and which ones she could skip, and promised to hold a chair for her. "We really should be a little bit out of sight," Sarah explained.

Jennie was still smiling to herself about Joe and Gwen searching for eggs in the backyard but when she saw him watching her with an expression of annoyance and warning, it occurred to her that the drive back to Mellingham tomorrow might be a little tense. She almost wished she hadn't gotten involved with Sarah to begin with—almost. Sarah was fun—a little bad—but totally fun.

All around Jennie the adults were chatting, gossiping, eating, talking, and all of a sudden nudging a child back into line, stopping to help a small child with her food, then returning to the conversation. When one little boy refused to take a seat on the bench with his parents, he stomped his foot and wailed. His mother and father stood nearby, listening and sympathizing with him, countering his arguments with patience and reason. After several minutes, as Jennie's plate sagged under the weight of her choices, the little boy threw his head back, gave a wail, then jerked himself straight and climbed onto the bench. The crisis was past, and a couple of women nodded their approval and patted the boy on the cheek. Jennie was transfixed by this display of parental skill, and it was only when she noticed everyone else was sitting and eating that she took hold of herself and headed to the chair next to Sarah.

"Do your parents ever get really mad at you for some of the stuff you pull?" Jennie rested her plate on her lap and leaned over it, hoping she could get through the meal without spilling half of it on her pants.

"Sometimes. My mom gets worked up, but my dad says I'm young and curious and nothing bad comes of it." Sarah snorted a chuckle. "He is so parental."

"I think Joe is upset—he might even be angry."

"Nah. He'll get over it."

"I hope so. I don't want to ride with him tomorrow if he's still angry."

"Your mom isn't." Sarah waved her fork at her. "You have to take the right approach here—it's all about strategy. First, the game has to be fun for someone—like the ducks and the eggs. Kids love things like that—it was just too bad that there weren't any around. How was I to know there weren't going to be any kids here over night to find them in the morning? Huh?"

"And they fall for that?" Jennie began to scowl. "My mom wouldn't."

"Yes, she would. Take that mirror. It was art—a painting."

"I thought it was a photograph."

"Same thing. Listen, Jennie. If you want to get away with these things, you have to make them like fun, then no one gets upset. After all, I'm just a kid really, in their eyes."

"You're seventeen."

"Why do you talk like that?" Sarah pulled a face, gave her a disapproving look, and brought her plate closer to her face. "Let's not worry about it. I'm going to drop the swing when they're setting out the ice cream. It is part of a celebration, after all. Did you check the ropes?"

Jennie nodded. "I had to be careful. There were people inside."

"Who? Everyone's outside once the food comes out."

"I heard your uncle Eddie talking to someone."

"Oh, him." Sarah hunched over and shoveled sausage into her mouth.

"He's not like the rest of your family."

"Forget him. We have to get ready. I figure in another hour they'll be so mellow." Sarah chewed vigorously.

For Jennie, keeping up with Sarah's moodiness, her changeableness and insistent defiance of her parents, took more energy than she would have thought. She wasn't ready to defy her mother on general principles, and often wouldn't defy her on any other grounds even if they were reasonable. She sometimes wondered why she was so different in this way from her peers— she didn't get a kick out of besting her mother in arguments or anything else, and unless pressed on a point of honor, she usually gave in. Her younger brother, Philip, was much more likely to argue and fight and demand, but even he never went as far as some of the other kids in town. Something in her held her back—and perhaps Philip also. She could feel it—hard and solid in the middle of her chest, getting harder and firmer and bigger when the pull from her friends grew stronger, more insistent. Sometimes it even felt like her feet were cemented to the ground and she couldn't have run off with them if she wanted to.

"Something's wrong." Sarah sat up, dropping her plate on the ground and scanning all the relatives in the back yard. "Omigod! You didn't set it right. It's too loose!"

Jennie began to protest but as she looked up at the attic window she saw what Sarah meant. There, loosening from its mooring, the swing with two figures began to fall to the porch roof below. But instead of settling as the girls had imagined, its two figures grinning madly over the crowd of relatives seated below, the swing continued to fall and slide down the second-floor porch roof, until it came to the eaves and fell over the edge, hanging down and bouncing back out when it hit the post, until it came to rest, dangling over the railing.

"Oh, my surprise is ruined!" Sarah jumped up.

Jennie reached out and grabbed her arm as she scrambled out of her chair. "Wait! It's not them!" And she was right.

Dangling over the porch railing, with ropes tied around his neck, was Uncle Eddie, his face turning purple, his arms twitching, his legs swinging. A woman screamed. Chairs tumbled away as men sprinted up to the house, up the stairs. Within seconds Joe pushed through the others and raced up the back stairs to the second floor porch.

Eight

Saturday Afternoon

The minute Joe saw Eddie dangling over the porch, he knew this wasn't going to be just a matter of pulling him back up, or lowering him down to the porch. Eddie's limbs were entangled in the rope strung through a wooden board, and he looked as though he had slid off a swing and hung himself. Getting him safely out of his situation was going to take imagination as well as physical strength. Safely, thought Joe. He shut his mind to the reality of Eddie's rapidly worsening condition and focused on rescuing his brother-in-law. On Joe's order, a cousin ran to call 911.

Joe climbed out onto the porch roof from the attic window, and began to work his way down the curled roof tiles. He'd patched this roof at least once as a teenager, but it looked like no one had done anything to it since then. Any tile could split and shred beneath his heeled shoe, sending him down the roof to the ground below.

"Joe!" Larry leaned out and tossed him another rope. "It's tied to the bed." Then he climbed out behind Joe, smearing oil from the window casing onto his cream linen pants.

"He's still alive." Joe wrapped the second rope around his waist and inched closer to Eddie. "You down there!" A younger cousin looked out over the railing, waving at Joe above him. "Two of you, grasp his legs and lift him up."

Eddie's contorted face rolled into view. Joe heard Larry gasp behind him, silence, then move down closer.

"I'll get his arm if you can get an arm around his torso. We can pull him up if they lift down there."

148

Joe nodded. Larry was sensible, a good man in a pinch, Joe'd always thought. And this was a time Joe never expected to come and he was glad to find he had been right about Lucia's husband. A gasp escaped from Eddie just as Larry reached down and fixed his grip on Eddie's arm. Joe leaned over, praying he didn't crash head over heels to the ground. He grabbed Eddie's side, lifting him closer, then onto the roof. He saw the hands holding Eddie's legs disappear and heard footsteps running up the stairs. Two cousins climbed out onto the roof, and the four men loosened the rope from Eddie's body, tossed it aside, and eased him up the porch roof and into the attic, laying him on the floor.

Someone moved behind Joe, placing an old torn cushion under Eddie's head. Joe eased his brother-in-law's head down, pulling his hand away, feeling the stickiness of drying blood on his fingers.

"Is he alive?"

Joe looked up to see Gino standing nearby. Joe nodded, stood, and looked around at the men bunched together by the doorway. "Gino." He repeated the name in a whisper as he waited for Gino to take heed of his circumstances. For a moment Joe was afraid he'd have two victims on his hands—one in shock, the other in a coma. "Gino. Get me that blanket." Joe nodded to a throw on a nearby bed. "Over there." Awkwardly Gino began to comprehend, turning his head stiffly to the side. He took one step, then another, and pulled off the worn blanket. He handed it to Joe, the ends trailing on the floor. Joe spread it over Eddie.

Eddie's eyes rolled up out of sight, and Joe quickly stroked his face and checked for a pulse. The injured man was breathing, but he was badly injured, Joe was sure of that. The rope had burned across his throat, chafed to the point of bleeding, marked a red path below his ear. As Eddie began to moan, Joe suspected there was a good chance the man's neck was broken. He listened hard for the sound of a siren.

* * * * *

Joe could see his sister far down in the yard, surrounded by relatives, Lucia embracing her. Someone set a chair behind her and helped Rosalie fall into it. Her body was rigid with disbelief and shock. Joe had seen far too many spouses facing the horrific news about a loved one—but this one was his own younger sister. She seemed to listen hard, confused, a tiny figure shrinking within as the crowd around her grew. She bent over, holding her head with her hands, her face pressed against her knees. Lucia knelt down, running her hand over Rosie's hair. Joe could imagine the words of comfort in English and Portuguese, murmurings to soothe.

The mood of the crowd changed. Joe took a step closer to the window. Whatever Lucia had said had startled Rosalie and she sat up. Lucia, thought Joe, always downplaying how bad things were. Rosalie, slow to catch on, but she always did catch on. She wasn't going to take this well, he could see. He headed for the stairs.

Joe braced himself when he saw Rosalie racing up the back stairs. She threw herself at him. "He can't be!" she screamed. "No no no no." She spun around, looking wildly at the back hall, before Joe grabbed her and pulled her into the kitchen, away from the sight of the EMTs running up the back stairs to the attic. She turned toward the sound of the heavy shoes on the treads and tried to snatch hold of the last one. She reached the hand railing and held and Joe had to peel her fingers from around the banister—she was nearing hysteria.

"They're taking care of him, Rosie. Let them do their job." He spoke softly into her ear, trying to find the younger sister who had always trusted him, always looked up to him, the one who would trust and listen now. "There's nothing we can do. Let's go back down. Come on." He pulled her toward the front of the house. If he could get her into the dining room and find a glass of whisky for her he could get her under control again—at least until the EMTs had a chance to do whatever they could do.

"Oh, no, I can't, I can't." She collapsed onto the floor and sobbed. "It can't be, it can't be. It's not fair." Rosalie wrapped her arms around herself and rocked back and forth, sprawled across the linoleum, incoherent with pain. Her face was a patchwork of red and smeared blue and black from her eye makeup, her nose running, her hair flying.

"They'll take care of him, Rosie. We'll follow them to the hospital, make sure he's all right. He'll get the best care." He glanced up at the faces peering in at the back door, at Larry's broad back holding the others at bay. Zaira slipped under her brother-in-law's arm and hurried to kneel beside Rosalie.

Joe shrugged; Zaira nodded and embraced her sister. In a moment Joe left and returned with a small glass of dark golden liquid and pressed it on Rosalie. She shook her head.

"Drink it!" Zaira commanded, taking the glass from Joe and pushing it into her sister's face.

When the EMTs were ready to move Eddie, Joe hoisted Rosalie to her feet and half-carried, half-dragged her into the living room and walked her over to a chair. Mae was ready with a shawl, wrapped her daughter in it and hovered over her. Rosalie bent over, pressing her face into her lap, wrapping her head in her hands and arms. Joe was glad to leave the stage to his other sisters and cousins and their ministrations—another shawl, a cup of warm water with sugar, hands warm and soothing on her back. To his surprise, he was embarrassed at seeing his sister collapse so completely.

On the back stairs, the EMTs brought Eddie down strapped onto a stretcher and carried him out to the ambulance. Joe wondered how long he'd last.

* * * * *

"We get calls like this every day this time of year." The EMT checked the latch on the ambulance door before turning to Joe. The family that had followed the EMTs and Eddie out to the ambulance was coalescing into smaller groups, of comfort, surprise, worry. "It's not the booze, in my opinion, it's all that feeling of summer—being free and having a good time and forgetting what a little impulsive fun can cost you. Too bad. You get too old to sit on a roof and wave to everyone, even if it does make you feel like a kid again."

"Where're you taking him?"

The man mentioned the local hospital and Joe promised to let Eddie's doctor know right away. "Some of us will be over there too—they'll follow you in probably." The man nodded and walked around to the passenger side.

Joe urged the rest of the family to return to the back yard. First, he had to get hold of Eddie's sons, since Rosalie was in no condition to hold vigil at the hospital while Eddie underwent whatever medical procedures were going to be attempted. Joe ran up the stairs, and made sure Zaira made the calls. Eddie wouldn't be alone for long in the hospital—both boys were nearby. When he heard her breaking the news, the cell phone clasped to her ear, turning away from him and walking over to the kitchen sink to stare out the window as she spoke, Joe allowed himself a moment of relief before heading out to the back porch.

The long tables, covered in faded flowery tablecloths, were mostly empty now, the meal in disarray, the older relatives confused and unsettled, or wearied and apathetic. The younger generations had sought comfort with each other, texting their friends and the cousins who hadn't attended—then gave in to the shocking reality of it all to sit and stare up at the porch to get a better view of the site of the accident.

But it had been no accident, of that Joe was certain. He could see the body tumbling over the shingles, the rope growing tauter and tauter. And when he reached Eddie, he had the same thought—this is not an accident. The way the rope was arranged around Eddie's neck, the light patch of blood on the back of his head, the palm and finger marks across his reddened cheek— Eddie had not merely stumbled through the window by accident. And he had lived through the fall and landing, entangled in a slapdash hangman's noose, only by the greatest good fortune. Joe grabbed a couple of young cousins, two of the many teenagers in the next generation, and set them on the driveway with a single duty. "No one leaves unless I say so. Got it?" The boys nodded and Joe left them to it.

With effort Joe persuaded his family members to reassemble at their respective tables, the older ones sitting bolt upright as they always did, but this time with an uneasy tilt toward the street outside, just in case there was more to come. Not all were so agreeable. Some complied after verbal skirmishes, others agreed but stood rooted where they were, unable to move. And still others couldn't remember where they were sitting and did it matter anyway? Moving from table to table, Joe let the conversation turn quickly and passionately to what might have happened. Once satisfied that they would engage each other for the time he needed, he headed for the garage.

"You!" he said to Jennie. She jerked her head up, and quickly looked around her, as if hoping he meant someone else, but she was alone. "Tell me what this was about."

Jennie opened her mouth and gulped; nothing else came out. She opened her mouth again, took a deep breath. "It was

supposed to be a, sort of, a celebration. It was Sarah's idea."
Again she looked to one side, then the other.

"I'm sure it was, Jennie. But she's not here and you are.
Tell me how it was supposed to work."

"Oh, Joe!" She slapped her hand across her mouth and tears
welled in her eyes.

"Not now, Jennie. There's no accusation here. I just need to
know what you set up to happen, how this was supposed to
work. We'll talk about culpability later."

Jennie nodded and took a deep breath, then began. "We set
up two figures—they were supposed to be your parents—and the
swing was supposed to come down and hang over the porch,
with them holding hands and kissing. Sarah set it up so that at a
certain time the sun would heat up a block of butter, which
would melt and that was just enough loss of weight so that the
line would slip . . . I'm not really sure. It sounded really clever
when she explained it." Jennie's eyes began to fill again. "Oh,
Joe, I'm so sorry." She covered her face with her hands and
started to cry. "We didn't mean to hurt anyone."

"Of course you didn't." Joe wrapped his arms around her,
gave her a squeeze, and pulled back. "We'll talk about practical
jokes another time."

"What's going on?" Gwen hurried up and pushed between
them, looking from one to the other. "What does Jennie have to
do with this?"

"She'll tell you. It's all right, Gwen. Jennie's not really
involved." He turned back to Jennie. "When were you last
working on this?"

"Late this morning, after everyone started arriving."

"Did you meet anyone up in the attic?"

Jennie shook her head. "I heard people when I was leaving
the last time, coming out through the kitchen."

"Who did you hear?"

"I could hear him—Eddie—he was talking to someone."

"Did you hear what they said? Anything?"

Jennie shook her head and looked like she was going to start
crying again.

"Did you see anything, anyone go up the stairs after you
came down?"

Jennie shook her head again. "I wasn't paying attention to
anything like that. I saw a jaguar drive up out the front window

and I couldn't stop looking at that. I just didn't pay attention to anything else."

"The jaguar was here while you were still in the house? And it parked out front?"

Jennie nodded. Gwen took a step closer and slid her arm around her daughter. Joe frowned and looked over the back yard, the families settling in to gossip and whispered explanations and theories, even a few jokes and nervous laughter.

"What was happening when you came out? Do you remember who was here?"

Jennie shook her head back and forth. "I don't really know everyone, Joe. Oh!" She brightened. "I remember the fish balls—Sarah said they were great. I should be sure to try them."

"So Sarah was out here with you."

Jennie nodded. "She quizzed me about how I left everything—she's very particular." Jennie frowned. "Like a real engineer. I wouldn't want to work for her."

"Was she satisfied, or did she want to fix it up herself?"

"Oh, no, I did exactly what she told me to do. Really."

Joe believed her, unfortunately. Jennie was, among other things, very dutiful. "Fish balls? Thanks." Joe shook his head, and gave Jennie's arm another squeeze before turning back to the picnic tables. "Stay nearby," he said over his shoulder as he walked away.

* * * * *

Lucia held her father by one elbow while her husband, Larry, held the other. Between them they struggled to get him into a chair, but he wouldn't budge—he wouldn't sit down and he wouldn't go forward.

"I can't do anything with him, Joe," Lucia said. She moved closer to her father, held him tighter, and urged him softly to take a rest, just for a moment. Joe caught Larry's eye, and the other man shrugged.

"He says he's not finished with what he has to do," Larry said over his father-in-law's head.

"Don't talk nonsense, Larry." Lucia broke off her whispered urgings to criticize her husband.

Joe moved in front of his father and gripped his hands. "Pae, tell me what this is about. What is it you have to do?" He waited for the old man to focus his eyes on him—dark brown eyes that had grown pale and rheumy over the years, as though they were fading away and when they were gone to pale beige, the old man would be gone too. Every moment of this visit had confirmed Joe's deepening understanding that his father was far older than he realized—he was no longer the old man who had lapses into incoherence, or reminiscences of experiences no one had ever heard about before, about times that went back to his childhood, stories that were laughed off when he came back to his old self, the father they knew and loved. Now, he was an old man who lived on the other side of his lapses and occasionally visited the world his family still lived in. His lucid moments were the interruption of his life lived elsewhere.

"If Paulo was here, he'd know." The old man looked beyond Joe as though searching for the other son. "Why don't you know, Jose? You're my son."

This is what they really mean when they say the years catch up with you, Joe thought. Not physical aging, but the questions and doubts left unresolved—they demand acknowledgment and resolution. "Is this about Gino? This is about Gino, isn't it?" Joe tugged at his father's hands, trying to bring him back. The old man studied him.

"Jose?" He squeezed Joe's hands in return. "I must talk to him—this time I must talk to him. Paulo told me all about this. He explained everything. One morning I am no longer confused and sad—it is all clear. Paulo is such a good boy."

"Oh, Pae." Lucia held him close and Joe was afraid to look at her, to see the pain of realization in her eyes at what had happened on this fine sunny day to her father. "Come on, Pae. Let's go over here." She and Larry returned to the task of moving her father along.

Joe left them to it and began to look for Gino. He'd left his younger brother at table when he'd seen Eddie sliding down the porch roof, and now had to remind himself where they'd been talking, the table filled with cousins gawking and grinning at Gino as only they could—delighted to see him, curious why he had stayed away, their good manners keeping them from prying too intensely. But some of the youngest cousins had rushed forward at the first sign of the accident and only now were finding their way back to their seats, clustering in tight knots of gossip and speculation. At the far end Gino and Melanie were still there, and both rose when they saw Joe approaching.

"I was just going to get something to drink," Gino said.

"Sit down, Gino." Joe glanced at Melanie, who gave him a nearly imperceptible nod and started to back away.

"You don't have to go, Melanie," Gino said.

Melanie rested her hand on Gino's shoulder, sighed, and said that yes, she did, and moved away, leaving the two men alone. Gino stood, the man who had run construction companies, climbed mountains, rafted down the Columbia River rapids, hunted everything that was legal in the west, was every inch the man his older brother was, but Joe sensed that even now Gino knew he was the younger brother still. Gino climbed back onto the bench.

"Pae is getting worse. His dementia is almost complete—he rarely makes sense," Joe said, sitting across from his brother.

"I noticed." Gino rolled his shoulders and watched his sister and her husband maneuver the old man across the back yard.

"But he's not completely gone. At least, he makes some sense; he says things I can figure out." Gino nodded. Joe leaned toward him. "Why does Pae want to talk to you now? Why does he say this time he has to talk to you?"

"Did he say that?"

"Why did you come back this time, Gino?"

"I missed my family." Gino sat up as though he were going to rise, but stretched and settled.

"You missed us for years. Why this time?"

Gino rubbed his large hands across the red painted rough wood of the picnic table. This was one he and Joe had repaired years ago, and someone else had repaired it a few times since then, or perhaps so many pieces had been replaced over the years that it was really a new table. But it was a table he knew—he knew the feel of the wood, the paint his mother always wanted, the weight of each bench. "I didn't have anything to do with Eddie falling."

"I know. You were out here—we were talking when it happened. And you aren't someone who would set me up as an alibi." Joe leaned forward. "But there's something behind your visit that only you and Pae know. And I have to know what it is."

"You're making too much of this."

Joe reached into his pocket and pulled out his badge, flipping open the black case. He slapped it down onto the table in front of his brother. "I'm a cop, Gino. I'm always a cop."

Gino stared at the shiny metal, moving inches closer as though he doubted its authenticity. "Yeah, you would be. You were always straight about things like that."

"Tell me now."

Gino pulled his hands toward himself and clasped them together, rapping them three times on the table, paused, then rapped them again three times. "Pae called me and begged me to come—as much as Pae could ever beg anyone for anything."

Joe could feel the rest of the family watching his back, wondering what he was talking to Gino about. He could imagine the speculations, the whispering, the friendly arguments, but there was nothing he could do about it—he had to get answers fast. "Why now, Gino?"

"He was getting old, he said. He wanted it settled, for his peace of mind, he said."

"What did he want settled?"

Gino opened his hands and spread them out, palms upward. Joe met his gaze, patient, still. "You know. Christina."

Christina. That was not the answer Joe expected. "Go on."

"He wanted us together again—the whole family." Gino sighed and began to fidget, shifting on the bench, swinging one way, then the other.

"What's the rest of it?"

"He wanted me to know that he never believed the rumors that I might have had anything to do with what happened to her." Gino paused and looked over Joe's shoulder. Scattered across the lawn were others who had never needed convincing back then.

"But he thought you knew something—and you did, otherwise you wouldn't have disappeared so completely as soon as you could," Joe said.

Gino nodded.

"You have to tell me what this is all about, Gino."

"It's about Deanie."

* * * * *

On the far side of the back yard Joe could see Deanie hold up a red high-heeled sandal and give it a good shake, then peer into the toe. She shook it again, and watched something fall to the ground before slipping her sandal back on. She glanced quickly over her shoulder and smiled at the man standing nearby, one of the many in-laws Joe didn't know. The man blushed

under her frank gaze before turning away, forcing a serious look
back onto his face.

Deanie. She had been such a quiet, thoughtful girl—until
the age of fourteen or thereabouts. And then she'd changed. Joe
tried to recall when he'd first noticed the change, but time was
fluid for him now. He remembered the change, but not when.
First she was withdrawn, then she was moody, and then she was
wild—dating the wrong boys, disobeying her parents, skipping
school. Joe could barely tolerate the thought inside his head—
disobeying her parents. It hadn't bothered him as much then as it
did now. This afternoon, with the smell of summer on the air, an
abundance of food, and a tribe of children all in good health, it
hardly seemed possible that anyone could have gone so wrong.
Deanie, Joe thought.

"What about Deanie?" Joe put the badge back in his pocket.
"I thought you barely saw each other."

"Not for years." When Gino looked up, his face softened
and Joe didn't have to turn around to guess that he had caught
Melanie's eye. She was good for him, Joe felt. She was an
uncomplicated woman who had simple desires and a good heart,
and she had settled on Gino—two confused people who had
bumped into each other and thanked their lucky stars for the
accident.

"You were very protective of her, when you were young."

"She needed protection back then."

"And now?" Joe wondered just how much Gino knew about
his younger sister. Gino leaned back, smiled, and the tension
seemed to leave him. He had passed through the dark moment, it
seemed, and now had marked his compass for a better course.

"If she turned against me, I'd need protection, serious
protection. She's not a little girl, Joe. She's serious business in
Las Vegas and wherever else she goes. She told me once she
made the best money in Monte Carlo. Can you see it? Deanie in
Monte Carlo?" Gino started to laugh and shook his head, but the
underlying sadness threatened to surface, and he pulled a face.

Joe could see it. He knew enough about Deanie's life over
the years to not be surprised by this little detail. Sometimes,
when he picked up a bit of news about her through his contacts,
he was surprised she had bothered to stay in the States. Life
wasn't nearly as glamorous here as it was supposed to be
overseas.

"What's all this got to do with Deanie?" Joe waved his hand to indicate the back yard and family surrounding them. "You said this had to do with Deanie."

"It does. Do you remember when Christina had her accident?"

Joe nodded. Everything seemed to revolve around Christina these days, and the persistent way her name kept coming up made him feel that in his determination to keep track of his family he had missed something obvious, something right in front of him. It irked him and worried him. He waited for Gino to continue. He seemed to have trouble getting started, and reached for an abandoned glass of water, pouring it down his throat without letting the rim touch his lips. "The accident upset her badly."

"She was fourteen when it happened."

"Yeah. I was sixteen, almost seventeen."

"What did this have to do with Deanie?"

"She got very fearful—you have to remember. She made me promise that I'd stick by her as long as it took, until she felt safe. I said I would."

"So when she ran off, you went with her."

"Yeah, like that." He smiled. "That was a long time ago—adolescents thinking we had the world on our shoulders."

"And you came back because you knew she was coming?"

"Oh, no." Gino shook his head. "No, I gave up on watching out for her years ago." His eyes began to twinkle, and for a moment he was the younger brother who liked joke books and good stories. "She called me once and told me she was worried about a guy she was dating. I was in Oregon, but I thought she was serious, so I got in my pickup and drove down to Tahoe. I walked in on her in this house on a hillside—bigger than three triple deckers put together. And there she was—looking gorgeous. I wasn't sure it was really her—the woman sitting there seemed so foreign to me. But she recognized me—I could see it in her eyes—while I was still trying to figure out what mistake I'd made. She was turning the pages of a magazine, standing at a large glass dining table, in pink silk pants and pink spikes and a white silk blouse. I never thought she could look like that—I never thought I would know someone who looked like that. And there I was looking like something too poor and stupid to even be hired to clear brush."

Joe felt the knot in his stomach tighten. He couldn't stand hearing his brother say these things about himself. "But you went when you thought she needed you."

"Things are different out there, Joe. She tried not to laugh at my showing up like that, but she had this little half smile on her face. I knew what I looked like to her. It made me think her phone call was more like remembering what we'd been years earlier, maybe she was just being kind or something. She was boosting my ego, I suppose, maybe being nostalgic. I don't know. I got in my truck and that was it. We talked on the phone once in a while after that, but I never believed she needed me anymore."

Joe watched Gino's face flicker with pain, anger, disappointment, and something else. Relief? "You're not telling me enough, Gino. There's something more. What is it?"

"What do you think? I've always felt guilty I wasn't around where I was supposed to be when Christina had her accident." Gino paused. "I went to see her. I was the one who found her in the bath—you know that. But some people thought it was strange I was there and maybe I'd—maybe I'd done that to her."

"No one here believed that, Gino."

"No, I guess not." He ran his hands over the rough surface of the table, leaned back and then in again. His right hand rose to his shirt pocket, touched it, then fell away. "I used to smoke. I gave it up years ago. You never smoked, did you? Can't bum a cigarette, I guess." He scanned Joe's shirt, the neatly pressed but empty pocket.

"Gino, this isn't a casual family conversation. Tell me about Deanie. She left. You left."

He nodded. "I know. I was glad to get out anyway, living with that—all that suspicion. I knew what people were thinking even if they weren't saying anything."

"None of us thought that."

"I know, I know. But you're family. And there's more to living here than family. And no one here ever forgets. For the rest of my life I'd be the one who might have . . . I didn't want that. That's what all of this was about, I guess. For me, anyway." He waved his hand at the now-empty tables and chairs. "Pae wanted me to come so he could tell me to my face."

"That makes sense, for Pae." Joe waited. "What's the rest of it, Gino?"

Gino looked across the table, a middle-aged man who had been dragged into the past. "I gave my word, Joe. No can do." He shook his head. "You'll have to ask Deanie. It's not my story to tell."

Nine

Later Saturday Afternoon

Joe crossed the back yard feeling the anger bubbling inside him. He had to be careful here, more than careful—it wasn't his territory, it was his family, it wasn't his gig, it was his brother-in-law. But he knew he couldn't hold back the inevitable much longer. Pretty soon his family would want to know more about what happened, and it wouldn't be long before someone let slip that Eddie had more than a rope entangled around his neck when he tumbled over the windowsill and along the roof. It was the bloody crack on the back of his head that worried Joe.

"Your father is starting to get strange, Joe." Gwen laid her hand on the back of Joe's shoulder as he started to pass by her. "I can't calm him down and your mother has disappeared."

Joe stopped abruptly and scanned the back yard. Gwen was right—she'd put her finger on something that had been bothering him for a while now. His mother might be inside with Rosalie now, but she had disappeared some time ago, something very unusual for her. She was always in the middle of the gathering, going from one table to the next, making sure everyone had what they wanted and needed, purloining one platter to serve at another table, shifting children around, sitting for a moment to counsel a niece or nephew looking less than cheerful. Where had she gone? And when?

"Pae!" Joe leaned over his father, placing one hand on the back of his chair and the other on the table in front of him, effectively embracing him in a box of solicitude. He began to rub the old man's arm and shoulder. "Everything's all right."

"No, no. It is not supposed to be this way." The old man shook his head, and Joe noticed a small tear dangling from a

162

dark eyelash. Joe felt a chill, the sinking feeling that his father knew more about what was happening than he would admit.

"I have to find Deanie, Pae. Have you seen her?"

"No! Not Deanie." He grabbed Joe's wrist. The old man's grip was like iron, as strong now as when he had fished in his prime. His legs might wobble and creak and occasionally collapse, his eyes sometimes didn't know what they were looking at, and sometimes he couldn't flex his fingers. But his grip could still break a man's arm in two. "She's not the one."

Joe reached behind him for a chair and sat close to his father. The old man knew something—or maybe he was as demented as Joe feared. But he couldn't take the risk of overlooking something important right in front of him. "Tell me about Deanie. Tell me what you know."

Pae turned a confused face to his son, releasing his wrist and raising his hand to Joe's chin. He brushed his thick fingers across Joe's face. "Paulo had stubble always. No one else ever did. I don't know why. He began to shave so young—but always the stubble."

"Tell me about Deanie, Pae. What does she have to do with Eddie?"

Pae pressed his hand down on Joe's shoulder and leaned his head into the pocket of warmth their bodies made. "Poor Gino. So sensitive, so kind, so loyal."

"You arranged this reunion to make something happen." Joe pulled his father upright.

"No, no. I want the truth to settle the lives, so much hurt. I remember how much Angela cried when it happened."

Joe sighed, and drew away from his father. The old man was slipping again—slipping back into the memories of Angela when Paulo had died, into the past so long gone that most of the living no longer had room even to fit in the memories. If Paulo had lived to marry and raise a family, that would have been different—he would have established a place among the adults his siblings had become, but they had left him behind with their childhoods and grown into people he had never known. And when they looked back on him, they looked back on younger selves forgotten and put away. "I have to find Deanie, Pae. I'll come back."

"Please, not Deanie."

The tone of his voice was wrong, Joe thought. The tone wasn't pleading, though the words were those of a plea. The tone was one of direction, as though Joe shouldn't be looking for Deanie but for someone else.

"Why not Deanie?"

"She will always be my little girl, Deanie." Pae smiled easily. "Do you remember—she was so quiet, such a little sweet girl."

"Yes, I remember, Pae." Joe stood up and leaned over to kiss the top of his father's white head. "Can you keep Gwen company for a while, Pae? She's comfortable with you." The old man looked up at him and grinned.

"Such a lovely girl, Gwen. A good wife. I tell her all about you as a boy." He looked around for her and Joe motioned her to come closer. He took her hand and kissed it before quickly moving away.

Joe knew he was right to be suspicious of Deanie, no matter how hard Pae tried to deflect him. He wove his way through the scattered relatives, dodging calls and waving arms, until he reached the driveway. A last arm grabbed him and tugged him closer.

"Joe! Joe!" Mrs. Perreira half rose from her seat. Nearby Christina dozed in her wheelchair. Joe promised to come back later and catch up on the news with her, then hurried down the driveway. The jaguar was still parked along the sidewalk, but it was empty. He tried the doors—all locked. He scanned the sidewalk in both directions, stepping out into the street, hoping against hope that Deanie was nearby, that she'd taken a stroll down the street to smoke a cigarette or chat with a cousin. Frustrated, he turned and slapped the jaguar with the palm of his hand.

"Hey, easy there."

He followed the sound of the voice. Deanie sat in the dark corner of the steps, just inside the front door, effectively hidden from the view of anyone passing by. He walked over and rested his foot on the first step, then stared hard at her.

"What did I do? Why're you looking at me like that? I'm just sitting here."

"What're you doing out here?"

"What's wrong with being out here?" She came to the top step, sat, and patted the step beside her.

Joe shook his head, but leaned on the railing, as though exhausted.

"So, Big Brother, which one of us is going to be carted off for Eddie's unexpected demise? Maybe I should be ready, just in case. You think?" Deanie opened her purse and reached in, rummaging among the contents. She pulled out a tube, unscrewed it, and began to apply lip gloss to her lower lip. "Better?" She reassembled the tube and dropped it back into her purse.

"I don't ever remember you liking makeup so much." Joe watched her close up her purse, felt his grip on the railing relax. "You were too pretty to even need it."

"Thanks, Joe. You should have told me that back then." She winked at him. "But then you were so serious back then. You've learned a few things since we were kids, haven't you?"

He thought about sitting on a lower step, blocking her way in case she wanted to get up and leave, but then he felt he'd give up some advantage of height and gravity, so he stood, leaning against the railing like a parent confronting a child, a teenage daughter home after curfew, but Deanie was anything but a saucy teenager, a sulky child. She was sophisticated, smooth, and scared. He could see it in the way she wouldn't look at him directly, the provocative remarks, the way she primped, then casually looked out on the neighborhood.

"Gino thinks you should tell me the story." Joe could almost feel the stab of terror his words inflicted on her. "He'll watch your back but he won't do the rest for you. Wasn't that how he was as a kid?"

Deanie began to curl up like a child, drawing up her knees, pulling in her arms, resting her chin on her folded hands. "I didn't have anything to do with what just happened to Eddie." She looked up at him, fierce, defiant. Joe waited. "You believe me, don't you?"

Joe felt an ache for the struggle in her eyes, her stoicism and determination not to give in to fear, swallowing it whole as though it were a live thing, but he couldn't bring himself to make that promise. He shook his head. "How do I know what I believe until I hear what you have to say?"

Deanie gave a single harsh laugh. "You would say something like that. But it's fair, I suppose." She pulled herself upright, stretching out her legs before plunking her feet flat on

166 / Susan Oleksiw

the step below where she sat. "He met me in the living room—
the old Eddie."

"The old Eddie." Joe could hear that phrase echoing down
through time—the old Eddie, the teen who was more than
rambunctious, more than pushy. She grew rigid, clasping and
unclasping her hands, rubbing one hand over her knuckles again
and again.

"You have to tell me, Deanie. I already know most of it, but
you have to get it off your chest and I have to be sure about
exactly what happened." He moved forward, almost kneeling in
front of her, but still standing, still above her.

"You followed me, didn't you?" She looked up at him, a
smile tickling the corners of her mouth. "I got arrested once,
years ago, and the cop told me he knew I had connections, that
they'd find out. That was you, wasn't it?" She gave a little laugh,
as though she had little to spare. "I knew you were watching me
from back here."

"I thought I was being pretty discreet."

"Oh, you were. It's the guys on the other end who were
blabbing."

"So let's hear it."

"You're right." She gripped her hands and looked up at him.
"I came back to have it out. I came back because Pae begged me
to—he has no idea about any of this." She paused, and the color
drained from her face. "Does he? Oh, Joe—"

"No, no, Deanie. They know nothing about you except that
you seem to have been successful. That's all."

Deanie closed her eyes and muttered a prayer. "Well, I'm
glad of that." She sighed. "Okay, fair's fair. I came back to have
it out with Eddie. I don't know what I thought I was going to
do—turn him in for . . ." She laughed. "It was so long ago. I
thought I'd really forgotten. I didn't think it would matter if I
disappeared forever—but when Pae kept calling . . ."

"It matters." Joe settled himself on the stairs and waited.

* * * * *

Joe willed himself to appear relaxed. He didn't have much
time before the local police showed up, asking about that bump
on the back of Eddie's head and all those ropes and how did he
get onto the roof in the first place? But if he rushed Deanie, he'd
get nothing. She was resilient in ways that surprised him—she'd
shut down and tough it out and he'd get nothing. She began to

rummage in her purse again, then gave it up and shut it, tucking it deep into her lap and pulling her knees up again.

"Eddie hates you." Deanie looked directly at him for the first time that afternoon that Joe could remember. "He always has. Jealous. He's like that." She pulled out her purse again and began rummaging in it. She pulled out a half crushed pack of cigarettes and slipped one into the corner of her mouth.

"I didn't realize you smoked."

"I don't. They're someone else's but once in a while I like one." She lit a match, nearly tearing it in two as she pulled it across the matchbook, watching it flare a few inches in front of her eyes, then drew it toward the dangling cigarette. "It's the most unattractive habit anyone could ever have, which is probably why I never took to it. Appearance is everything."

"There are other reasons not to smoke, Deanie."

She flicked her wrist and the flame disappeared, a thin plume of smoke snaking its way to the sky above her. She glanced at the match, as if to reassure herself that it was indeed out, and tossed it toward the sidewalk. It landed on the bottom step, and she stared at it, as though wondering if she should get up and retrieve it or leave it there. "Not for me, at least not one that counts as much."

She took a long drag, exhaled, and watched the flow of smoke float away from her mouth and billow into a cloud over the steps before blending into nothingness. "Appearances have ruled my life—and Gino's." She flicked the ash and again looked at Joe, but this time with a smile. "You didn't know that, did you? And you don't believe it either, do you?"

"Convince me, Deanie."

"I sometimes wondered why you didn't feel guilty about Christina after she had her, well, accident, I guess we say. I thought when people started whispering about it being a botched suicide, you'd say something, do something, anything. But you never did. You felt bad, you said, but nothing more."

"And?" That had been so many years ago that he was surprised she even remembered him talking about it. He didn't actually remember a specific conversation, but he must have said something to her because that was how he felt, or rather didn't feel.

"You said you weren't worried about what other people said about you for not going back and staying with her and all that."

The cigarette was unfiltered and Deanie began to pick little bits of tobacco from her lower lip, glance at it on her fingertip, and flick it off into the air. "I never could feel like that. Gino could, but I couldn't."

Joe listened, wondering if she knew how disconnected her expressed values now were with the life she had lived for as long as he knew. And where was she going with all this talk about Christina?

"It wasn't an accident. That thing with Christina."

Joe felt a chill go all through him—he wouldn't have believed he could feel so suddenly like ice. In all those years he had never for a second believed she had tried to kill herself. And he had never considered any other possibility. And now, confronted with a past more real than the present, he wondered how much his determination not to profess a guilt or regret he did not feel had blinded him to the truth. "Deanie, you have to be really clear here."

"I know what I'm saying. Christina didn't slip and fall in the tub. She wasn't supposed to ever get out of the tub alive." Deanie took another drag on her cigarette before slipping it beneath the toe of her sandal and twisting her foot to extinguish it. She moved her foot to look at the remains, the dirty white paper and ash and bits of tobacco crushed flat, then she kicked it away with her toe.

"You're making a very serious accusation."

Deanie cocked her head to one side, smiled, and nodded. "I know. Pae was right. I did have to come home. Maybe it is worth it."

"The police report said Christina slipped in the bath tub, tried to get out, and knocked off a hair dryer, which shorted out and shorted out the wiring in the house, setting off an alarm in the box in the cellar."

Deanie nodded. "Yup. All that happened. Except that she didn't slip. She was pushed down and left for dead."

"How do you know this?"

"I think he told me."

Joe grabbed her wrist and wrenched her towards him. "Are you talking about Gino?" He was about to say he didn't believe her, but the shock in her eyes was answer enough. Not Gino. Joe squeezed his eyes shut to regain control. He was losing it—this was too close to him.

"Because someone saw Gino coming out of the house when the alarm was going off?" Deanie shook her head. "I sent him over there to give him something to do—go over and check it out, Gino. I don't need you, not really. I'm okay."

"Deanie, what are you talking about? You're not making any sense?"

"I know." She dropped her head into her hands, then looked up at him. "I never wanted anyone to know—I just wanted to get past it and forget about it and Gino promised he'd stay with me and back me up. That's all I wanted."

Joe waited. Deanie pulled out the cigarette pack and peered inside it, then crushed it in her hand and dropped it back into her purse.

"Eddie came into the Lopes's house—he saw me on the porch. I saw him coming out of Christina's place, by the back door; he saw me and came over. Gino was supposed to come pick me up—I was babysitting and Mrs. Lopes was on her way home and it was late and I had to get home to get my homework done. Gino said he'd be there right away. But Eddie saw me watching him coming out the back door of Christina's parents' house and he came straight up the steps to the back door and came right in. I knew he liked Christina—I heard he was going to ask her out after you two split up. He was so angry when he came in but I didn't think about it. He was just angry and, anyway, I pushed him away. I just thought he was being a jerk, not serious, just roughhousing, or something. That made him angrier. He said I was as bad as Christina but he didn't have to take it from me. It was summer—I wasn't wearing a lot—a cotton dress. I remember it."

Joe moved to sit with Deanie and put his arm around her.

"You don't have to do that. I'm okay. Everybody seems to think I should burst into tears, but I'm not going to. I'm not a teenager anymore. It was awful, but it was over years ago." She paused. "Gino found me—he passed Eddie on the way out of the house. Gino saw me but the alarm was going off next door and I sent him over there to find out what happened. I took some of Mrs. Lopes's clothes so I could get home. That's when someone saw Gino at the back door of Christina's house and thought he had something to do with what happened to her. But it wasn't Gino." Deanie rubbed her palms together. "Telling you now is like recalling an old movie—maybe I should feel more, but I don't."

"It was Eddie." Joe gripped her hand. "Deanie, do you have any idea how dangerous it is to confront someone like that?"

She began to laugh. "Do you have any idea how much courage it takes to confront someone like that? More than I have, Joe." She sat up straighter and smiled at him. "More than I have."

"But you talked to him today."

"Oh, yes, in the living room. But after I saw him and saw what a looser he is—sure, he has money, but Joe, he's a loser, a real loser. Realizing that—it was like a kind of release for me. I just wanted to get out of there. I might have said something if I'd had the chance but I could hear people in the next room so I turned around and headed out the front door."

"That was probably the smartest thing you ever did, Deanie." For a while they sat in silence on the steps, listening to the sounds of traffic flowing along the streets around them. "Deanie, you said you heard someone in the next room. Do you know who it was?"

"It was Mrs. Perreira. I didn't recognize her voice at the time, but someone told me later who she was." Deanie brushed back her hair. "I forgot how much older everyone would be. I just passed an old woman in the driveway and I nodded and smiled and didn't realize who it was."

"You're sure it was Christina's mother?"

Deanie nodded. "She looks so old. God, I hope I don't end up looking like that. But I suppose she's got a lot on her plate." Deanie sighed and began rummaging in her purse again. She pulled out a compact and snapped it open. "Oh, God, Joe. Stop talking to me. I look awful."

* * * * *

The last thing Joe wanted to do was dredge up the past with all its rotting resentments, ugly secrets, and coulda-woulda-shouldas. But he didn't have much choice, and if he didn't do it now, someone else, with far less sensitivity, would be sure to do it for him, corralling every possible relative and eliciting every resentment, every sin, no matter how minor. It would be an avalanche that would crush everyone and cleanse no one.

Joe scanned the backyard for a wheelchair and spotted it beneath a tree. The teenagers had gathered the food onto one table and were making fast work of it; the little kids had escaped to the garage and its special discoveries, and the adults were huddled in small groups, trying to make sense of it all, nibbling here and there, and sighing heavily.

"You're looking tired, Mrs. Perreira." Joe moved up behind the wheelchair, surprising the old woman. She let the lap rug fall from her curled fingers as she stood up. Her face was criss-crossed with deep lines beneath the powder, and rows of rings dangled loose on her fingers, held in place by arthritic knuckles. He had known her when she was young and graceful, with delicate hands and a petite figure, known in the neighborhood for her children's parties and volunteer work for the Portuguese-American Club. But that woman was gone, along with everything else except her daughter and her own half-life.

"You didn't come over here to tell me that. What do you want?" Mrs. Perreira scowled as she began to rearrange the shawl on Christina's shoulder. Joe noticed that the old woman didn't look at her daughter, but treated her as though she were a mannequin and her outfit needed adjusting. There was a roughness in her handling, an emotional fidgeting seemingly beyond her conscious control.

"You had a talk with Eddie this afternoon."

Mrs. Perreira glanced down at the figure in the wheelchair, looked over the lap rug and shawl, gave each one a little tug, and patted her daughter on the shoulder. "Just sit, now, Christina. I won't be far." The old woman moved stiffly away from the wheelchair and turned her head one way, then another, deciding where she would go. Joe nodded to an empty table with chairs scattered around it. She led the way. "Straighten that one out," she said to Joe, pointing to a chair tipped on its side. He picked it up and placed it near the table. She pulled it toward her and sat down, testing the chair as it rocked beneath her. "Flimsy."

Joe pulled up another chair and sat facing her. "You've given her as much of a real life as anyone ever could." He meant it. Mrs. Perreira was considered a marvel even among her own generation as well as the ones who came after.

The idea seemed to intrigue her and she let her head swing toward the wheelchair. She pulled a face and returned her attention to Joe. "So? It's what I have."

"Is that what you told Eddie?"

"Eddie?" She tipped her head to one side and studied Joe. "You never married."

"What did you want to talk to Eddie about this afternoon?"

"Why do you think I wanted to talk to him?"

"Someone saw you, heard you, going into the living room."

Mrs. Perreira nodded, her face softening, though not quite smiling. "You must know why by now."

"I want you to tell me."

"Your mother is a good woman, a good woman." She nodded her head forcefully. "So, I will tell you. She thinks of Christina like I do. She remembers her when everyone else has forgotten her. Did you know that?"

Joe nodded. He guessed some years ago. His mother would have gladly had more children if they had come to her; helping a friend care for a disabled daughter would not have been an unwelcome burden.

"She brought me a photograph of the whole family from a few years ago—such a nice one. I was in it, so she wanted me to have a copy. I took it to the nursing home to show Christina, to show her how her old friends had grown, the new grandbabies, my friends." Her shoulders stiffened and she clasped her hands, her arms rigid against her body. "I pointed to each one—this is Lucia, and see that wonderful man she married even though we didn't like him at first. And here, see Zaira and her daughter, Sarah, she looks more like her father than Zaira but she's still pretty. And look, here's Rosalie and her husband, Eddie. Sad they have no grandchildren."

"And?"

Mrs. Perreira took a deep breath. "I am always telling the nurse she must be careful what she says in front of my daughter because she understands. It is unkind to think otherwise because then you do cruel things without meaning to. What do you think, Joe? I said Eddie's name and pointed to his picture and she got so agitated—so upset and excited and I couldn't calm her. It frightened me." She bowed her head and pressed her fists against her forehead. "Eddie. I never thought . . ."

Joe leaned forward and pulled her hands away from her face. "Did you take another photograph over to her?"

"Your father gave me one. I told him I needed it. I needed to know. He gave me what I asked for."

"And you showed it to Christina and got the same reaction."
It was a statement, not a question. Joe could see it all now—the
long-serving mother watching her paralyzed, barely conscious
daughter rocking wildly in her wheelchair at the sight of an old
friend in an old photograph. "And you believed . . ."

"I knew it, Joe, I knew it. I told him I knew and . . ." She
gasped, then took a deep breath, determined to remain in control,
her chin lifting. "I told him I knew, but I also told him he was
pathetic. I told him Christina had identified him, that I knew for
certain and I would go to the police."

"You threatened him with the police?" Joe was incredulous.
He could imagine the frail Mrs. Perreira challenging Eddie, a
man twice her size but no match for her righteousness or anger.

"I was ready to do worse, much worse." She dropped her
hands into her lap and spread them wide, palms upward. "Look
at me. An old woman. But for her . . ." She glanced over at the
still figure in the wheelchair. "For her I would do anything." She
looked again at Joe. "Anything. But something stopped me, and I
thought first, is he worth it?" She shook her head. "I wanted to
kill him." She pulled the small purse that had been dangling
across her chest in front of her, pulled the zipper, and squeezed
the purse open, pointing the gaping mouth at Joe. There, nestled
among the tissues and lip gloss and car keys was a small knife.
"Are you shocked, Joe?"

"Mrs. Perreira, that's not what I expected." He couldn't
believe that this eighty-year-old woman had planned a murder—
until he looked into her eyes. She had endured with her iron will.
If something in her said murder was the answer, she would do it.
"But you didn't use it."

She shook her head. "No, no. I came ready. I knew he
would be here. I knew no one would notice an old woman or
anything she did. But when it came time, no. He repulsed me and
I could feel Christina calling me, needing me. We are so close,
Joe. I can tell when she needs something—she doesn't even have
to look at me, or cry or moan. I just know. I looked at him and
my hand was inches away from the knife, but I could feel her
needing me. And I knew if I did what I wanted to Eddie, I
wouldn't be here to take care of Christina. I planned this meeting
for almost two years, every day thinking how I would do this
accounting, freeing my daughter from his memory. But when I
faced him all I could feel was my daughter calling to me. He

thought I was a coward—he laughed at me. I was just an old woman who couldn't get even. I was disgusted with him—but I wouldn't give him the satisfaction of ruining my life. I'd take care of Christina and I'd go to the police."

"He didn't admit to anything, though." Joe felt a tinge of hope burning along the edge of her words.

"Hah! I knew what he did and he knew I knew. 'What are you going to do about it?' he said. 'Who will believe you now? It was years ago. Go on, tell anyone. No one will believe you. Go back to your daughter. I'm going upstairs to see what's going on up there. I'm here to enjoy myself. I've been watching those girls going up and down those stairs—must be something going on.' He blew me a kiss. He was laughing at me." The gnarled hands began twisting again, the thin shoulders trembling with rage. Joe could feel it too—Eddie could be coarse and cruel and think nothing of it.

"So he went upstairs? Are you sure about that?"

"Oh, yes." She gave a harsh laugh. "He was right. I was just an old woman, impotent. What could I do? But I have my Christina and she needed me. I came back out to her."

Joe rubbed his hand across his face. He could take the knife and have it tested for blood and DNA, but when he examined Eddie briefly, surreptitiously, so as not to attract attention, he hadn't noticed any knife wounds. And he didn't see how she could have stabbed him with such a small weapon and carried his body up the stairs to the third floor. No, Mrs. Perreira would be a great suspect—if she were thirty years younger and about a hundred pounds heavier—and better armed.

"For the first time in my life I felt sorry for Rosalie." Mrs. Perreira shook her head. "Always she is making the wonderful dishes for her family and for Eddie and he is so vile. I wanted to stop and tell her what a good wife she was, so much better than he deserved, but all I could feel was my Christina wanting me. So I passed her by."

"What do you mean you passed her by?"

"In the kitchen, putting out her platters."

"Rosalie was in the kitchen when you were leaving after talking to Eddie?"

Mrs. Perreira nodded, but she was no longer interested in Joe. She kept turning her head toward her daughter in the wheelchair, turning her body slightly to face her across the lawn, tipping her head to hear better in case her daughter made a sound. "She is calling me, Joe. I must go to her." She pressed a curled hand onto the table and steadied herself as she rose, then hurried back to her daughter. In a few years she would no longer be able to push the wheelchair, help with bathing and feeding, or even drive to the nursing home. Joe wondered if both women would fade away together, lying beside each other in the nursing home, the one following the other's call into darkness.

* * * * *

Joe didn't have much time left, and he knew it. He found Gwen sitting at a table near the back porch, both Jennie and Sarah sitting opposite her. Gwen was uncanny in her intuition of what was going on, even if she couldn't articulate it. Right now she was guarding those girls—they weren't going anywhere without her no matter what.

Both girls leaned on the picnic table, looking over their shoulders, up at the porch, out toward the traffic on the street, barely talking—they were restless and worried. They had little to say, considering their great prank had led to disaster and possibly death. Sarah was the first to notice Joe coming and turned around to watch him. He knew that look—a frightened craziness barely under control, her emotions under siege, her mind going blank. This wasn't the reaction he would have expected from her— something else must have happened, something he didn't know about—yet.

Joe slid onto the bench beside Gwen and looked across at the girls. They stared at him, waiting for him to speak. The longer he waited, the more strained Sarah began to look. He couldn't be wrong about this.

"Gwen, why don't you and Jennie take a moment and see if Mae's all right. I haven't seen much of her this afternoon, and if I go to her now, she'll start asking questions. I'm hoping she'll be easier with you and Jennie." He paused. "She likes Jennie."

Gwen looked at him for a moment, then smiled. "Good idea. Come on, Jen." She climbed off the bench and waited for Jennie to follow her up the back steps.

"Maybe I should go too." Sarah began to get up. Joe reached out and held her hand.

"Sit." He waited. "When was the last time you were up in the attic, Sarah?"

"I'm really sorry about that, Tio. It was just a joke. I never thought . . ." Her head trembled and he was afraid she would snap. He reached across the table and held both her hands.

"Were you up there when Tio Eddie went up? He heard someone up there and went up to take a look. Were you up there?" Oh, God, thought Joe. You were. You were up there all alone with Eddie, not knowing, not knowing. Playing a prank. Not knowing what he was capable of. Her lower lip began to tremble, vibrating like a child trying not to cry—but that's what she was, a child frightened and terrorized. "Tell me what happened, Sarah. It's all right." He began coaxing her, calming her and nudging her to tell him just enough so he could be sure. He had to be sure, even if his instincts told him he didn't need anything more than what he could see in front of him. The cop pushed aside the uncle, and Joe pressed his niece for information.

Sarah shook her head, repeating no no no, turning her head away, but gripping his hands as tightly as if she were hanging on a cliff.

Once again he reassured her she was safe, this was her home and her family all around her. There was nothing to fear— Eddie would never come near her again. But once again Sarah was firm in her denial, rigid in her fight against tears. It stymied Joe. He couldn't understand why she would deny what was so obvious to both of them—she had to know that he knew what had happened.

"How long were you up in the attic?"

"Not long. I just went up to check the balances, that's all."

"How long did it take?"

"Just a few minutes."

"Who was in the living room when you went through?"

"I don't know. I came in the front door—I didn't want anyone to see me. It was supposed to be a surprise."

"Did you hear people in the living room?"

She nodded.

"Who did you hear?"

"Tio Eddie and a woman."

"Anyone you knew?"

She shook her head.

"Mrs. Perreira was in there talking to him."

"It wasn't her. I know her. She comes over to see Avô."

She comes over to see Pae, thought Joe. Not Mae. Pae. "Was it Tia Deanie? You met her today for the first time."

"Maybe." She wouldn't look at Joe now, just at the table between them.

Joe ran his eyes over her outfit—jeans and a bright yellow shell with a long-sleeved low-neck white jersey over it. She was tall and lanky like all her cousins, with thick dark hair and skinny legs—she reminded him of a grasshopper sometimes, all limbs and elbows. There was a tiny smudge on her shoulder— he'd noticed it when he'd approached earlier, before sitting down, but otherwise she was dressed as he had first seen her earlier in the day, and her clothes weren't torn or badly stained or dirty. For a moment he heard a prayer of thanks fall from his lips.

"What?" Sarah peered at him.

"Nothing. I was just thinking." He smiled. "You're all right, aren't you?"

She nodded slowly.

"Frightened. He scared you badly. Threatened you too maybe."

She shook her head. "He didn't threaten me."

Joe waited. Behind them other family members were gathering up the remains of the meal, packing up their pickles and breads and sausage loaves and fish cakes and scallops and coriander potatoes and more. With all this food, Joe thought, no one should ever be unhappy or needy. But life was full of spoilers too. He watched her. She was frozen in the moment, her chin jerking higher as she struggled to recover her sense of safety in the world, her child's confidence that she could venture out and explore and somehow still be safe. He could see the change in her, the puckish teenager morphing into a sad little adult. He had seen this before. He remembered Deanie when she was fourteen.

"Ow!" Sarah pulled at her hands.

"Sorry." Joe released his grip. "I was thinking about something—and it made me angry."

"I guess." She managed a weak smile.

"Listen to me, Sarah. I have a pretty good idea what happened." He raised his hand to forestall her protests. "I want you to tell me parts of it. You don't have to tell me the worst of it. But I want to know what he said to you. What did Eddie say to you?"

Sarah's face collapsed into a pout, like a child now caught and unable to get away with a lie about the cookie jar, the broken bicycle, the lost homework. She screwed up her face and lowered her head.

"All right. What stopped him? You got away from him—I can see that."

"Oh!" Sarah sat up straight, her face composed. "How can you tell?"

"I can tell, Sarah. I can tell."

To Joe's surprise, Sarah found that a great comfort and she began to relax and smile, letting tears flow while she dug through her pockets for a tissue. "Yeah, I got away."

"How, Sarah, how did you get away?"

She held the tissue in front of her, studying Joe, deciding whether or not to answer. "I just did." She blew her nose with abandon, obviously feeling much better.

It was happening all over again, only this time no one was in danger of being suspected of Eddie's supposed accident. This time the victim was shielding the guilty party, the one who had sent Sarah away and dealt with Eddie alone.

"It won't take long to figure it out, but a lot of people—your family, Sarah, everyone who loves you—will go through a hard time while we're at it. And the police here will be on it in no time. They're at the hospital right now trying to figure out what happened to Eddie."

"Is he dead?"

"No, I don't think so. But he's in a bad way." Joe wasn't surprised that she was unmoved by that thought. She had no reason to feel sympathy for him—Joe certainly didn't. "I want to spare the family as much anguish as possible, but you have to help me."

"I can't."

Let her dig in her heels, Joe thought. There are only so many options here. He went over the possibilities in his mind, thinking of his large and ungovernable family—his sisters and their husbands, their children and grandchildren, the cousins who were like siblings, the Mortons who were childless but had never been without children in their home, the spouses who sometimes sat like stunned war veterans watching the chaos around them, the loud and passionate greetings to anyone who arrived a half hour late even if they had visited the day before. He imagined each one taking the stairs to the attic, seeing Eddie at his worst, perhaps already knowing who he was at his worst, and stepping in to save Sarah and exact revenge—for Sarah, for Christina, for Deanie.

"Rosalie," he said in a whisper.

"I promised, Tio, I promised I wouldn't tell." Sarah began to cry, crushing the tissue to her face.

"You didn't tell." Joe stood up, patted her cheek, and took her inside to be with Gwen and Jennie.

Ten

Saturday Evening

The rows of chairs with their sad and suffering partners seemed to go on forever, but Joe knew that was more his feeling about the emergency room than what he was actually seeing. Still, it was more than he wanted to see right now. The chaos and quiet moans and occasional shouts yanked him back to an earlier life, to his years working in the city with all its attendant miseries. He had no desire to be here any longer than absolutely necessary. He paced down the hallway toward the entrance, feeling a tunnel separating himself from the rest of humanity. He hated these places—except when they saved Gino from a burst appendix and when his uncle had a stroke.

The twilight softened the bleak scene of empty cars waiting in the parking lot, the aging buildings beyond, the patients shuffling across the tarmac, their canes dragging along. Rosalie would leave this way—she wouldn't try to sneak out the back or side—she wasn't the sort. She lacked a certain calculated deviousness, survival instincts that drove the less decent. Joe stuffed his hands in his pockets and stared through the glass, seeing nothing but recalling everything from earlier in the day.

A woman bustled past with tightly curled hair and a half smile on her face, humming to herself as she pushed through the double glass doors. Happy, he thought. Happy. Relieved of a great worry, so, happy. A race apart. That's how he felt. People who were happy, the rest of the world, he imagined, were a race apart—he was cut off from them, had been all weekend. Gwen was one of those—quietly settling into the background while the family drama played out, not asking anything of him except that she and Jennie emerge unscathed. That's just about all he wanted too—about all he was beginning to see would be possible. This weekend was a lesson—he was no longer the one his family would call on when something went wrong, and he was no longer taking up any worries even before he was asked. This was a different moving away.

He checked his watch and turned back to the interior of the hospital. The staff would throw her out soon, as soon as they could. They hated having relatives underfoot, but they would feel they had to let her stay until the emergency surgery was over and Eddie was on the mend, or at least out of imminent danger of death—if he was.

The anger clenched and unclenched in his gut. Eddie. His own brother-in-law. He gave a heavy sigh to push away the thoughts that came afterward—the three girls he had damaged. (Who knew if there had been more?) Sarah had been lucky, and Jennie luckier still. Surprised at how the rage had built in him when he was talking to Sarah as he realized Jennie's narrow escape, he looked around for a place to go. The emergency department was crowded, noisy, miserable. He turned abruptly and pushed open the door, heading out into the humid twilight. He started to walk briskly around the parking lot, out to his car and back again, then over to the medical building, around the lot, stopping once more at his car, keeping an eye on the main door as he went. Thank god he hadn't had to sit down with Gwen and tell her . . .

He checked his watch again—closing in on eight o'clock. He leaned against the car and waited. After a while he was rewarded with the sight of Rosalie coming through the doors. She stood uncertainly on the sidewalk, looking one way, then the other, as though expecting someone to drive up and collect her. He crossed the lot and came up on the near side.

"Rosalie." He called her name softly and waited for her to turn.

"Joe." She sounded surprised, but smiled. "You came. That was nice of you."

She walked toward him and wrapped her arms around him, leaning her head against his chest. "He's in a coma."

"Yes, it's a shock. Not dead, in a coma." He could see her in the back yard, getting the news that something had happened to Eddie, the way she had to be told twice—not dead, alive, but just barely.

After a moment, she pulled away and stepped back. Her face was pale and splotchy but her makeup was intact—not ruined by tears. She stood with her feet planted wide apart as though to steady herself.

Joe took her arm and began to walk her towards his car.

"I'm parked over there." She nodded in another direction.

"Someone will pick it up." Joe held onto her and pulled her along with him.

"I think I'd rather take my car, Joe." She tried to pull away but he held his grip. "Joe, what're you doing?"

"I'm keeping you with me, Rosie." They reached the car and he turned to her. She had always been pretty but Eddie's money had made her beautiful and sophisticated. She was the best dressed, the best coiffed, the most luxurious of his sisters, except now for Deanie. Deanie was in another category altogether. "I talked to Sarah."

Rosalie's eyes flashed for a second, so quick that Joe doubted for a moment that he had seen anything at all. But he had, for a split second. "What about?"

"Rosie, in a few minutes I have to make a call to the local force and let them know what I've found out."

Rosalie stared at him. He could see she was thinking, trying to get a grip on what was happening, wondering just how much he did know, what did he know, was it too late for her, could she still get away with it. "He's alive. What're you so worried about?"

"He's in a coma, barely alive."

"I didn't know you cared about him so much."

"I always wondered why you did."

She tried to laugh. "I've had that conversation with myself every day for how many years. I wish I knew."

"If you go to the police with me, things will go better for you."

"You believe that?"

"Yes, Rosalie, I do. And I'll be with you."

"Lucky me."

"Tell me what happened, Rosie."

"I thought you knew everything."

"Let's stop dancing."

"Let's stop dancing." She smiled and lifted her shoulders and spread her arms out as though about to twirl around.

"I hate doing this, Rosie, you know I do. I have no choice."

"The judge will say everyone has a choice, even you."

"Tell me what happened."

"You know, the American Indians believe that people come into their maturity in their fifties. I think it's life catching up with you—settling scores before you can go on to the next big thing—old age. If only he'd . . . we might have made it into our later years."

She sounded so innocent and wistful, as though the revelations of the day, the violence of the evening, hadn't happened.

"You never liked him." She drew herself up straight, pulling in her arms, and glared at him. "Ever since you got into that fight years ago—when you were still in school."

"Why do you even remember that?"

"Eddie remembers that. He beat you and you never got over it. That's what he said."

"He beat me?" Joe couldn't decide if he should be furious or amused. He shook it off and took a deep breath. "Rosie, he attacked Christina all those years ago. And Deanie. And . . ."

"Christina? He attacked Christina? Are you saying . . . He was the reason she . . ."

"Yes. He's the reason."

"Oh." She began to sway, her eyes opening wide, then her face shuttered, as though something was dying inside. "Does anyone else know?"

"Pae does, and Mrs. Perreira."

"That's why she—I heard her arguing with him in the living room. But she left. When I went in, he was gone. Upstairs. I heard him go up. I went up to see what the argument was all about—she's such an old friend and she didn't even speak to me when she left. I was worried something had happened. But when I got upstairs . . ."

"Yes?"

"I forgot." Her voice was so soft and scratchy Joe could barely make out what she was saying. "I forgot what I wanted to say to him. I only saw him—and Sarah. He was pulling up her jersey and she was, she was freaking out." Rosie crossed her arms across her breasts and bent over as though in pain.

"So you went in to stop him."

"I pushed my way between them and sent Sarah away—she ran. She didn't have to be told to get out of there."

"And Eddie?"

"He laughed at me, and then he got angry. He threatened to teach me a lesson like he had Deanie. The minute he said it I knew what he meant—I knew what he had done. It was like it had just happened. I knew it all—why she'd changed all those years ago, why she couldn't bring herself to ever come back here. I knew it all—everything made sense. It was Eddie! My husband! The man I . . . " She began to cry, sputter, but her words grew in rage. "He started to walk away—like I was . . . I grabbed a hammer—it was just lying there—and I hit him and he fell. One blow and he was down, lying there, still. And it was so quiet up there. I didn't know what to do—I didn't want to touch him, to have anything to do with him. But I couldn't leave him there—in my house, my house, Joe, my house. We played here, we grew up here. This was our place, this attic, this house. He couldn't be here, he couldn't. So I got him into the swing and I pushed him out the window. I didn't want him in my home or anywhere near me. I just wanted to be rid of him. I wanted it all to go away—like it never happened." She squeezed her eyes shut and huddled tighter. She lifted her head, eyes shut, took a deep breath. "What happens if he dies?"

"Pray he doesn't." Joe took her by the arm and eased her into his car.

* * * * *

Joe drove slowly down the gravel and dirt driveway to the clearing in front of the garage. The backyard was tidy now in the night tinged with the afterglow of the late sunset—the tables folded and leaning against the side of the porch, the chairs stacked in a pile on the ground nearby. His sisters would collect their own parts of the assemblage later in the week, after they spent a few good hours deconstructing Rosalie's behavior.

He put the car in park and looked over at the empty seat. The world can change in an instant, his father often said. But he'd been talking about fishing and how suddenly danger could come upon a man at sea. It was carelessness that was the worst threat, he'd say.

And rage, thought Joe. Unchecked, thoughtless rage.

At least he had one thing to be grateful for—Rosalie had walked quietly, matter-of-factly into the police station. After she got out of the car, she never looked him in the eye again, not when he led her to the detectives' office, not when he called an attorney, not when he sat her down in the chair to make a statement, not when she was led away, not when he said goodbye to her across the room. She was gone from him more thoroughly than he could have imagined possible.

The car door squeaked, bringing him back to the yard in the gathering darkness. He climbed out and slammed the door, half hoping the sound would rouse his parents and save him the trouble of looking for them. But nothing about this was going to be easy. He climbed the back stairs and walked through the kitchen and dining room, into the living room.

Pae sat in his worn upholstered chair, staring into the fireplace, a newspaper folded beneath his clasped hands, and beneath them his summer cap with the bright green logo of a local farm. Joe stood in the doorway, waiting for his father to acknowledge him, gave it up and stepped into the room.

"I have something to tell you, Pae."

The old man nodded. "I am waiting for you to tell me."

On the drive back, Joe had prepared himself for this, the most difficult moment of his life as this man's son, when he would have to tell him that his beloved daughter Rosalie had been arrested and would probably be convicted of attempted murder—and Joe had helped bring it about. The man who had pressed into the investigation, followed each story no matter how threatening or condemning it grew, had moved forward hour after hour pushing away the second thoughts, the warnings to slow down, the whispers that he wouldn't like what he found. And then there was the other voice—the one he knew well and never doubted—until now. No matter how loud that voice got in his head—duty, the right thing to do, the law above all else—he was washed with an acid sorrow. He looked back down a long tunnel of years of blue and begged life to be different, begged to be someone else with different choices and different losses.

"Tell me," the old man said. "I am waiting."

"Eddie's fall, his injury, wasn't an accident."

Pae nodded, as though this was what he expected to hear. Still he kept his eyes fixed straight ahead. "I know this. Go on."

Joe pulled up an ottoman and sat in front of the old man. "I talked to a lot of the family this afternoon—everyone who saw Eddie when he arrived, while he was in the house." He almost said, "right here in this room," as he looked around, realizing how much of what he'd heard had taken place where he and his father were sitting right now. "I spoke to everyone who had seen him or talked to him."

Pae nodded, his lips crinkling like dried leaves.

"I talked to Rosalie." Joe paused, wishing he didn't have to go further, knowing he did. "She told me how it happened. She has a good lawyer—Eddie threatened her."

Pae raised his hand. "He was no good—never was he any good."

"She heard him talking to someone else and he said things that drove her over the edge." Again, the old man nodded. His eyes grew pink around the rims but his gaze remained steady.

"I have to ask you, Pae. Why did you want Gino and Deanie to come home? Is there something you're not telling me?" Joe watched for a telltale twitch, for a blink or spasm—some sign that his father was deeply aware of what he had set in motion—but he didn't flinch, gave no sign. Perhaps he hadn't suspected, Joe thought; perhaps, it was all about a father who was old and desperately wanted to see his children together again before it was too late.

"Mrs. Perreira said she knew who had done this to Christina—it wasn't an accident. She knew who had hurt her daughter. She wanted to prove it, she said, and she asked me to help. How could I say no? Her only daughter like that?"

"Did she tell you who she thought it was?" Joe asked.

He shook his head. "But I knew Gino was innocent. I knew if he came back, all those lies would die. I knew it. I have always known it. He is my son. I wanted him to have that, that triumph, to have back his good name."

"And Deanie?"

The old man's face softened, but still he didn't smile or flinch. "Gino would not come without her—I knew that. They had something extra as children—some trust between them. I had to get her here to get him here. She came and so did he." He took a deep breath, his rock-hard chest filling and deflating. "I like his wife."

"Yes, Melanie's a nice woman."

"I knew it wasn't Gino." His hands began to tremble, and Joe kept himself from reaching out to comfort him and still the tremor. "I never thought more than that. I never thought if not Gino, then who? I didn't care."

"But Mrs. Perreira did. And then, when she found out and confronted him, she no longer cared. Having the truth out in the open was enough." The irony of it would be the poison of his father's later years—that Mrs. Perreira, who had put all this in motion, should walk away from the confrontation she had craved and prayed over for years.

"I knew it wasn't my Gino." He pulled his arthritic hands apart and picked up the cap, turning it around with his thickened fingers. He found the logo and placed the cap on his head, pulling it down firmly onto his skull, over his thick white hair. He picked up the newspaper and tucked it under his arm, then braced himself, and pushed himself up.

"Shall I get Mae to help you?" Joe rose.

His father waved him away with the back of his hand and shuffled off to the front door, which he pulled open. In the hallway a number of coats and sweaters hung from a coat tree. He pulled off a light jacket, and fumbled his way into it. Joe watched, not quite believing his eyes. The old man slipped the newspaper into the pocket and turned to Joe. "Which station?"

"Pae, you don't have to go tonight. The lawyer will try to get her out on bail in the morning. Her boys are on the way."

"No, tonight. I must go to her. She is my daughter. Where is she?" The old man stared hard at him, and Joe felt his stomach lurch. He thought he knew his father, knew the man he had worked with and loved for his entire life, but now Pae was looking at him as though he were just another man in the neighborhood—someone who could help or hinder, nothing special. "She is fragile. She needs me." He made his way down the stairs and, reluctantly, Joe followed him.

* * * * *

The neat, dark ranch house sat low among the shrubs, its porch light glowing in the damp night, its shine picking out the pinks and yellows and blues of the garden flowers. Joe pulled into the driveway of his sister Zaira's house, coasted close to the garage, and came to a halt. He shut off the engine and leaned back in the dark car, trying to let go of the image of his father sitting on a hard folding metal chair in the police station, officers greeting him as they passed, marveling at the old man's fortitude.

Through the lit window he could see his sister Zaira standing over the sofa talking to someone, probably Lucia. He'd noticed her car farther down the street, parked in front of a friend's house. A man crossed in front of the window and flopped into a chair, and Zaira turned and spoke to him. Joe could imagine her telling him not to put his feet on the footstool without a newspaper beneath them, or some other minor order for proper behavior. Zaira, who never let anyone get past her, never shirked what she regarded as her duty as the eldest. And that was why Joe was here. They probably already knew—news of Rosalie's arrest would travel fast—but Joe felt obligated to tell them himself.

"Oh, Joe." Zaira grabbed Joe's arm as he stood on the threshold and pulled him into the house. "What awful thing this is. Lucia is crying and drinking and I'm crying and drinking and Larry is just drinking." Zaira started to look over her shoulder, as though expecting to see her husband, Gray, standing there with a bottle. "Larry's in the other room calling a lawyer friend. I called a friend on the force and he said no, we can't all come down there. Come on. Tell us what happened." She led him into the living room with a hand on his back. She was right—about Lucia at least. Her tear-streaked face looked up at him, her eyes stunned and almost senseless.

"Over here, Joe." Gray motioned to a chair.

"No, no, he's fine right here. Sit there, Joe." Zaira pointed to a spot on the sofa. "I want you there where I can see you better and hear you better." She put a hand on Joe's shoulder until he sat. For once in his life he was deeply grateful for his sisters' fussing—they could go on like this all night, and the longer they went on, the less he would have to say because they would fill in all the little details and gaps with their murmurings and suggestions and quizzical looks and assumptions until they had the whole story, in a sort of accurate form, and he was relieved of the painful duty of spelling it out for them.

"Thanks, Bernardo." Joe reached up to take the beer his nephew handed him. He rarely got to see Lucia and Larry's son, somewhere in his mid-thirties—and living off in the Berkshires.

"I made him come." Lucia crossed her arms and her lip trembled as she lost herself in her own misery.

"She was drinking too much to drive." Bernardo found a chair near the dining room and settled back down, the dutiful son. He was plain looking, with dull brown hair and short fair eyelashes and soft features, and everyone remarked on it because he and his wife had three gorgeous daughters.

"Why did she do it, Joe?" Lucia stretched a hand across the sofa, imploring him. "Why didn't she come to me, to Zaira, to you? What will happen to her?"

Joe didn't want to think about what was going to happen to Rosalie—she wasn't young and she wasn't someone who had ever willingly faced hardship, but she had thrown away everything she'd built up and seemed barely conscious of it—a single moment of rage and self-discovery had changed everything for her. Lucia curled up against the sofa back, drawing up her legs and resting her head against the cushion. Her question had been rhetorical, and she went on crying.

"I want to know." Zaira sat down on a stool in front of him. "You figured it out, didn't you? I saw you talking to people all afternoon, going from Gino to Mrs. Perreira and some of the others. What were they telling you?"

"I don't want to start any rumors, Zaira. Rosalie is in for a hard time and the less talk about her the better."

Zaira sat bolt upright. Despite the few lines on her face, she could pass for a much younger woman—her posture, her bearing, her demeanor warned anyone to dare call her old. She walked with a determination that made people turn their heads at the sound of her footsteps and move aside to let her pass. She wasn't sentimental, but generous, not intellectual but curious. "Why did she do it? You can tell me that."

"I can't tell you anything of the sort, Zaira. I came here because I wanted you to know directly from me—not from some gossip."

"Mae called me." Zaira studied him. "She's with Gwen," she added when she saw the alarm in his eyes. "Gwen'll take care of her. She's sensible."

"It's about Christina, isn't it?" Lucia gazed over at Joe. "It has to be. Mrs. Perreira was making such a fuss for the last few weeks. She was like a cat waiting on the fish pier."

"I don't think she'd like that simile." Joe finished the beer and put the bottle on the table.

"Another one?" Zaira turned to Bernardo. "Your uncle wants—"

"No, I don't. This is fine."

"So you came to tell us what we already know." Zaira slapped her hands onto her thighs as she prepared to stand up.

"No, he didn't, Zaira. Give your brother a chance."

Zaira turned her gaze to her husband as though he had never been known to speak before this. When he refused to respond, she turned back to Joe. "All right, Joe, the floor is yours."

This wasn't exactly what he wanted. He'd much rather sit on the sidelines and watch a Mr. and Mrs. spat, or listen to one sister making up explanations to comfort the other one, or listen to one of them boss around Bernardo, who was unlucky enough to be the only offspring there. But they were more focused than usual, and they wanted answers.

"I want you to make sure that Deanie and Gino stay here for a while. We're going to need their testimony and I don't want to have to chase them down. You and Lucia have to make them feel we want them to stay."

"But we do." Lucia sat up straight. "But we do. They know that."

"After what happened this afternoon, we may have to work harder to persuade them." Joe looked from one sister to the other. "Will you do it?"

"Of course." Zaira gave a sigh and stood up, stretching out her stiff legs as she did so. "I thought you were going to have something to say about my menopausal child, whom at this moment I do not want to call my own. And don't you start defending her, Gray."

Gray held up his hands in a sign of surrender. "She's my daughter and I will always defend her, but if you say not to, I'll keep my mouth shut. Joe's not going to condemn a teenager for a prank that someone else abused, are you, Joe?"

"Of course not," Joe said. "There wasn't anything malicious in what they tried to do."

"Kind of sweet, actually." Gray smiled, then caught his wife's eye and turned away, settling back into his wheelchair.

"All right, Joe. Lucia and I will make sure Deanie and Gino stay here for a while, and we'll also make sure that they want to come back, won't we, Lucia."

"Of course, Joe, of course." Lucia nodded slowly, then sat up and put her feet on the floor. "What an awful end to such hope Pae had. Awful. And Mae too. How will they survive it, Joe? I called Mae as soon as I heard—I just dropped off the

platters next door—and came in here and Zaira told me. We
were going to go right back and we called and Mae said not to
come tonight. Come tomorrow. I said we would. But why? Why
didn't she want us with her tonight? Tonight of all nights?"

* * * * *

Mae leaned over the table and pressed the folded cloth
harder, putting her entire weight behind the effort. She had been
scrubbing the table for a good ten minutes already and when she
stopped to mark her progress, she was breathing heavily, sweat
beading across her forehead and upper lip. The back of her neck
was damp and her arms ached. The stain on the wood table was
unchanged. Ink, she thought. It spoils everything.

The kitchen door squealed and she looked up into her son's
face. Ah, Jose, she thought, so grown and now grown older—
with gray hair. I don't like seeing my children looking old—it
isn't right. He should be young. But he was always serious and
earnest when he was young—not flighty or puffed up like some.
Like he was already an old man. He gave her a quizzical look
and she wondered if she had forgotten to speak. Sometimes the
voice in her head was so engaging she realized she wasn't
talking, just thinking.

"He didn't come back with you." She walked over to the
sink. She turned on the faucet and rinsed out the rag, ringing it
hard before spreading it out on the counter to dry, half of it
draping over the edge. "No, he wouldn't." She stared into the
black mirrors of the window over the sink. "I'll go to her
tomorrow. She will want to talk to me, to explain. She doesn't
have to."

Joe crossed the room and gently put his arms around his
mother. She leaned her head against his chest for a moment, then
pulled back. She patted his chest and began to look around the
kitchen for something to do.

"I didn't realize you were alone." Joe led her to the
doorway, toward the living room.

"I haven't been alone. Gino and his wife were here—nice
lady she is. Nice lady. And Deanie was here." She stopped in the
doorway, heard the television in the living room and two girls
laughing, then slipped out of his arm and went back to the
kitchen table, pulling out a chair and sitting down. Joe followed
her. "I think he is going back out west. But he promised to come
again. He's a good boy. She makes him happy."

"And that's all you want." Joe smiled. She watched him thinking about what he would say next. She knew he would come home and tell her all that had happened, but she already knew. She had seen it in his eyes during the afternoon when he'd gone after Gino, then Mrs. Perreira and Deanie and Rosalie. She'd seen it in the way he moved around the family. At first she'd been angry—how dare he not be her son, how dare he betray the whole family with this business of making sure he knew what happened. Let them take Eddie away and say it was an accident, let him spend his life in a nursing home if he lived, and if he didn't, well, good riddance. She was almost afraid that all his poking and prying and proving would bring Eddie back. She didn't want him back. She didn't like him, never had. But he was Rosalie's choice and a daughter must have something that is her own. Mae couldn't understand Rosalie—didn't know where this strange choice had come from, but she had accepted it.

"A mother wants to see her children happy. What is there? Are you happy, Jose?"

"Yes, Mae. I'm very happy." He moved his chair close enough to touch her. "There's something I have to tell you."

He would have to talk until he got it all out. She knew that—it was the way he was. He was a good boy and he never did anything seriously wrong, but when he made a mistake he would come home and explain to her in quiet, straightforward terms, in a soft voice, what he had done, why he thought it was wrong, and what he thought he should do about it. It was left to her and Pae to agree or not—they always agreed. It was a little confusing to her that a thirteen-year-old boy should weigh his actions so deliberately and decide to give up his bike for a week in penance. She thought he would grow out of it, but he never did, and now she wanted to crush his heart into hers to hold onto the one part of him she could understand.

"Yes, tell me what I already know." She didn't like talking about these things. Why should anyone put into words the uglier sides of life if we all knew they were there? It was good to talk, to tell what another didn't know and needed to know, but not this. Eddie was lying near death if not already dead in a hospital. Perhaps he deserved it—he probably did. And poor Rosalie was sitting alone in a cold place with her father sitting nearby to comfort her. But she would never be comforted.

"I don't think you know this, and I'm telling you because I believe it will clear the air and perhaps make the future easier. We both want Deanie to be part of this family again, and that means she has to feel that she is accepted entirely, without reservation."

"And her mother doesn't feel that already?"

"She will always be uneasy, but after I tell you, she will look at you and know that it's all out in the open. The two of you always seemed to read each other's minds."

She nodded. Yes, she had always known what was going on in Deanie's head, at least in her early years. And maybe she would again. She nodded and told Jose to go on, she would listen; she always listened.

"It's about Christina and Eddie."

"Ah, yes. What he did to her—he deserves what he got even if it's forty years late." She grew sad thinking about her best friend's child; such a beautiful girl she had been and such joy to think that she would become part of the family with Jose. But it was not to be. She couldn't understand that—he had left and not married and there she had been, so vulnerable, so damaged. "Why did you stop loving her?"

"Mae? What did you just say? Do you understand that Christina's condition isn't the result of an accident? It was Eddie."

She nodded. "Eddie was always jealous of you. And she was a good girl."

"Are you saying you knew? How?"

How did she know? She tried to think back to the first moment when she'd been certain that he was the reason she was so injured. When had it come to her? Had she been talking to Mrs. Perreira? Had she been visiting in the hospital? Had she been talking to Eddie's parents, who said how much Eddie liked Christina? Somewhere in those first few months after the accident, she had known—instinctively, pulling together little bits of truth here and there until they cohered into a shining beam of light that fell straight on Eddie. "I don't know, but I always knew. Always."

"Well, maybe that'll make the rest of it easier."

"You mean Deanie?" Yes, she could tell by the sudden widening of his eyes that he was now talking about Deanie. Yes, she knew they had to be connected, one injury leading to the next. She had seen and marked the change in Deanie, but the girl wouldn't talk to her—she grew silent and watchful. The other girls never stopped talking, but Deanie never really got started. So it was Eddie. She had always wondered. She had watched him once passing behind the chair where Deanie was sitting and how she had leaned forward, perched on the edge of the chair, glancing over her shoulder as he squeezed past her in the crowded dining room. It wasn't necessary to move so far away. She had wondered about that. And she'd noticed other times when Deanie left the room as soon as Eddie came in. "He did something to her, didn't he?"

She let him take her hands and hold them in his—his were large and still fine and hers were old and gnarled and hardly her own anymore. "Yes, Mae, he . . . he assaulted her." She squeezed her eyes shut and shook her head. Eddie deserved what he got. "Yes, I should know this. She'll be able to tell if I know or not. So now I know." She lifted his hands to her lips and gave them a quick kiss.

"There's more, Mae."

Poor Jose, she thought. He looks so tormented. His jaw is going to come unhinged if he grinds his teeth any harder. "I know the rest."

"I mean why she left."

"Oh, yes. Her life in the casinos with all those men. The ones she escorted and the gamblers." Yes, she knew all about them. At first she hadn't understood what the word escort meant and had to find magazines in the library to look at and novels to scan to find out what this business was. But then she understood. The letter was meant to be unkind—no signature, no reassurance that her daughter was well, nothing but the insidious story of what Deanie was doing to make money. Yes, she knew all the rest of it and someday she might even find out who sent the letter, who would want to hurt an old woman and her husband. But he hadn't seen the letter. She would never let him see it. Deanie was his baby and he believed in her and she would make sure he went on believing in her. Poor Jose. He's so surprised. "I knew about it from way back."

"How did you find out? I had a really hard time tracking her down through friends in the police forces out there."

"It's not your business how I know. But your father doesn't and you are not to tell him. You do as I tell you, Jose."

Perhaps I have been too stern, she thought. Jose was starting to laugh and shake his head and the tears in his eyes could be pain or sorrow or relief. But he's a good boy. He will do what I tell him. He will keep the secret from his father. It's a good family. My children are alive and healthy. I have a roof over my head and food to serve. I am blessed. Tomorrow I will thank Our Lady for her blessings on all of us.

* * * * *

The sound of his own footsteps seemed ominous, foreboding, when in fact the worst was over, at least as far as Joe was concerned—he had sent his sister to a certain prison sentence, pushed his frail father closer to the end, driven apart the close relationships he had known all his life, and listened to his mother's decades-long burden of heartache carried alone and in silence. She would not say how she had come to know the truth about her youngest child—she was impervious to his questioning, but also apparently to the pain of Deanie's life. The family reunion had ended in catastrophe but also honesty—for the first time since he was a young man there were no secrets, no fears about the truth coming out. And yet, the heaviness of his shoes scuffing on the bare, unfinished wood of the stairs as he climbed to the attic room seemed appropriate.

As he stepped into the attic he studied the remnants of the teenage prank—the ropes and costumes torn from Eddie's body. The moonlight streamed in, washing over the straw-filled humps that had been his parents' images, the board they had been tied to and that had then been tied to Eddie, all of it piled neatly near the window, to be delivered to the police. Joe looked it over and closed the door. He went back downstairs.

Joe rapped softly on the bedroom door before he entered. Gwen lay curled up on a small sofa with a book. He knew Gwen was watching him, wondering what his mood was—if indeed he had a mood other than his usual professional calm. He wondered too.

Throughout the entire day and evening he had done his duty, chased down the truth from relative to relative, brother to sister to friend to sister, never stopping to think that this was his family, his sister he was questioning, his brother he was probing. And now it was done—he had handed the police a woman ready to confess, and had walked away. How did he feel? Truthfully? He wasn't sure—didn't want to know—not yet.

He walked back toward Gwen. She closed her book, not bothering to mark her place, and dropped the book on the floor, pushing it aside with her toe. She smiled and sat up, stretching out her long legs, leaning back, and patting the cushion beside her.

"You weren't in the living room."

"No." She shook her head, tipped it back to rest on the pillows. "Where were you?"

Joe reached out to the sofa back and eased himself down. He was tired, achy, but he knew there was nothing wrong with him. "Talking to Mae."

"How is she?"

"Awesome as Jennie would say. And she'd be right." Joe rested his head on the pillows and closed his eyes. He could feel Gwen's fingers brushing the hair from his forehead—they were cool and gentle and he felt the stress flowing out of him, being brushed aside as gently as the strands of hair. The night was quiet—cars passed slowly if at all somewhere on a side street, a breeze crinkled through the leaves and was lost before it could reach the open window. In the far distance he thought he heard a telephone ring, then decided it must be a neighbor's television— the ladies in the neighborhood liked to sit up late on a Saturday night and watch old movies, black and white with slender women in long slinky dresses and men in black tie and tails, accents that swallowed half the word.

"She's a strong woman." Gwen rested her arm on the sofa back and continued soothing Joe's forehead. After a moment of silence, she whispered, "Are you asleep?"

Joe shook his head, kept his eyes closed. "I think I realized tonight just how strong she is. She has known for years about Deanie—what she does for work, I mean." When Gwen's fingers paused, Joe opened his eyes and looked over at her. "I didn't tell you everything, did I?" Gwen shook her head. No, he hadn't told her, hadn't thought he would ever want to or have to. He had never let his thoughts travel that far into the future, to a time when Deanie's ill-managed life would have to be laid bare to anyone here. But the time had come. He told Gwen about Deanie's escape to the west, her life among the men and casinos, the reasons for her flight. Hearing himself describe the entire sad history made it seem like he could pile it all into a little box, close it up, and be done with it. But nothing was as tidy as his recitation of it. They listened to the night sounds around them while Gwen absorbed the tale.

"Not the restful fun weekend I promised you," he said.

She laughed softly, then turned and pushed back into the sofa, snuggling into his arms. "We are very afraid of our secrets, aren't we?"

"I wonder, now that it's all out in the open, at least among the family, and soon to be among everyone else, I wonder what we were so afraid of. If we hadn't lost Deanie, would any of this have happened? Rosalie wouldn't have married Eddie, that's for sure. Deanie wouldn't have felt the need to flee and get so caught up in another life. And Gino, he wouldn't have felt he had to go with her, to protect her."

"But he met Melanie, and they're very happy together."

Joe smiled. Gwen was determined to see the best in every situation—it was her way of surviving some very dark times. He didn't bother arguing with her. "Deanie was very afraid of her secret, yes. Very afraid."

"I'll bet she's glad it's no longer a secret." Gwen closed her eyes and savored the smell of Joe, the feel of his shirt beneath her fingers, against her cheek.

"Pae is at the station with Rosalie—he insisted on staying with her. He's probably sitting outside, within shouting distance, I suppose." Joe gave Gwen a squeeze as he spoke. "He's old, Gwen. I'm worried how much this is going to take out of him."

Gwen snuggled deeper into his arms. "You don't have to worry about him, Joe."

"No?"

"You know what he said to me this afternoon, while you were off talking to everyone?"

Joe pulled away just enough to be able to see her expression. She turned to him. "He saw you going into the house, brushing by everyone, people who wanted to chat with you. You were on a mission, it looked like." She paused, as though wondering at the deepening silence. "He was watching you and he said to me, 'This is something you should know. Perhaps you already know.'

"I didn't know what he was talking about, Joe. But he looked me in the eye and he said, 'The truth will hurt, but it won't hurt you.' And then he said he was going to take a nap."

-End-

About the Author

Susan Oleksiw is the author of the Mellingham series featuring Chief of Police Joe Silva, who was introduced in *Murder in Mellingham* (1993). Oleksiw introduced Anita Ray, an Indian American photographer, in a series of short stories, including "A Murder Made in India" (*Alfred Hitchcock Mystery Magazine*, 2003). Anita Ray's first book-length adventure is *Under the Eye of Kali* (2010). She also appeared in *The Wrath of Shiva* (2012) and *For the Love of Parvati* (2014).

Also known for her nonfiction work, Oleksiw compiled *A Reader's Guide to the Classic British Mystery* (1988), the first in a series of Reader's Guides. As consulting editor for *The Oxford Companion to Crime and Mystery Writing* (1999), she also contributed several articles.

Oleksiw trained as a Sanskritist at the University of Pennsylvania, where she received her PhD in Asian Studies, and has lived and traveled extensively in India.

www.ingramcontent.com/pod-product-compliance
Lightning Source LLC
Chambersburg PA
CBHW072353190626
46811CB00019B/724